The
Plot Is
Murder

The Plot Is Murder

V. M. BURNS

KENSINGTON BOOKS
www.kensingtonbooks.com

KENSINGTON BOOKS are published by

Kensington Publishing Corp.
119 West 40th Street
New York, NY 10018

All Kensington titles, imprints, and distributed lines are available at special quantity discounts for bulk purchases for sales promotion, premiums, fund-raising, educational, or institutional use.

Special book excerpts or customized printings can also be created to fit specific needs. For details, write or phone the office of the Kensington Sales Manager: Kensington Publishing Corp., 119 West 40th Street, New York, NY 10018. Attn. Sales Department. Phone: 1-800-221-2647.

Kensington and the K logo Reg. U.S. Pat. & TM Off.

eISBN-13: 978-1-4967-1182-3
eISBN-10: 1-4967-1182-3
First Kensington Electronic Edition: December 2017

ISBN-13: 978-1-4967-1181-6
ISBN-10: 1-4967-1181-5
First Kensington Trade Paperback Printing: December 2017

10 9 8 7 6 5 4 3 2

Printed in the United States of America

I dedicate this book to my mom, Elvira Burns.
I miss you each and every day.

Acknowledgments

There were a host of people who helped bring this book to reality. So I apologize if I miss naming anyone. I want to start by expressing my gratitude to Dawn Dowdle, Blue Ridge Literary Agency, and Editor-in-Chief John Scognamiglio, Kensington Publishing, for believing in me.

Thanks to my Seton Hill University family and support network, starting with my mentors, Barbara Miller, for your insight, guidance, suggestions, and support; and to Patrick Picciarelli for allowing me to tap into your crime fighting knowledge and expertise. Thanks to my critique partners and friends Dagmar Amrhein, Stephanie Wieland, Michelle Lane, Tricia Skinner, Lana Ayers, and Jessica Barlow for slogging through the muck of first, second, and third drafts. Special thanks to Patricia Lillie for reading, editing, and then rereading and re-editing, but especially for listening. I am so grateful for your help and the website design. A special shout-out to my SHU Tribe for all of the encouragement and support. Repeating our motto helped get me through many hard times.

Finally, I want to acknowledge with gratitude the love and support of my family—my dad, Benjamin Burns, for listening to me and for always being there when I needed you. Thanks to my sister Jackie; my nephew, Christopher; and my niece, Jillian Rucker. In addition to my family, I have been blessed with wonderful friends, Sophia Muckerson and Shelitha Mckee, who are like family to me. You have listened, prayed, cried, supported, encouraged, and celebrated with me. Without your support (and the occasional kick in the pants), I would not have made it through all of the ups and downs and definitely wouldn't have seen this dream come to reality.

Chapter 1

North Harbor, Michigan

"Victor Carlston, don't you think it's wicked to sit here enjoying yourself while your dearest relative lies at death's door?"

"That's a good start," I said out loud, even though there was no one to hear. "Although, I don't know about Carlston. It doesn't sound British enough. Maybe Worthington? Weatherby? Or Parkington? I think I like Worthington." I rolled the name around in my head and scrolled back up to make the change, reading aloud as I made the edits.

"Victor Worthington, don't you think it's wicked to sit here enjoying yourself while your dearest relative lies at death's door?"

"Hmmm . . . I wonder if Worthington is too British. Maybe I should go with something simple, like Brown." I was about to try out yet another surname on my hero when the doorbell rang. My toy poodles, both moments earlier curled up sound asleep on an ottoman, barked and raced downstairs to greet our visitor.

I peeked over the stairs and saw my sister Jenna's reflection in the glass. I considered ignoring it and sneaking back into my office until my cell phone started vibrating in my pocket. My family and the Borg from *Star Trek* had a lot in common. Both demanded complete assimilation and resistance was definitely futile.

"Darn it."

My sister wouldn't leave me a moment of peace. It was just a matter of time before she tracked me down like a blood-hound.

I girded my loins, tramped down the stairs, and opened the door.

Like a blustery autumn wind, Jenna Rutherford blew through the doorway and marched up the stairs, talking a mile a minute.

"Have you talked to your mother?" She stopped at the top of the stairs, turning, and looked at me. "What's taking you so long? Do you have any tea?"

Resistance truly was futile. I closed and locked the door and went upstairs. She already sat at the breakfast bar, waiting for her tea. I stepped behind the bar, grabbed the kettle, and filled it with water from the sink.

"Hello, Jenna."

"Your mother. When is the last time you called her?"

It was always "*your mother*" when Mom was annoying.

"I talked to her this morning," I said slowly and deliber-ately. I knew where this conversation was going.

"Oh. Well, your mother called me all upset."

"Hmm." Little input was needed on my side of the con-versation. She was on a roll. I placed the kettle on the stove and took tea bags from the cabinet.

"Sam, it's been six months. You've got to snap out of this," she droned on.

This was an old song I'd heard before, but that day some-thing snapped.

"Six months. Is that the deadline?" Anger rose. "Leon and I were married for thirteen years. He was my best friend."

Perhaps Jenna sensed we were on dangerous ground when

my voice got softer and each word became more pronounced. Unlike most people who got louder as they got angrier, I tended to get softer and I enunciated each and every syllable.

"Is six months really the cutoff for mourning?" I took several deep breaths to regain my composure. "Jenna, I know you mean well. Everyone means well."

What neither my well-meaning sister, nor the rest of my family, understood was that mourning was actually comforting.

"The first month after Leon died, I don't think I felt anything. The shock was so painful, I was in a daze. Afterward there were so many things to do. Decisions had to be made. I didn't have time to think. I barely had time to breathe. I definitely didn't have time to grieve." I paced behind the counter while I talked.

Thankfully, Jenna sat and listened, something she rarely did where I was concerned.

"After the shock wore off, the pain started. It felt like a part of my body had been cut off. It's only now, six months later, that I feel like I can mourn. I have finally allowed myself to feel again and the heaviness, the grief is actually comforting."

The look on her face said she didn't understand.

"I know it sounds crazy, but it's like when your foot falls asleep. At first you can't feel anything, so, you keep shaking it to wake it up. Eventually, you get the prickly tingles right before your foot wakes up completely."

She stared, but at least she wasn't talking. I shouldn't be angry with her. None of it was her fault.

"Jenna, I'm fine," I said calmly.

Her skeptical expression was enough for me to backtrack.

"Okay. I'm not *fine*." I sighed. "But I will be."

She looked into my eyes as if the truth was there behind my irises. Who knew, maybe it was.

"Okay. But we care about you and we're all worried, especially *your* mother."

"I know, and I'm sorry. I don't want you or Mom to worry."

The kettle whistled and I poured the boiling water into the mugs and handed my sister the box of raw sugar she liked, which I kept in the cabinet especially for her.

"Anyway, what were you doing?" Jenna asked.

I perched on the stool next to her and sipped my tea.

"Writing," I said shyly. The fact that I was actually attempting to write a book was a deeply held secret I shared with very few people. Until recently, my sister and my husband were the only people I'd entrusted with my precious dream. Talking about it was still scary.

Leon and I were both huge mystery fans. We met in the mystery section at a chain bookstore. Leon liked hard-boiled, private detective stories and I was more of a British cozy person. Regardless of the types of mysteries, we both loved the genre. Even our dreams revolved around mysteries. I fantasized about becoming a successful mystery writer, while Leon dreamed about owning a bookstore that specialized in mysteries. We spent countless hours talking about our dreams—dreams that seemed light years away. Leon worked as a cook at a diner and I was an English teacher at the local high school. We worked hard but lived hand to mouth and paycheck to paycheck. We knew our dreams were just that—dreams.

By the time the doctors found the cancer that caused the pain Leon complained about for more months than I could count, it was too late. With only a few weeks before he died, he made me promise I would buy the brick brownstone we walked past weekly and talked about *"one day"* or *"when we hit the lottery"* how we would fix it up and have our bookstore. He made me promise I'd take the insurance money and buy the building and write my book.

I sold the three bedroom home we'd purchased and renovated over a decade ago. It held too many memories. Every room was a story about our life together. My family and friends tried to talk me out of making major changes. Maybe I'd regret selling the house one day, but Leon suggested it. He knew me so well. He knew I'd never be able to move forward as long as I continued living in the past.

"Earth to Sam."

I pulled myself off memory lane. "I'm sorry. What did you say?"

"I asked how the writing was going." Jenna took a scone from the tiered plate on the counter and inspected it.

I knew what she was looking for. "Don't worry. There aren't any raisins in that batch."

She spread clotted cream and strawberry preserves on her scone, took a bite, and moaned in delight.

"The book is coming along pretty well, but I'm just getting started. I have a long way to go. I have my main characters, Penelope and Daphne Marsh and Victor Carlston—or Worthington. I'm not sure which name I like best."

"I like Carlston," Jenna said with a mouth full of scone.

"I like it too. Maybe I'll keep it." I reached for my fourth scone of the day.

"And when is the grand opening?"

"Supposedly in two weeks."

"Why 'supposedly'?"

"I'm still waiting for the last set of bookshelves. I've got boxes and boxes of books that have to be inventoried and shelved and my new point-of-sale system isn't working yet. I also haven't gotten the final okay from the health department to open the tea shop."

"Well, the tea shop can wait. You don't have to do everything at once. You could get the bookstore opened first. Then once it's open and running, you can open the tea shop later."

My sister always adopted a condescending tone when she talked to me. It annoyed me. The fact that she was right made it even more annoying.

A couple of scones and two more cups of tea later, she left. I loved my sister, but spending time with her left me emotionally drained.

I wasn't exactly in the mood for more writing. I sat at my computer and reread what I'd written so far, hoping it would help me get back to a relaxed frame of mind.

❦

Wickfield Lodge, English country home
of Lord William Marsh—1938

"It seems wicked to sit here enjoying yourself while your dearest relative lies at death's door."

Victor Carlston might have taken Daphne's statement more seriously if he wasn't laughing uncontrollably. Lord William Marsh was the dearest relative, who was, according to Daphne, a breath away from death. Not a callous man, Victor didn't laugh at Lord William's ill health, which placed him at "death's door" once every three months. He always pulled through. His *illnesses* always followed a night of rich food and extensive enjoyment of the fruit of his vineyards. No, Victor laughed at Daphne's dramatic manner. She fussed and fidgeted as if she was about to go into hysterics. He'd read of a fellow who kissed a girl to stop her from hysterics. Maybe this was his opportunity.

Daphne was bewitchingly beautiful, and he'd barely had two seconds alone with her all night. That obnoxious American, Charles Parker, kept popping up.

The slippery Parker was confident, cocky, and overdressed in tails. Daphne didn't appear to mind.

Speak of the devil. Parker's "How about a dance, Daphne old girl," was more a statement than a question. Before she had a chance to reply, Parker pulled her to her feet and into his arms and spun her off to the dance floor set up in the parlor of Wickfield Lodge.

Damn it! He'd missed another opportunity, and there Daphne was, dancing and laughing as though whatever Parker whispered in her ear was the most hilarious thing she'd ever heard. Where was her concern for Lord William now? Victor sat in brooding silence and smoked.

"Perhaps if you weren't so obviously in love with her, she might take you more seriously." Victor hadn't noticed Penelope in the seat recently vacated by Daphne, until she spoke.

"Am I that obvious?"

"Even a blind monk could see you're in love with her."

Penelope held out a cigarette, which Victor lit. For a few seconds they smoked quietly until Penelope broke the silence.

"You know what your problem is, Victor?"

"No. Do tell."

"You make your love too easy. There's no challenge."

"Challenge?" Victor laughed. "You talk of love as though it was a game or a battle to be fought in war."

"It is a game and a battle. Haven't you heard?" Penelope leaned back and looked at Victor through lazy, dark eyes, with a smug smile.

He stretched his legs in front of the fireplace. "I was never good at playing games." The stretch felt good. He'd been sitting far too long and the knee he'd injured in the war was stiffening up.

"If you want Daphne, or any woman, for that matter, you'll have to learn to play the game."

"Perhaps you can enlighten me on the rules." He swallowed the lump that had developed in his throat when Daphne and Parker glided out of the room onto the terrace behind the parlor.

Wickfield Lodge, the ancestral home of Lord William Marsh, had a lovely back terrace with magnificent sweeping views of the rose garden, hedge maze, fountain, and the wooded copse below. At this late hour, none of the grounds were visible by moonlight. Obviously, Parker wasn't interested in admiring the foliage.

"Victor, you're tall, dark, and handsome. You're rich, which is always a plus, and you've got brains. That's more than I can say about most men your age."

He raised an eyebrow at the backhanded compliment and stood, performed a sweeping bow, and sat back down.

"Don't be an ass." Penelope spat the words.

"Given the qualities you mentioned, one would expect me to be the one out on the terrace with the beautiful Daphne, instead of sitting here with . . ." He stopped, but not quickly enough.

Penelope knew what he was going to say. He could tell by the way her eyes flashed and the flush that went up her neck. For a moment, he thought she'd cry, but Lady Penelope Marsh was made of sterner stuff.

A moment was all it took for her to regain her composure.

"I'm an ass! I'm terribly sorry. I didn't mean—"

Penelope held up her hand. "Yes, you did mean it, and it's okay. It's true. Everyone knows Daphne is the beautiful one in the family. Golden hair, blue eyes like sapphires, and skin like cream. She's a goddess. I'm not stupid. I know my sister got the beauty and I the brains. It's all right."

Victor tried again. "I'm really sorry, Penny."

"No need for apologies." Penny gazed at him. "I'm going to put my brains to good use. I've decided to help you."

Puzzled, it took a few moments to grasp what she'd said. Eventually he'd recovered enough to ask, "Help me? What are you going to do, drive a stake through Charles Parker's heart? That's the only thing that can help me." Victor tossed back his drink and brooded.

"I'm going to help you win Daphne's heart." Penelope accepted a drink from a nearby waiter.

"And how do you propose to do that? I gave my heart to Daphne a long time ago." He grabbed a drink from the waiter and took a sip. His desperation echoed in his ears. He winced.

"Exactly. No woman wants something that's given so easily. Daphne knows she has but to snap her fingers and you'll come running. You are the ever faithful, ever loyal, always to be relied upon, Victor Carlston."

Tossing his cigarette into the fireplace, he tried to hide his anger, but there was an edge in his voice. "You make me sound like a dog."

"Exactly my point. Why should Daphne waste her youth and beauty on someone who's always here? She can have you any time she wants. A woman wants a challenge."

Victor laughed.

"Why are you laughing?" Penelope perched on the edge of her seat like an eagle.

"You have such a way with words. You make love sound like a battle."

"It is a battle. What other challenges does a woman of Daphne's station, breeding, and class have? She can't go to war. She can't work. And there are only so many cushions a well-bred lady can stand to embroider."

Something in her tone made Victor wonder if there was more to Penelope Marsh than he'd seen before. He looked at her as a woman, and not simply Daphne's sister. "You sound like you've thought about this a lot."

"What else do I have to do but think? I have no talent for sewing cushions." Penelope's eyes flashed. Perhaps it was the firelight or her anger but, for an instant, mousy Penelope exuded a passion that transformed her dark eyes and complexion. In that moment, Victor Carlston made a decision that would forever change his life.

❦

"That's enough for one night." I closed my laptop. It was getting late, and I had a busy day coming up, the last day of school, for the children and for me. I would leave the stable security of a regular paycheck, insurance, a pension, and the union that had dictated my life for the past twelve years to embark on a new adventure.

Following your dreams sounded like an exciting journey, but for a widow in her mid-thirties, it was a bit scary. As a society, we were encouraged to work hard, invest for retirement, and make sound financial, practical decisions. Maybe it was my working class upbringing, or maybe it was the Midwestern work ethic. Whatever the reason, I found myself waxing nostalgic about the daily grind of teaching our nation's youth. On the wall hung the motto from Henry Ford that Leon liked to quote,

> *If You Always Do*
> *What You've Always Done,*
> *You Will Always Get*
> *What You've Always Got.*

I knew what I had to do. Change was scary, but if Leon's death taught me anything, it was that life was short, sometimes too short. Tomorrow wasn't promised. I needed to do this for Leon and for myself. I consoled myself with the knowledge I could teach nights at the community college if I truly needed money.

I'd been very frugal with both the insurance money and the money from selling the house. In our original plan, Leon and I envisioned converting the upstairs of the bookstore into living space, which we could rent out to help pay the mortgage. Near the end, when Leon thought I needed a clean start, the idea of my living in the space took shape. The upper level of the soon-to-be bookstore was a large, open loft with beautiful oak hardwood floors, brick walls with seventeen foot ceilings, and windows stretching from floor to ceiling. The renovated 2,000-square-foot space contained a nice kitchen area, living room, two bedrooms, and two bathrooms. Track lighting and skylights made the space bright and inviting. I enjoyed the space more than I imagined I would. My new home was just right for me. There was even a detached garage at the back of the lot, which I accessed through an alley. I'd had a fence installed and created a small courtyard perfect for my dogs, Snickers and Oreo.

I decided to turn in. I needed all of my mental and emotional strength to get through yet another change.

Chapter 2

I parked my Honda SUV in the staff parking lot of North Harbor High School. The message board outside the school not only proclaimed the prowess of the North Harbor Wildcats and congratulated the graduating class, but also wished me a fond farewell. It wasn't often you got to see your name in lights. So, I reached into my purse and grabbed my cell phone to take a picture of my name scrolling across the sign and a tissue to wipe away the tears I couldn't blink back. A quick look in the mirror showed the tear tracks were ruining my makeup, and my mascara was already gone. It was going to be a long and difficult day.

Inside, signs from grateful students covered the walls. GOOD-BYE, MRS. WASHINGTON—WE'LL MISS YOU. My favorite was PARTING MAY BE SWEET SORROW, BUT IT STILL BITES. There was a picture of our mascot, Willie the Wildcat, taking a bite off the bottom of the sign.

The principal was waiting for me when I walked through the door and walked me to the gymnasium. Streamers, balloons, and confetti decorated the large room and the bleachers were full with students, teachers, janitors, and secretaries. Even the cafeteria staff was there with their hairnets and smocks. Everyone stood and cheered as I entered. I got misty eyed thinking about my students. They were truly the best group of young people I'd had the pleasure of teaching. I'd miss the entire tattooed, pierced, and multicolor-haired bunch.

The day was filled with cupcakes, cookies, punch, and gifts. Tears were shed. I would treasure the store-bought and handmade cards, notes, and letters of thanks for years to come. The principal surprised me with a beautiful first edition Rex Stout. Leon would have drooled. At the end of the day, I needed two students to help me carry my things to the car.

I backed out of the parking lot and drove away from school. I cried like a baby.

Pulling into my alley, I noticed several cars in the small parking lot I shared with the church next door. Technically I owned the parking lot, but when I closed on the building, I learned about the *gentlemen's* agreement that had existed for close to thirty years. The previous owner permitted the church to use the lot for Sunday services, and the church paid half of the cost of plowing the snow from the lot for the winter. The agreement seemed more than fair to me. I would have allowed the church to use the lot for free, especially since I wouldn't be open on Sunday, not initially anyway. Later, if I decided to open on Sunday, it wouldn't be until after their service was over, so it seemed like a win-win to me.

Struggling to carry my boxes without my student helpers, I fumbled with the door. I finally managed to adjust the boxes, opened the door, and stepped from the garage into my backyard.

"SURPRISE!"

Startled, I dropped my purse and all of the boxes. The sound of breaking glass told me my favorite porcelain coffee mug was now history. Family and friends packed my yard.

Snickers and Oreo barked and pounced on me. A banner and streamers decorated the yard, and a large cake sat on the table.

"What're you all doing here?"

In answer, my family hugged me, kissed me, and wished me well.

My nephews Christopher and Zaq picked up my boxes and my purse and gave me a hug. I couldn't help but smile as I watched them. The boys are identical twins. As babies it was almost impossible to tell them apart. However, now at twenty, their differences were much more prominent, not only in their facial features and mannerisms, but also in dress. Christopher tended toward a look that I would describe as preppy while Zaq was much more edgy. Both were blessed to have inherited their father's height and metabolism. At well over six feet and slender, they were well-mannered, handsome, and intelligent. Of course I might be slightly biased.

I guided my mom and my grandmother to a table where we could sit and talk. Two more different women were hard to imagine. My mom, Grace Hamilton, was about five feet even and one hundred pounds sopping wet. Her eyes were light and her head full of fine, soft white hair like cotton candy. While Nana Jo, aka Josephine Thomas, was about five foot ten and two hundred-fifty pounds with young and flirtatious dark eyes and a head full of thick auburn hair. My nephews inherited the best of both worlds, getting their height from their dad and Nana Jo and their slim figures from my mom. I, at five four and closer to my nana in weight than I'd ever admit publicly, in-herited the worst traits of both. Short and pleasantly plump was how I described myself.

"Were you surprised?" Mom asked.

I kissed her check. "Definitely. How did you manage all of this?"

"I didn't know if we'd be able to do it, but Mama and

Jenna thought we could, so . . ." Mom waved her hand with the queenly flourish that drove my sister mad. With one twirl of her hands and a shrug of her shoulders, she implied my sister and grandmother merely brandished their magic wands and this party was the result.

"Well, thank you all so much. This has been an incredible day." I sat down at the picnic table laden with presents and delightful-smelling glass containers.

Near the back door, my brother-in-law, Tony, grilled burgers, chicken, and hot dogs on a portable grill. The delicious aromas wafted their way toward me, and my stomach responded with a loud growl. Everyone within earshot laughed.

Several hours later, the guests were gone and I was able to relax and enjoy the peace and serenity of my home. Most of the food went home with family, although I kept enough chicken to tide me over for a few meals. Pouring the last of the mango margaritas, I turned my television to the jazz music channel and walked downstairs to the bookstore.

I was preparing to live my dream, unfortunately, without Leon. I'd quit my job, sold my house, bought a building, and was about to open an old-fashioned bookstore during a time when electronic readers were more popular than old-fashioned books. Major bookstore chains were going bankrupt, yet there I was.

"I must be crazy," I said to Snickers and Oreo.

Oreo's adoring eyes assured me he'd love me even if I was a few nibbles short of a rawhide. Snickers simply sniffed. She'd known all along I was crazy, and it didn't matter to her as long as she continued to live in the manner to which she was accustomed.

We used to call this the Gargoyle building when I was a kid. The builder had placed several hideous-looking gargoyles around the top of the building on the inside ceiling. I was surprised to find more of them upstairs as well. I'd even found a couple in a box in the basement when I first moved in.

Two large bay windows, with display space, flanked the front door. I loved the thick brick walls, which the previous owner sandblasted to a lovely light shade of beige. The dark wood plank floors creaked. The lower level had the same high ceilings and exposed duct work I loved in the upper level. My realtor recommended an Amish craftsman whom he knew to build sturdy bookshelves. They weren't fancy, but they were solid and would hold the weight of the books still piled in boxes all over the room. The back of the store had a small kitchen. The area, the only one where Leon and I had disagreed, was still unfinished. Leon wanted a traditional coffee bar with espressos and lattes. I wanted a British tea shop.

Like many cozy mystery lovers, my introduction to mysteries was through British writers, like Agatha Christie. In books, my heroes and heroines had tea with scones and treacle tarts. It wasn't until my first trip to London, a thirtieth birthday present from Leon, that I learned a scone wasn't the dried-up things served at coffeehouses across the United States. I developed a love of clotted cream (a cross between whipped cream and butter) and discovered the correct way to pronounce treacle (tree-kell), which was basically molasses. High tea at Brown's Hotel or the Ritz Carlton in London was an event to be savored, and I wanted to bring the experience to mystery lovers in North Harbor, Michigan. I decided to try a compromise. I'd serve tea and scones, along with coffee, but no espressos or lattes—at least not yet anyway.

Beyond the coffee area, a door led into a hallway. Across the hall, another room would serve as an office. The office was small but had one redeeming feature, a glass garage door leading out to a small patio area. Initially I'd thought of making the office area the tea shop and having both indoor and outdoor seating, but the cost of moving the plumbing quickly changed my mind. Since I lived in the building, I liked the idea of a private courtyard for me and my dogs.

Surround sound speakers in the store meant I was able to hear music both upstairs and downstairs. My bookstore was almost perfect. If only Leon was here. . . . It was best to not travel that path. I'd end up crying and hugging Snickers who, despite her sassy attitude, was a bigger comfort than Oreo when I was sad. Leon wasn't there, but in what I hoped would be a matter of weeks, I would open my mystery bookstore. Standing in the back of the store, I wondered if anyone would come. Just as I decided I'd have to wait and see, a knock sounded at the front door.

I wasn't open for business. While Snickers and Oreo barked a lot and sounded quite formidable behind a solid door, two toy poodles were absolutely no protection. It was still fairly light outside, so I made my way to the front of the store, peeked around a bookshelf, and saw the one person I'd hoped never to see again, Clayton Parker.

I edged my way to the door, glared at him through the glass, and pointed to the CLOSED sign.

"I need to talk to you." Parker pulled at the door handle.

The thought of that man entering my store made my blood boil. I prided myself on being professional and always behaving in a ladylike manner, but I wasn't feeling very ladylike. I stuck out my tongue.

The blood rushed to Parker's face. He looked as though he might explode.

I was in control of my destiny. I had the keys and a ton of papers declaring the building belonged to me. I didn't have to talk to anyone I didn't want to, and I didn't have to allow the likes of Clayton Parker in my store. Clayton Parker could talk to my lawyer if he had anything further to say to me.

I walked, nay, strutted to the back of the store and up the

stairs, and left Parker seething outside. I went to bed and slept well without a second thought of Clayton Parker. I woke up refreshed and energetic.

Two staircases led to the upper level. On the parking lot on the side of the building, a door led to a back hallway. Visitors entering through that door would find two doors on each side of the hall. On the left, the first door opened to a small but functional bathroom. The second door on the left went to my office. The first door on the right led upstairs to my living space and the second door to the back of the store.

My morning routine typically involved getting up, showering, and dressing while listening to the news. Snickers wasn't a morning dog. Preferring to get eighteen to twenty hours of sleep per day, she stayed in her bed at the foot of my bed until I was dressed and ready to leave for the day, at which time she stretched and slowly made her way downstairs to take care of business. Oreo, on the other hand, was so concerned he might be left out of some important event, he jumped up every time I rolled over during the night. Like the energizer bunny, Oreo darted around the room with speed and zeal as if saying, *Is it time to get up? Huh? Time to get up?* His exuberance resulted in modified sleeping arrangements. While Snickers slept in a dog bed, free to come and go as she pleased, Oreo was crated at night. I tried to allow Oreo the freedom to live without the crate, but he preferred the safety of his crate, which was fine with Snickers and me.

After sleeping in, our norm on weekends, we completed our basic morning routine and headed downstairs. Snickers and Oreo ran to the office door and then the door to the enclosed backyard, where they could sniff and run free without leashes. Their goal was to find just the right blade of grass to leave their scent on and take care of business at their leisure.

As usual, they reached the door ahead of me. I wasn't surprised at their barking, although the growls were unusual.

Thinking a squirrel or a bird must have entered their domain, I opened the door cautiously. So far, they'd never caught any of the interlopers, but I didn't want to take a chance. One look outside told me the source of their angst wasn't animal.

Well, not technically.

In a heap on the grass near my patio lay the crumpled body of Clayton Parker.

Chapter 3

Amazing how a person could live in a town for almost half a century without interacting with local law enforcement.

Despite my love of mysteries, the closest I'd come to the police were the men and women who directed game day traffic near the football stadium at the local university. I wasn't sure what I expected. North Harbor bore no resemblance to New York or Los Angeles, with their densely populated skyscrapers and bumper to bumper traffic. Nor did North Harbor resemble the idyllic tranquility of the fictional Cabot Cove.

Located on the shores of Lake Michigan, North Harbor was a small town of less than fifteen thousand people. Whether due to urban decay or other social factors, the town had seen better days. North Harbor sat on a beautiful stretch of beach that drew tourists to the neighboring towns during the summer months. In the 1950s and 1960s, North Harbor thrived. Local plants, about a hundred miles up the road from the Motor City, produced parts for the then-booming auto industry and provided high-paying jobs. Victorian homes grandly looked down upon the smaller working-class towns, like South Harbor, located on the same Lake Michigan shoreline. The two cities are separated by the St. Thomas River, which winds through the cities and flows into Lake Michigan. When the lucrative manufacturing jobs either went south or sailed across our borders, North Harbor simply withered up and died. The death was slow and lingering. First, yards were left untended. Then homes, former majestic displays of wealth and opulence, were abandoned and boarded up. Those wealthy enough to leave, did. Those who stayed fell into two distinct categories. Those idealistic enough to believe that North Harbor could be turned around, the socially minded do-gooders who stayed to fight for good schools, commerce, and a better quality of life, and those too poor to leave. When Leon and I married, we vowed to stay in North Harbor and be a part of the change we believed would surely come.

In the police at my door, I saw the toll of economic decline and crime. The weariness and cynicism that kept these civil servants going from day to day was palpable.

They came in surprising numbers, for a town this small. Surely every police car the city owned was parked on the street in front of my building, blocking the busy Saturday morning traffic on Main Street. They came and they photographed. Through the window, I watched as they collected every blade of grass, every gum wrapper, and everything that might in any way resemble a clue. For about five seconds, I felt bad I hadn't scooped the dog poop or bothered to clean too vigorously after the party. The feeling vanished when one of the detectives smashed the impatiens I'd planted not two weeks before.

Holding out his hand, the policeman introduced himself. "Mrs. Washington, I'm Detective Brad Pitt," he said in between chomps on his chewing gum.

Detective Brad Pitt was absolutely nothing like the famous actor of the same name. Detective Pitt was short, fat, and balding. He wore polyester pants about an inch too short, a too-tight polyester shirt, and aftershave that was too strong.

Unable to stop myself, I grinned, thinking how totally opposite two people could be.

Detective Pitt raised his hand in the rude *talk to the hand* gesture popular with my high school students about five years back. "Spare me the jokes. No. I don't know Angelina Jolie or Jennifer Anniston." He flipped through his notebook without making eye contact.

I believed he'd asked a question, but I was so angry I didn't hear. It might have been his rudeness that rubbed me the wrong way. Maybe it was the way he spoke to me while chewing gum like a cow with a cud. Or, maybe it was my lack of coffee or the memory of him trampling my flowers. Whatever the reason, the teacher in me rose to the surface. I threw back my shoulders, straightened my back, and lifted my head. Looking down my nose at Detective Pitt, I gave him the glare that never failed to produce silence in the classroom and held out my hand. I waited. Silence could be a powerful weapon.

Detective Pitt deposited his gum in my hand.

He mumbled an apology.

I dropped the gum in the trash, walked over to the desk, and indicated he should sit. When he did, I took my seat behind the desk.

"Now, I believe you wanted to ask me some questions?" I didn't spend over a decade teaching rambunctious, unruly teens, as well as some of the brightest and most caring kids in the nation, to be disrespected by a man whose salary was coming out of my tax dollars, especially in my home.

"Can you tell me what happened?" Detective Pitt asked.

"Well, I don't really know. It must have happened last night when I was asleep."

"Did you know Mr. Parker well?"

There was the question I dreaded.

"No." I paused. "Not well. We met a few months ago when I purchased this building. He was the listing agent."

Detective Pitt scribbled in his notebook. I thought the note taking was purely for show since I'd repeated the same thing I told the last two officers, who asked the same question. . . .

"Were you expecting Mr. Parker last night? I understand you had a party. Was he one of the guests?"

"No!"

Detective Pitt raised an eyebrow. My response might have been too emphatic.

"Look. Clayton Parker and I weren't friends. Neither do I believe we were enemies. He listed this building for sale and I bought it. In my opinion he was a spoiled, pampered, arrogant, self-centered bigot."

"Sounds like you two must have gotten pretty close for you to have formed such a strong opinion."

"I learned about his true personality after my offer was accepted. At first all was well. But, as we got closer to the closing, he changed. He claimed he had another buyer with a higher offer."

"How is that possible? I thought the sellers were under contract with you?"

"Exactly. But to Parker, the fact the sellers were already under contract with me didn't seem to matter. He claimed his buyer was simply submitting a backup offer in the event my deal fell through. Apparently there is nothing illegal about that. However, the shady part came later. Parker then did everything in his power to sabotage my ability to close on the property, including sending e-mails to my banker questioning my ability to afford the mortgage. He even tried to prevent the inspector from completing the building inspection, which was the final condition on the loan."

"What did you do?"

"I got fed up with all of the delays and the double-talk. I ended up hiring an attorney who forced the sellers to meet their contractual obligations, and I was eventually able to close."

"That must have made you angry." Detective Pitt leaned forward, as though he were about to pounce. It dawned on me he actually thought I murdered Clayton Parker.

"Hold on. I'll admit the entire experience left me angry and bitter. But, I didn't kill him."

Detective Pitt wrote in his notebook, but he looked as though he wasn't buying my explanation.

"Look. Clayton Parker lacked integrity. But ultimately, I won. I closed on the building. I've moved in and that is that. I didn't kill him."

Detective Pitt flipped through his notes and scribbled. "You told Officer Klein Mr. Parker showed up at your door last night. Why?"

I was sorely tempted to ask if he meant, "why did I *tell* Officer Klein that Mr. Parker showed up at my door? Or why *did* Mr. Parker show up at my door?" I didn't think I should antagonize the police too much.

"I have no idea."

"Well, what did he say?" Detective Pitt asked as if he was speaking to someone who was a bit daft.

I was losing patience. "As you know from my statement, I never opened the door. It was late. I was tired, and I didn't want to talk to Clayton Parker. So, I pointed to the sign, indicating I was closed, and walked away."

"Just like that?"

"Just like that!"

"Was Mr. Parker distressed?"

"What do you mean distressed?" This was getting redundant. He asked questions and I responded with the same question but different emphasis.

"Well, was he asking for help? Did he seem afraid in any

way? Did he behave in a way that might indicate he was being pursued or in danger? Was he looking for help?"

His questions humbled me. Was it possible Clayton Parker came to my door in search of aid? And I, who professed to be a Christian, turned my back on him? Was there a chance I could have saved his life if I'd opened the door? The thought crashed down on me like a load of bricks and settled in my stomach. Add the image of Clayton Parker's bloody corpse to the equation and the result was a mad dash to the bathroom. I barely made it to the porcelain throne in time. I hadn't eaten, but the dry heaves felt worse than if I had. When I finished, I cleaned myself up. Although I still looked a little green, I re-joined Detective Pitt in my office.

"Are you okay now?" Score one for Detective Pitt.

I nodded and returned to my seat. In that moment, I made the decision to do anything and everything I could to find the person who left Clayton Parker to die on my patio. I knew nothing would bring him back, but perhaps, in some small way, I could make amends.

"Okay, Detective Pitt. I'm ready to answer your questions now."

Chapter 4

I moved in with my mother in the tiny villa she moved to after my father's death. As the saying goes, *after three days fish and company both begin to stink.* My mother was exceptionally kind and accommodating, but two toy poodles, two grown women, and eight hundred square feet would be a bad combination under the best of circumstances. It was worse in my case.

After four hours in my mother's presence, I transformed. The change was subtle. I rarely saw it coming until it was too late. At some point, I ceased to be the confident, intelligent, independent woman who could quail a classroom of disorderly youth with a single glare. I turned into the awkward, unsure, immature teenager who locked herself in the bathroom and cried because neither life nor her parents were *fair.*

After three days, it was time to go.

"There is no homicidal maniac lurking in the alley just waiting to stab me as he or she did Clayton Parker." I repeated my mantra over and over as I drove over the bridge from my mother's South Harbor villa to North Harbor, where I belonged. For the first time, I found myself wishing I had bigger dogs, like pit bulls or German Shepherds, rather than the cute but totally ineffective for protection poodles I lived with. If attacked, the best I could hope for was Oreo's incessant barking would give me fair warning, and the killer would stumble over Snickers as she lay at his feet on her back, waiting to have her belly scratched.

My first few hours home, I jumped at every noise, every car horn, and every voice I heard on the street. Strange how acute your hearing became when you were waiting to be murdered. My nervous energy made Snickers and Oreo even more skittish than normal.

"This is crazy," I said, glad to hear my voice break the silence. "I can't live like this." Out loud, the words sounded solid and rang true.

"I need a distraction."

I made a cup of Earl Grey tea, turned on the jazz station, and decided to lose myself in the English countryside.

<hr>

Wickfield Lodge, England—1938

"You have got to be kidding!" Victor's face reflected the utter incredulity of his words. "That's it? That's your grand scheme?"

Penelope's neck colored. Her eyes flashed.

"Forget it." She spat the words and rose to her feet, knocking over the table and Victor's drink. She stomped out of the room.

Victor ran to catch her and barely missed knocking over a waiter on his way to clean up the mess she'd created.

He caught up to her on the terrace and grabbed

her arm. "Look, Penny, I'm really sorry. I didn't mean it as an insult."

Penelope turned away, but not before a tear made its way down her cheek.

"Go away! You want her. Good luck!"

"Penny, I just meant, that, well, I was expecting something a bit more . . . well, a bit more complicated. That's all. I didn't mean any disrespect to you." He handed her a handkerchief.

She flung it back at him.

Penelope faced the stone wall of the house and refused to turn around. She shivered, but he wasn't sure whether from anger or the cool summer evening. He draped his jacket over her shoulders. She didn't toss it to the ground. That was a good sign.

Even as a child, Penelope had a short fuse, but she was also the last person to hold a grudge. Her temper ignited, and then extinguished as rapidly as it started. Daphne, on the other hand, was slow to anger, but once she was angry, she remained so. As children, Victor made a comment about Daphne that angered her enough she refused to talk to him for a full six months. It was the quality he liked least in her, but she was so incredibly beautiful, one small flaw was easy to overlook.

"Look, Penny. I just don't see how your plan can work. I mean—"

"But that's the beauty of my plan. It's so simple."

"How are we going to make Daphne jealous? Honestly, I doubt she cares enough about me for that," he said.

"Oh, she cares. Trust me. But, she's never had to wonder what life would be like without you. You've always been there, steady, reliable, and ready to marry her whenever she snapped her pretty little fingers." Penelope's voice held a slight edge. "If she thought you weren't going to be here, at least not for her, if she thought there was a chance that you could love someone else, especially if that someone else was me . . ."

Daphne and Penelope had a fierce sisterly rivalry. Penelope excelled with books and sports, while Daphne was the most beautiful debutante of the season and more popular, especially with the boys.

"Besides . . ." Penelope pointed.

Victor followed the direction of her finger to the rose garden. Charles Parker and Daphne stood under the moonlight, engaged in a passionate embrace.

"—what have you got to lose?"

At the sight of his beloved in the arms of another man, Victor swallowed hard. "Okay. How do we go about this?" His voice faltered.

For the remainder of the night, Penelope and Victor danced only with each other. Victor was Penelope's ever-present, ever-attentive companion. They were inseparable. The hardest part was trying not to notice Daphne. He had his doubts the strategy would work until he prepared to take his leave.

At the door, Daphne approached him, her beautiful lips in a pout. The expression made her look young and irresistible. Victor's stomach did a somersault.

"You certainly have been inattentive tonight. You barely spoke to me all evening," she whined.

His heart fluttered. Could he go through with the plan? Penelope had warned him to not capitulate too early.

With all the strength he could muster, he shrugged

and laughed. "Well, I know when I'm beat. Far be it for me to stand in the way of true love. I guess it's time for me to move on. You two make a rather good match."

At the look in her eyes, his knees almost buckled. Had Penelope not joined them at that moment, he would have given in.

"You were about to leave without your hat." Penelope pulled his hat from behind her back and put it on his head at a rakish angle. She beamed, bright and confident.

"Perhaps I was hoping for an excuse to come back," Victor said.

Daphne's gaze was fierce. If looks could kill, both Penelope and Victor would have dropped dead on the spot.

"You don't need an excuse. You're always welcome," Penelope spoke softly and stared into Victor's eyes.

Heat rushed to his face. Here he was, a grown man of nearly thirty blushing like a schoolgirl.

Daphne stamped her foot.

"You'd better go," Penelope whispered into his ear and gave him a quick hug.

"Good night, ladies." Victor tipped his hat and walked off. He thought long and hard about the look in Daphne's eyes and concluded he hadn't been mistaken.

"This plan might just work," he muttered to himself. With a smile and a whistle, he strode to his car.

All week Victor made daily visits to Wickfield Lodge, the estate of Lord William Marsh, the 8th Duke of Hunsford, and home to Daphne and Penelope.

Lord William was the firstborn son and therefore

inherited the title and the land of the estate. Daphne and Penelope's father was Peregrine Marsh, his younger brother. Daphne took after her fair-haired and dashing, spoiled and accustomed to having his way, but friendly and likeable father. Penelope resembled her dark-haired and dark-eyed mother, Lady Henrietta Pringle. Their union was a happy one, albeit rather short. Not long after Daphne's birth, both were killed in an automobile accident.

Victor's home was about three miles down the road from Wickfield Lodge, where he found an excuse to visit nearly every day. Not unusual, considering he often visited when he was home on leave from the military. For the past year, he was stationed in West Africa. He took a bullet in the leg and required several surgeries but was on the mend. Now that the empire was enjoying a moment of peace, Victor was thankful to be home with only a slight limp and a few nightmares.

He'd spent so much of his life chasing Daphne he was practically a permanent fixture at Wickfield Lodge. The unusual part was he now spent his time with Penelope, rather than fawning over Daphne. He poured all of his attention onto Penelope. Charles Parker was there to adore and worship Daphne. Strangely enough, Victor caught Daphne glancing at him much more than she had in the past. She seemed much less enamored of Parker and much less inclined to laugh at his jokes. She was also short-tempered and pouted and complained a great deal more than he remembered.

He enjoyed his time with Penelope more than he imagined he would. She was intelligent and well read, not normally traits a gentleman expected a woman to possess, but quite refreshing nonetheless. He found her conversation stimulating. She was a good sport and listened. She enjoyed riding and didn't care if the bottom of her frock got muddied or her hair mussed. She was kind, thoughtful, and pleasant. Victor found the time they spent together pleasant. Perhaps if things had been different, but no, it was only a game, and a game that he might stand a chance of winning. Daphne was showing distinct signs of jealousy.

Penelope and Victor sat together in the parlor after dinner. Victor leaned in close and whispered, "Why is Daphne in such a foul mood?"

"Some tragedy about her maid's inability to style her hair in a way she'd seen in a Hollywood magazine."

Daphne was curt, petulant, and sulky. Parker tried to please her. He was attentive and eager to fulfill her every whim. He threw out compliments at the speed of a train. Nothing helped. Daphne was determined to be unhappy. Penelope and Victor ignored her and enjoyed a game of cards, which Daphne declined to join.

"You will be here tomorrow evening?" Penelope peeked sideways to make sure their conversation wasn't overheard.

"Of course. I wouldn't miss it for the world."

"I've been thinking. I think it's time for something big." She absentmindedly placed cards on the table.

"What do you have in mind?" He made sure Daphne and Parker were still out of earshot.

"Well, I think an announcement is in order." Penelope blushed.

Even though they had discussed it, he was a bit surprised she was still willing to go through with that particular part of the plan. "Are you sure? Won't that be a . . . well, won't it be awkward for you?" Victor knew it was old-fashioned, but he worried that breaking an engagement would make him appear a cad and Penelope rather pathetic.

"You're worried about me? Well, don't be. We're in this together, and if we're going to do this, then we need to do it properly."

Penelope had a unique ability to read his mind. "What do you mean?"

"You must put your heart into it. No wearing the mask of the wounded lover. We must be convincing. Daphne may not be an Oxford scholar, but neither is she a fool. She'll see right through you unless you're careful. You'll need to guard yourself."

"Don't worry about me. If you're able to keep up the charade, then I am too."

The night of the ball was especially beautiful. The weather was cool but pleasant. The drawing room at Wickfield Lodge was brilliantly lit and exquisitely decorated. Lady Elizabeth, Lord William's wife, had excellent taste and threw wonderful parties. The orchestra played lively tunes from the Jack Hylton band and other American jazz favorites and drew people to the dance floor.

Daphne was a goddess in a soft white gown that flowed like gossamer. Penelope wore a gown of rich red that contrasted with her skin and hair. Normally, Daphne was the center of attention, and men swarmed around her like moths to a flame. That night, things were different. Daphne was beautiful, like a marble statue, cold and distant. Penelope looked like a Gauguin painting, fiery, vivacious, and alive.

Victor wasn't the only one who noticed. Men who

normally barely noticed Penelope surrounded her, but it was Victor's night. He nudged his way through the crowd and took hold of her. He held her close, twirled her around the room, and staked his claim.

"Beautifully done." She laughed.

"Thank you, m'lady."

Penny and Victor floated across the dance floor.

"Daphne looks beautiful, don't you think?" Penelope studied Victor's face.

"I never noticed."

Penelope laughed. "Well, I think we made an impression. Just about everyone is staring at us." Penelope looked around the room. "Everyone except the cellist. He can't seem to take his eyes off of Daphne."

Victor swirled Penelope around so he could look at the cellist. "Fellow is a fool."

The flush that rose into her face heightened her cheeks and added sparkle to her eyes.

Victor looked into her eyes and gasped. He pulled Penelope closer and they danced until perspiration beaded both of their foreheads.

They spotted Charles Parker heading toward the terrace. Daphne followed not long afterward.

"I think they managed to beat us outside." Victor nodded toward Daphne.

"Well, it's rather warm in here. Perhaps we should go and get some air too. Besides, this is where you propose."

The aroma of jasmine and roses wafted from the gardens, and the air on the terrace was cool and sweet. Penelope left to powder her nose, and Victor enjoyed a smoke in the moonlight.

A woman screamed.

Victor froze, trying to get his bearings and determine where the sound originated. It sounded like Daphne. He squinted through the darkness. A white form emerged from the hedge maze. In the glow from the moon, it appeared to be a ghost. Hesitating only a moment, he ran down the terrace stairs toward the maze. The bright moonlight allowed him to quickly make his way to the edge of the maze.

"What happened? Are you hurt?"

Her response was merely a whimper before her legs gave out. Victor scooped her into his arms and carried her to the house and through the doors to the study. Thankfully, the room was empty. He gently placed her on the sofa in front of the fireplace and rang for the butler. Thompkins, prim and proper, appeared promptly.

"There's been an accident. Get Lady Penelope and Lady Elizabeth," Victor ordered. "And bring some towels."

Thompkins retreated to carry out his commands.

At the sideboard, Victor grabbed a glass and filled it with brandy. He held Daphne's head and put the glass to her lips.

Penelope appeared. One look at Daphne, and the color drained from her face. She staggered.

For a moment, Victor was afraid she was going to faint. "Come on, old girl. I can't do this alone. I need you."

Penelope steadied herself and rushed to the sofa. "What happened?" She carefully checked Daphne for wounds.

"I have no bloody idea. I was out on the south terrace smoking and heard a scream. I looked down and Daphne staggered out of the maze. I ran to her, and she collapsed in my arms. I picked her up and brought her here."

"She doesn't appear to be injured," Penelope said.

"Then whose blood?" He motioned toward her blood-soaked dress.

She shook her head.

Lady Elizabeth arrived and kicked Victor out of the room so she and Penelope could perform a more thorough examination.

Unable to block the sight of Daphne's pale form illuminated by moonlight and covered in blood from his mind, he needed to find the answer to the question he asked in the study.

In whose blood was Daphne covered?

Chapter 5

"Hmmm . . . Whose blood is it? I'll have to figure that out later."

Snickers and Oreo barely looked up when I mumbled. They napped on the nearby chair until a knock at the door sent them both into a barking frenzy.

Peeking over the open banister, I saw Nana Jo and her latest beau and ran down to open the door.

Nana Jo reminded me of all the characters from the television sitcom *The Golden Girls* rolled into one. She looked the most like Dorothy, the tall character played by Bea Arthur. She flirted like Blanche, played by Rue McClanahan, and had the sharp wit and an even sharper tongue than Sophia, played by Estelle Getty. Her background was most like that of Betty White's character. Like Rose, Nana Jo was born and raised on a farm in Minnesota. I used to wonder if the writers had met my nana.

"What on earth brings you out on a night like this?" I kissed my grandma and noted her latest hunk carried a suitcase. "Don't tell me you're running away."

Nana Jo was a quick-witted, wisecracking woman who

liked to have fun and didn't take crap from anyone. "I'm moving in. Your mama said men were dropping dead in your backyard, so I figured I'd better come and grab a few before all the good ones were gone." Nana Jo laughed so hard she had to wipe tears from her eyes.

Momentarily shocked, I gasped but couldn't help laughing too.

It wasn't funny. It wasn't right to laugh at the death of a human being, but it was the first time I'd laughed in days. Besides, I wasn't sure I'd have classified Clayton Parker as human three days ago. I might be committed to helping our pathetic police force catch a murderer, but there was no point in turning a sinner into a saint simply because he was dead.

Nana Jo's friend deposited her case in my guest room and politely made his exit.

"Seriously, why are you here?" I inquired as politely as I could once we were upstairs and seated on the sofa.

"You'd think it was a crime for a woman to visit her favorite granddaughter." Nana Jo laughed.

When I was with Nana Jo, I was her favorite granddaughter. When my sister was with her, Jenna was the favorite granddaughter.

"It's not a crime. I'm just a little suspicious of your motives." Taking both of her hands in mine, I looked in her eyes. "I am happy to see you, but why are you here, really?"

"I'm here to catch a murderer, of course. I know my granddaughter, and the North Harbor police are idiots. I figure it's just a matter of time before you go sleuthing. So, here I am."

"What do you mean?"

"You can't honestly expect to figure this thing out on your own? Everyone needs help. Sherlock Holmes had Watson. Hercule Poirot had Captain Hastings. Nero Wolfe had Archie Goodwin. And you, my dear, have got me!" She patted my knee. "Besides, you might need some protection," she said with a straight face.

I wasn't surprised my grandmother knew the great literary detectives. She was a huge mystery fan. In fact, she was the one who started me on my love affair with mysteries. She bought me my first mystery, an Encyclopedia Brown book. I devoured it. No, my grandmother knew her mysteries, all right. What amazed me was that she was even contemplating the two of us as real-life sleuths.

It was absurd. I struggled to formulate my response. "But, Nana Jo . . . I mean, how?"

"I don't know what you're planning to do, but I know you can't and *shouldn't* do anything on your own. There are crazy people out there. With two of us, we should be able to put the pieces together and figure this thing out."

I was touched my eighty-something grandmother was looking out for me. At least, I was touched until she reached into her purse.

"Plus, I'm the one that's packing heat." She pulled out a gun.

I nearly choked. I wasn't a big proponent of guns and my grandmother was waving one around in my living room. I didn't even know she owned a gun.

"Nana Jo, you put that thing away! Where on earth did you get it?"

"I've had it for years. Your grandpa bought it for me." She looked at the gun lovingly.

"Do you even know how to shoot it?"

She looked at me as if I'd suddenly grown a second head. "Well, of course, I know how to shoot it. I grew up on a farm, didn't I? I've been shooting since I was ten. I used to be pretty good too." Nana Jo aimed the gun at a picture on my wall, cocked her head to the side, closed one eye, and looked down the barrel. "I won the Junior Annie Oakley Competition three years in a row and Best Shot for Lauderdale County, Female Division, my senior year of high school." She must have noticed my shock and, I must admit, awe.

"Didn't I ever tell you?"

"Ah, no. You must have skipped that part."

"Well, one day when you come to the house, I'll show you my trophies. I've still got most of them. Used to keep 'em in the display cabinet, but I got tired of dusting. They're in a box in the attic now. I thought you knew." She put the gun back in her purse.

"I don't think you're going to need that." I couldn't take my eyes off her handbag. How long had she been carrying that thing around?

Geez, live your whole life and you think you know someone, and then they come to your house wielding a gun and you realize you don't really know them at all.

"I hope we won't need it. But, better safe than sorry is my motto."

"Right. Well, I'm not planning to go out and get myself killed. I just want to do some research. I thought I'd find out about Clayton Parker. Hopefully, I can do most of it on the Internet and won't even have to leave home." I wanted to convince my nana sleuthing wouldn't be the exciting adventure she was looking for.

"Good. I already Googled him and have some of the girls at the village working on his real estate company."

"The village" was the retirement village my grandmother moved to after Gramps died. Unlike my mom's villa, my grandmother moved into a retirement community that offered hiking, martial arts, Zumba, and waterskiing. Yes, waterskiing. Those seniors were certainly nothing like Miss Marple, who gardened and knitted sweaters. I didn't think my grandmother knitted, but she took Aikido.

"Really? What did they find?" I was intrigued, in spite of myself.

She reached into her bag again. The muscles in my stomach tensed until she pulled out an iPad.

"You have an iPad?" I tried really hard to keep the envy out of my voice.

"Sure do. I bought it a few months ago, and I have to say, I really like this thing. It's fantastic. You don't have one?" She sounded surprised. "I thought everybody had one."

I tried not to drool. I wanted one but couldn't justify the expenditure. "No. *Everyone* does *not* have one." I didn't even try not to snipe, but Nana Jo didn't seem to be listening.

"Well." She absentmindedly looked at her iPad and swiped through pages of information. She stopped swiping and adjusted her glasses. "Irma found some interesting stuff. It seems Clayton Parker had his own real estate company until he sold it rather suddenly a few months ago."

"What? You mean he doesn't own Parker & Parker Real Estate?" When I bought my building, I thought Clayton Parker owned the real estate company. He acted like he owned the place. But then, Clayton Parker acted like he owned the world. "Was she able to find out why he sold?" I was intrigued that Irma had found the information already.

"He used to own Clayton Parker Real Estate, but he sold it and went in with his dad's company, Parker & Parker. One of Irma's great-grandsons is a realtor. She sent him an e-mail and asked him to come by on Sunday. She'll pump him for information then."

"Really? That's great." I was genuinely amazed.

"And Ruby Mae has a daughter who used to clean house for Robert Parker."

"Robert Parker?"

"Robert was his dad. He started Parker Realty about forty

years ago. His brother George joined the company a few years later. That's when it became Parker & Parker. Robert owned the majority of the company. George handled the books. He's an accountant." Nana Jo scrolled through her notes, and I looked over her shoulder.

"Are they still with the company?" I asked.

"Robert died a couple of months ago. I think George's still there."

"What else have the girls found out?" No skepticism in my voice that time.

"Well, Dorothy has a son who works at the country club and a nephew who works at the yacht club. She's going to a wedding on Saturday. She should have some information for us by Sunday or Monday, at the latest." Nana reached the end of her notes.

"Wow. You guys are fast."

"Honey, at our age, you have to be, and Freddie, the hunk who just dropped me off, has a son who works for the state police. He's going to get him to pull the police report so we can find out what that nincompoop detective has done so far. He said it may take a couple more days, but he should be able to get it."

"That's amazing. I was just planning to go to the library and look through old newspaper articles and surf the Internet for anything I could find." Reluctantly, I had to admit Nana Jo and her girls might come in handy after all.

"So, we're a team?" Nana Jo's smile lit up her whole face.

"We're a team."

We shook on it for good measure.

"Great. Now, let's go across the street to Murray's Ice Cream Shoppe, get some ice cream, and get to work." Nana Jo grabbed her purse and headed downstairs.

I grabbed my wallet and keys from the counter, along with

leashes for Snickers and Oreo, who raced after Nana Jo when they heard the magic word—*ice cream*.

"Get a move on girl—we've got a murderer to catch," Nana Jo yelled.

I headed down the stairs.

Chapter 6

The next few days were busy. Andrew, the Amish craftsman building the bookshelves, dropped off the last set. He wore the traditional black and white clothes of the Amish. His face, the part that wasn't covered by hair, looked like that of a sixteen-year-old with skin as soft as a baby's. Were it not for the long dark beard, you might mistake him for an adolescent.

Northern Indiana, less than an hour's drive from North Harbor, had quite a few Amish. The community coexisted peaceably with the modern society of rural Indiana and Southwestern Michigan. Passing a horse and buggy on the road or parked at a shop right next to a car or motorcycle wasn't uncommon. Amish men, known for exceptional craftsmanship and woodworking, were highly sought after for building projects. Amish women were sought out for their excellent baked goods and quilts.

The bookshelves Andrew built weren't fancy, but they were sturdy and beautiful in their simplicity. The shop smelled of freshly cut wood and wax, and I couldn't wait to load the shelves with books.

I hired my two nephews, off from college for the summer, to help. They shelved books, swept, and cleaned. They got my new computer and point-of-sale system up and running. Between the two of them, they scanned and sorted all of the books within days. The actual shelving took a little more time. I was still unsure of how to organize the shelves. I toyed with the idea of sorting the books into subgenres, like British Cozy or Police Procedural. Ultimately, alphabetical order won out and, within three days, we had most of the books shelved. It actually began to look like a real bookstore, and I was both excited and nervous to open the doors to the public.

Nana Jo, surprisingly, was quite helpful in organizing and shelving the books. Despite her age, she was active and energetic. I struggled to keep up with her. I would have been embarrassed that, at more than half of her age, I was so out of shape, if not for the fact my twenty-year-old nephews, Christopher and Zaq, also struggled to keep up with her.

It was Saturday before I had time to think about Clayton Parker again, and then only because Detective Pitt came by the store to ask more questions.

Nana Jo, a retired teacher, remembered Detective Pitt. As a child, he was called Stinky.

I wished I had a camera to record the look on Detective Pitt's face when he swaggered into the store, opened his mouth to speak, and was halted at the sound of Nana Jo yelling, "Well, bless my soul if it isn't Stinky Pitt."

I ducked behind a bookshelf to keep from laughing in his face. Christopher and Zaq weren't as quick. Zaq laughed so hard tears streamed down his face. Christopher tried to stop laughing but couldn't.

"Mrs. Thomas! What are you doing here?" Detective Pitt sputtered.

Nana Jo came around the corner and stood in front of him with her hands on her hips. "Working. This is my granddaughter's bookstore, Stinky. What are you doing here?"

"I'm investigating the murder that took place here," Detective Pitt said with as much dignity as he could muster.

"Well, Sam, you never told me Stinky Pitt was the detective investigating this murder." Nana Jo turned her back to Detective Pitt and winked at me.

"I'm sorry. I didn't know you two knew each other," I managed to squeak as I peeked around the side of the bookshelf where I had retreated.

"Well, few people call me that name anymore, Mrs. Thomas. I'm Detective Pitt now, ma'am." He stood straighter.

Nana Jo was a much better actor than I gave her credit for. She smiled innocently. "Really? Well, that's nice. But you'll have to forgive an old woman. After almost thirty years, it may take some time for me to stop thinking about you as little Stinky Pitt."

The color rose in Detective Pitt's face.

"May I help you, Detective?" I tried to alleviate a little of his discomfort.

"Ah . . . yes. I was hoping you could answer a few more questions." Whether it was fear of his old math teacher or fear we would spread his childhood nickname around the police force, whatever the reason, Detective Pitt was much kinder to me this time around.

We retreated to the office, and Detective Pitt stepped over the boxes still piled everywhere and sat in the guest chair.

"I was just wondering if you remembered anything that might assist us in our investigation."

"No. I really haven't, Detective."

"You weren't perhaps planning to meet Mr. Parker here to discuss anything?"

I was puzzled. "No. I definitely wasn't planning to meet Mr. Parker here or anywhere else. We weren't exactly friends. But, you know that already. Why do you ask?"

Detective Pitt pulled a note in a plastic bag from his coat pocket and handed it to me.

The note was written on a napkin. The writing was simple, block print, rather than cursive.

MIDNIGHT AT GARGOYLE BUILDING

I shook my head and handed the note back. "Sorry, but I haven't seen that before. You think he planned to meet someone here at my shop?"

"That's the way it looks." Detective Pitt returned the bag to his pocket.

"That means this wasn't an accident, doesn't it? No chance it was a mugging gone terribly wrong or a robbery. Someone planned to kill him."

"That's certainly the way it looks."

"Who was he planning to meet?"

"I was hoping you could tell me." Detective Pitt stared at me.

"Me? I have no idea."

But, it sure did leave me a lot to think about. Who could possibly have come to my shop to murder Clayton Parker? The plot was definitely thickening.

Chapter 7

Victor grabbed a torch from the closet and headed out to the hedge maze. He had no idea what he expected to find but needed to be careful not to disturb anything important.

The moon shone exceptionally bright. He grew up playing in the maze and knew his way by heart. It didn't take long to reach the center. Just beyond two marble statues stood a fountain big enough to swim in, which he had as a child. Near the fountain was a bench.

In front of the bench lay Charles Parker.

If the large knife next to the body and the amount of blood on his clothing were any indication, Parker was dead.

Victor thought he hated Charles Parker, but seeing the man lying on the ground changed his attitude. He might have disliked Parker, his sense of humor, his cocky self-assured manner, and especially the way he walked in and swept Daphne off her feet, but whoever did this must have really hated Charles Parker.

"I can't leave him like this, but the police need to

be called. Maybe Thompkins . . ." Victor stared at Parker, unsure of his next step.

The orchestra played softly in the distance. Crickets, bullfrogs, and owls croaked, hooted, and chirped with the music. The spot was perfect for a romantic liaison. Had Parker planned to meet Daphne at the center of the maze? Was that how she'd come to find him? How had she gotten so much blood on her dress? Surely she wouldn't . . . couldn't have.

Rapid footsteps on the gravel path heralded someone who knew where they were headed. Victor blocked the sight of Parker's body, and Penelope made the last turn into the center of the maze.

"Did you find out—Oh, no!" Penelope looked past Victor to the body on the ground. She swayed, and Victor grabbed her to keep her from falling.

"Steady on, old girl! Don't fall apart on me now," Victor whispered. He held her closely, noting how nice she smelled.

Penelope stopped shaking and pulled away. "I guess there's no question about him being dead?" Her voice trembled, but only slightly.

"Afraid not."

"But how? Who?"

"I have no idea, but someone needs to go inside and call the police. Can you manage?"

"Victor, not the police. That's . . . ghastly." She paled.

"I'm sorry, but it has to be done."

She shuddered. "Shouldn't we move him? I mean, it seems indecent to leave him here like this."

"No. We can't move him until the police arrive."

Penelope seemed to gain strength from Victor's calm, matter-of-fact attitude. She stood straight. "All right. I'll call."

"Good. I'll stay here and keep guard."

Penelope turned to go but looked over her shoulder. "Any possibility this was an accident?"

"I don't see how it could be," Victor said.

Penelope's shoulders sagged. "I was afraid you'd say that." She hurried away.

It took hours for the police to complete their assessment of the scene and remove the body. The darkness hadn't made their job any easier. The guests were questioned briefly. No one saw or heard anything useful. They left their names and addresses and were allowed to leave.

Dr. Haygood gave Daphne a sedative and prevented her from being questioned. Detective Covington, who appeared to be in charge, didn't seem happy, but since she was the niece of a duke, the situation was extremely sticky.

On the terrace, Victor sat with his legs stretched out and smoked. He reviewed the evening's events, still unclear about what had happened.

Penelope joined him on the terrace. She peered at him. "What has you in such deep thought?"

Victor ensured there were no policemen still lurking around before responding. "Did Daphne say anything about what happened?"

"Nothing. I tried to ask. She was too distraught."

"I need to talk to her before the police do." Victor's tone brooked no opposition.

"She's out for the night. Dr. Haygood gave her a strong tranquilizer. You might as well stay here tonight. It's late. Or rather, early." The sun would soon rise. "I'll have Thompkins get a room ready for you. You'll be able to see her first thing." She wearily rose from her seat.

"Thank you."

She left to see to the arrangements.

Victor didn't expect to sleep, but exhaustion won out. He slept like the proverbial log until an early morning lark's song woke him.

The clothes Thompkins had left for him must have belonged to Daphne and Penelope's distant cousin, Lord Edgar Worthington. Slightly too tight and a mite too short, they were still far more appropriate than the tuxedo he'd worn to the party.

Victor dressed in short order and headed out. He nearly collided with Penelope.

She stood outside his door, hand raised as if she were just about to knock. Still in her dressing gown, she looked as though she hadn't slept.

"Penelope, what are you doing up at this hour?"

"I've been sitting up with Daphne. You wanted to talk to her first thing."

"How is she?"

"She had a fitful sleep and woke up asking for you."

"Well, then lead on." Was his shock evident on his face?

Penelope looked like she wanted to speak, but she led him to Daphne's room in the west wing without a word. Someone, most likely Thompkins, must have carried Daphne from the study into her bedroom. Victor hadn't been in Daphne's bedroom since they were children. He remembered the room filled with dolls and stuffed animals, but that was a million years ago. Flowers and lace and pictures of fashionable women wearing the latest styles, pulled from *Harper's Bazaar*, filled the bedroom of the young lady out in society.

Daphne turned her pale face toward Victor. Her eyes were wide and slightly wild. Her hair was mussed from tossing and turning. Yet, in all her despair, something childlike and innocent remained. The room was hot. Despite the warm weather, a fire had been laid.

"Victor, you must help me." Daphne reached for him.

"Of course, Daphne." Victor sat at her bedside and clasped her hands.

Penelope remained quietly by the door.

"Penelope, please wait outside. I must speak to Victor alone," Daphne said.

"Of course. I'll be right outside if you need me." Penelope pulled the door closed behind her.

"Victor, please, you must help me. You must," Daphne said.

"But of course," he repeated.

"They will think . . . they will question me and they may think . . . what did you tell them?"

Victor wanted to reach out and hold her, but he restrained himself. He focused on her question. "I told the police the truth. I heard a scream and saw you come out of the hedge maze and that you collapsed. Then I carried you to the study."

"Did you tell them about my dress?"

"Yes. I had to. I'm sure they'll want to see it."

"But they can't. That worried me so much, but I took care of it."

"What do you mean?" Victor hesitated. "How did you take care of it?"

"Well, I thought it might make them think I had something to do with Charles's death, so I got rid of it," Daphne said.

"You got rid of it? How?"

Daphne looked down demurely and plucked at a nonexistent thread on her coverlet. "When Penelope thought I was asleep, she stepped out. I burned it."

She waved toward the still smoldering fireplace. "Which was such a shame because it was a Norman Hartnell, and it cost a king's ransom. It really suited me so well, don't you think?"

Victor stared, openmouthed, "But—you can't do that. That gown was evidence."

"It was my gown. Besides, it was ruined. I would never be able to look at it again, let alone wear it." Daphne went from petulant to matter of fact. "Now there won't be anything to tie me to that horrible man. Don't you see?"

"Yes, I think I do see." Victor spoke slowly. "Look, Daphne, what really happened last night?"

"I don't remember much, really."

"Please. It's very important."

"All right." Daphne sighed. "We were supposed to meet on the bench at the center of the maze. I got a note."

"You got a note from Parker?"

"Yes. You see, it was in the pocket of his jacket. We were dancing and I got hot. We went outside to get some air, but then I got chilly. He gave me his jacket." Daphne gave Victor a coquettish look. "He'd written the note and placed it in his pocket. That's where I found it."

"What did the note say?"

"Meet me at the bench in the center of the hedge maze at midnight."

"Did you ask Parker about the note?"

Daphne blushed. "No. I just thought it was a sort of game. He often left me little love notes."

"Do you still have the note?"

"I burned it with the dress."

Victor gawked in stunned silence. He took several

deep breaths and regained his composure. He needed the full story. "What happened next?"

Daphne stared at the ceiling as though she were reliving the moment. "We danced several times. Right before midnight, I was dancing with James Hampton and saw Charles slip outside. I thought he was going to wait for me at the bench. So, I finished the dance, made some excuse to James, and hurried outside." Daphne hesitated.

"What happened next?"

She scowled. "I got to the center of the maze and tripped over him. I think I might have screamed. Then I saw the blood and ran. That's all I remember."

"Did you see or hear anyone else?"

"No. I wasn't really paying attention, though."

"You'll have to make a statement to the police. Tell them the truth," Victor said.

"But what if they don't believe me?" Daphne grabbed the lapels of his jacket and looked into his eyes. "Victor, you must help me. I can't bear the thought of going to jail." Daphne verged on hysterics.

"You won't go to jail," he reassured her.

"Do you promise?" She buried her head on his chest.

"Well, I can't promise, but if you didn't kill him, I'm sure it will be all right."

"You will look out for me? You won't let them take me away, will you?" Real fear shone on Daphne's face.

"No. I won't let them take you away."

Victor had a sinking feeling in the pit of his stomach that his promise might come at a heavy price.

Chapter 8

I spent the next two days taking care of the ordinary things of life, including church and dinner with Mom and Nana Jo. One of my few rituals was spending time with my mom on Sundays. I picked her up for church, and we went out for dinner afterward. Sunday was supposed to be a day of rest. For my mom, who hated cooking, that meant eating out. Usually, dinner with Mom was Cracker Barrel or Red Lobster. We chose Red Lobster this Sunday. We'd done it for so long, the servers all knew us by name. Nana Jo came too. Afterward, we spent the day shopping.

Monday ended before I realized it had begun. From the time I got up, I was on the run. I almost forgot Snickers and Oreo had grooming appointments and rushed to make them on time. I dropped off the dogs and made trips to the dry cleaners, the city building permits office, the health department, the post office, the bank, and the grocery store. I picked up the dogs, and the day was over.

Tuesday, on the other hand, was much more noteworthy.

Tuesday was Senior Citizens' Day at local restaurants, and Nana Jo and "the girls" were fond of the half-price buffet at

Randy's Steak House. In an attempt to avoid the rush, we arrived at eleven. It didn't work. I wove between seniors with canes, walkers, and wheelchairs and in and out of multiple buffet lines. I felt like a schoolgirl. Normally, I wasn't fond of buffets. I preferred food that didn't sit out all day for men, women, and children with varying levels of cleanliness to handle. However, servers stood at all of the food stations assisting customers, and I had to admit Randy's seemed sanitary. The food was also noteworthy. The roast beef and barbecue ribs were so tender you could cut them with a fork, and the mashed potatoes—made with actual potatoes, not instant—were creamy and delicious. Randy's was well-known for their delicious, warm Banana Pudding. After two helpings, I decided I might need to check the place out again the next Tuesday.

We finished eating, sat at the table drinking coffee, and got down to business.

"All right, ladies. Let's get this party started." Nana Jo pulled her iPad out of her large bag. "Irma, why don't you start? What were you able to find out?"

Irma Starczewski was a petite woman, probably in her mid-eighties. Decades of heavy smoking, which she still indulged in, gave her a deep, raspy voice. She wore her head full of jet-black hair in a beehive. I puzzled over how she slept with that mountain on top of her head until I learned from Nana Jo that Irma's beehive was a wig. She took the beehive off when she went to bed.

"My great-grandson is a realtor, and he said Clayton Parker was a bad little mother—"

"Irma!" Nana Jo interrupted. "Watch your mouth."

"Sorry," Irma croaked and broke into a coughing fit. "Well, my great-grandson Ernie said he wouldn't even show properties listed by Parker. Parker was taken before some board of realtors multiple times and would have lost his license if he hadn't been so rich and his family so influential."

"Did he know why Parker sold the business?" I asked.

"Ernie said there were some questionable real estate deals being reviewed. He didn't have all of the details but promised to look into it and will let me know when he finds out."

"Great. Nice job." Nana Jo typed notes into her iPad. "Now, Dorothy how was the wedding?"

Dorothy Clark was about six feet tall and three hundred pounds. She might have been a linebacker for the Chicago Bears in a previous life. Despite her appearance, she had a certain appeal. Dorothy, like Nana Jo, was a hopeless flirt.

"My youngest son, Albert, works at South Harbor Country Club. He's an accountant. Graduated top of his class, you know." Dorothy beamed.

"Yes. We know," Nana Jo said.

Irma and Ruby Mae rolled their eyes. Dorothy's eyesight wasn't that great. I doubted she saw them.

"Did Albert know Clayton Parker?" Nana Jo continued typing.

"He didn't know him personally, but he did say the Parkers had been members of the country club for years. And, the older Parkers were well respected and paid their dues on time, unlike their son. Clayton was far behind. Al actually had to send him several letters encouraging him to pay up."

"Well, the rotten little bast—"

"IRMA!" Nana Jo and Ruby Mae both yelled.

Irma clamped her hand over her mouth.

"Geez! I'm sorry." Irma broke into another coughing fit. She sounded as though she was about to hack up a lung.

I handed her a glass of water. She declined and reached into her purse, pulled out a flask, and took a swig.

"Go ahead, Dorothy," Ruby Mae said.

"That's about all Albert knew, but my sister Joyce's boy, Danny, works at the Yacht club and he said virtually the same thing. Danny works in the dining room. The older Parkers were always good at paying their dues, but Clayton wasn't and he never gave tips," Dorothy finished.

"Good work, Dorothy. Very helpful." Nana Jo patted Dorothy's hand. She turned to Ruby Mae. "Your turn. Did you have a chance to talk to your daughter?"

"Yes. She told me quite a lot about the family."

I loved Ruby Mae's southern accent. Of all Nana Jo's friends, Ruby Mae Stevenson was my favorite. I'd learned her story from Nana Jo years ago. She was the youngest of the girls, only in her mid-sixties. She was African American with dark chocolate skin that always reminded me of coffee with a touch of cream. She had salt and pepper hair that was more salt than pepper, which she wore pulled back in a bun at the nape of her neck. She was born and raised in a small town in Alabama; she moved to Chicago to live with her older sister after both of her parents died. Ruby Mae married a plumber. One day he said he was going out to get beer and never returned. She raised their nine children alone. To support herself and her children, she cleaned the homes of Chicago's wealthiest citizens, including some well-known politicians. Ruby Mae was proud that all nine of her children graduated from college and were all doing what she called *tolerably fair*. However, her greatest joy seemed to come from knowing that, with a Master's degree in Business, her youngest daughter, Stephanie, chose to run Mama Ruby's Cleaning Service.

Ruby Mae pulled a ball of fluffy pink yarn and knitting needles out of her shoulder bag and started casting on. "Stephanie always investigates clients who request live-in maid service. She likes to make sure her workers are safe. She said Robert Parker was a good man. He was kind to the workers and always paid his bills on time. His son, Clayton, was another story." Ruby Mae pursed her lips like she was sucking on a lemon. "She had to threaten to take him to court if he didn't pay his bill. He was almost six months behind."

"I'll bet he didn't like that," I said.

"He sure didn't. He got ugly and called her names. Threatened to ruin her business." Ruby Mae's outrage showed.

"The nerve of the little—" Irma caught herself before breaking into yet another coughing fit.

"Stephanie doesn't scare easy. She got right back in his face and dared him to try. She told him if he wanted to start trouble, then her brother the lawyer would be more than happy to finish it. Then my two grandsons went by and had a chat with Mr. Clayton Parker." Ruby Mae's eyes twinkled. "Those boys are linebackers for State's football team, and they don't take kindly to anybody messing with their mama." Ruby Mae snickered and we joined her.

"That shut him up pretty fast. She said he 'bout fell all over hisself trying to apologize. Paid his bill in full after that. She also said he was a womanizer. Cheated on his wife and she knew it. But he had all the money, so she put up with it."

"You ladies are amazing." I was truly astonished. "I can't believe how much information you found in such a short period of time."

"Well, we aren't done yet. I haven't given my report," Nana Jo said.

"I'm sorry. Please, go ahead." When had she had time to go out sleuthing? She'd been with me the past three days. She hadn't said a word about getting any information, and she'd had ample time to mention it if she had. But then, Nana Jo did like a bit of drama in her life.

"As you know, Freddie has a son that works for the state police. Mark said there was an old file on the Parkers."

"What kind of old file?" Dorothy asked.

"It goes back to just after the war."

"The war? You mean Vietnam?" I didn't see how anything that far back would help with Clayton Parker's murder.

"No, honey, World War II," Nana said as if it was obvious.

"What kind of file would the police save for that long? I can't believe they have records that go back that far."

Nana Jo ignored me. "There were three Parker brothers. Robert was the oldest. George was next."

"He's the one who works in the real estate office, right?" Dorothy said.

"Yes. That's him. Then there was the youngest, David. He was the one who was always getting into trouble. I vaguely remember him," Nana Jo said.

"They were trouble, those boys." Irma shook her head.

"Seems like I recollect the father used to do plasterwork in some of them big houses in North Harbor." Ruby Mae counted her cast-on stitches. "He used to be pretty good when he could stay away from the bottle."

"Apparently, he couldn't stay away from the bottle," Nana Jo said. "He was the town drunk. Later he got into bootlegging. The mother, well, she ran off not long after David was born."

"I forgot about that until you mentioned his name. He was real trouble." Another coughing spell hit, and Irma took another drink from her flask.

"Well, you have these three brothers, all dirt poor, who leave to fight in the war. They get shipped overseas. When they come back, they aren't poor anymore. Robert buys the biggest house in town and starts buying up buildings left and right. He opens Parker Real Estate and becomes successful. George buys a big house and goes off to college. He gets an education and comes back and opens a bookkeeping office. He wasn't as successful as Robert. Later he joined his brother's real estate business." Our server had brought more coffee, and Nana Jo took a drink.

"What about David?" I asked.

"He's the one puzzle. He came back but got in some trouble and hightailed it out of town under suspicious circumstances. No one has heard a thing about him for years."

"People don't just disappear," I said.

"Yes, they do," Ruby Mae said, her voice sad. "People disappeared all the time back in them days. Honey, it just depended on what they'd done. Back then, if you had enough money or power, you could make people disappear."

Irma and Dorothy nodded. Nana Jo patted Ruby Mae's arm. I felt awkward. I'd obviously brought up some painful memories.

"Mark had to do some searching, but he found out David was accused of getting some young girl in trouble. He ran. He eventually turned up in Arizona. He was involved in a bank robbery. A guard was killed. He's been in prison until . . . six months ago."

"Six months? That seems to be when Clayton Parker started having money problems," I said. "Where is this David now? Do you think he's back?"

"Freddie didn't say. I'll see if he can find out. If he was released from prison, you'd think he would have to check in somewhere," Nana Jo said.

"That's a lot to think about. But what does it all mean?" I said.

"It means Clayton Parker was a womanizer who cheated his clients and he cheated on his wife," Nana Jo said.

"We know he was having money problems," Irma said.

"And we know his money problems started right after his uncle got out of prison," Dorothy added.

"So, the list of people who might have wanted to kill Clayton Parker is quite long," Nana Jo said. "Looks like we've got our work cut out for us."

Chapter 9

Nana Jo and the girls had changed my opinion about senior citizens forever. Gone were visions of the befuddled elderly with walkers and wheelchairs and drool running down their chins. Not only were these women creative and intelligent, they were active, vibrant, and lively. Lunch at Randy's Steak House was only the beginning. The buffet was followed by half-priced hairstyles at the local beauty college. Double value coupons led to a mad dash through no fewer than three grocery stores and an SUV filled with toilet paper, toothpaste, and soap. The girls believed the maximum limits printed on the bottoms of the coupons were a challenge to overcome by visiting as many stores as possible.

I had to admit, I was happy to get a half-price oil change and free car wash by letting Nana Jo drive my car through Mr. Quickies's Oil Change and Car Wash. Half-priced Margaritas would have been much more enjoyable, if I had been able to partake. However, as the designated driver, I drank Diet Coke while Nana Jo and the girls got wasted. The nonstop activities left me exhausted, but it was hours before I could convince everyone it was time to go home.

Dorothy hooked up with a guy young enough to be her son and short enough to be her grandchild. It took all kinds of promises from me and threats from Nana Jo before she reluctantly agreed to get in the car.

Thoroughly exhausted, I lay in bed and sorted through the information they had uncovered. The question of wealth was particularly intriguing. Where did the Parkers acquire their wealth? How did three dirt-poor brothers go off to war and come back with enough wealth to become pillars of the community? I doubted I'd ever know the answer, and I wasn't sure if the answer mattered. It was close to seventy years since the war had ended, and if there was a connection, there was no way it involved Clayton Parker. He wasn't born seventy years ago. No. As interesting as that puzzle was, it had nothing to do with Clayton Parker's death.

What did I know for certain? Something changed six months ago. Up until then, Clayton Parker paid his bills on time. He might have swindled his clients, but that didn't appear to be unusual for him. I was sure he'd swindled them for years. Six months ago, his uncle David was released from prison. Was there a connection? The dates were too close to dismiss. Tomorrow, I'd do a bit of snooping on my own. I needed to find out as much as I could about Clayton Parker, and the place to start was with my realtor. He was tuned in to everything going on in the community. Not to mention, I couldn't let my nana and her elderly friends show me up.

Sleep eluded me. I needed something to settle my racing mind and help me relax. I needed a distraction, and I knew just the thing.

⌒

"Darling, I knew I could count on you. You've always been such a gentleman. I knew you wouldn't let the police bother me." Daphne pouted. "Although, I had hoped you wouldn't mention the bit about my dress or that you saw me coming out of the hedge maze. But, we can fix that." She put her head on Victor's chest and snuggled up to him like a kitten.

For the first time, Victor really did see.

"I knew I could depend on you," she said. "You are my knight in shining armor, riding in to save a damsel in distress."

Victor caught a glimpse of himself in her dresser mirror and was glad Daphne wasn't looking and couldn't see the look of dread he saw staring back at him. He had what he thought he'd always wanted. He held Daphne. The scent of her perfume filled his senses and made him lightheaded. She called him her knight. She was everything he wanted. Or was she?

After a brief knock and a discreet cough, Penelope entered the room. Victor fidgeted to free himself from Daphne. Unsure why Penelope witnessing their embrace bothered him, he stood, unable to make eye contact.

"Detective Inspector Covington is here. He's downstairs and he's asking to speak to you." Penelope addressed Daphne. "It might not look good if he finds you two together." She avoided looking at him.

Victor thought nothing could shake him more than the look on Penny's face when she saw him in her sister's arms until Daphne said, "Whyever not? We're going to be married, after all."

"Death by person or persons unknown." Penelope relayed the coroner's verdict to her aunt and uncle.

"Well, that was rather expected, Penny dear."

Lady Elizabeth knitted in a chair by the window. "The poor man was found stabbed, after all."

A stately woman in her mid-fifties, Lady Elizabeth Marsh exemplified the quintessential British aristocracy. She knew the right people to invite to any function. She wore the right attire. She always behaved in a respectable fashion. Her intelligence, however, often came as a surprise to those not well acquainted with her ladyship.

"Right. Right, ol' girl. The coroner could hardly come back with a verdict of suicide, at least not nowadays." Lord William clamped his teeth onto his pipe. His voice held just the slightest hint of regret for the good ol' days when the aristocracy commanded respect and fear and messy murders were swept under the carpet. He shrugged and smoked as he watched his wife knit and his niece pace.

"That Parker was a bit of a scoundrel." Lord William was pleasantly plump, in his early sixties and fond of rich food, good wine, and his pipe. His family knew he often paid for his fondness with gastric attacks, like the one during the recent ball. The attacks were responsible for his rare instances of bad humor.

"I was surprised to hear the American police followed him all the way here," Lady Elizabeth said.

"It seemed odd. I've never heard of the police going undercover like that. Imagine getting a job in an orchestra to keep an eye on a suspect." Penelope continued to pace.

"He obviously wasn't watching closely enough," Lord William said.

"Person or persons unknown, my foot." Penelope stamped her foot, just as she had when she was frustrated as a child. "That person won't be unknown for long. It's only a matter of time before that inspector identifies a person. He's going to arrest Victor. I know he is!"

"Sit down, girl. You're making me dizzy." Lord William's growl was friendly rather than a rebuke.

"Yes, do sit, Penelope. You'll wear a hole in the carpet." Lady Elizabeth beamed fondly at her niece.

"I'm sorry, Aunt Elizabeth." Penelope perched on the edge of a chair. "I'm sorry, but you should have seen him. Victor sat there like some lost puppy. He's going to let them arrest him. He thinks he's protecting her." Penelope choked back her emotions.

"Victor always did have a chivalrous nature, even as a boy." Lady Elizabeth paused in her knitting. "I always liked him."

"Ugh. I can't believe she's going to let him take the blame for this. Of all the selfish, self-centered, spoiled . . ." Penelope popped up and resumed pacing.

"I know, dear, but you can't honestly believe Daphne killed that poor man." Lady Elizabeth cut to the heart of the matter without dropping a stitch.

Penelope halted in front of the window and pondered her aunt's words. She shrugged and returned to her seat. "That's just it. I can't believe she did it. I mean, Daphne would never do anything that horrible. Besides, she would never risk ruining a new dress."

"I can't imagine the girl cares about anyone other than herself. She certainly wouldn't care enough to kill." Lord William's tone was kinder than his words.

"I don't believe she did it. She wouldn't. It's just too cruel." Penelope strode to the window.

"I won't go quite that far. Daphne can be cruel.

But I agree, she didn't care enough about Charles Parker to kill him." Lady Elizabeth counted stitches.

Penelope strode from one end of Lord William's bedroom to the other, and back again. "Then why won't she talk to the police? Why is she avoiding them? And, why did she burn that dress? And why . . ."

Lady Elizabeth finished Penelope's sentence, "is she marrying Victor?"

"Well, *yes!* She doesn't care two pence about Victor. Why agree to marry him now?" Penelope asked.

"The important question is not why she's doing it. The important question is what are we going to do about it?" Lady Elizabeth unwound yarn from her skein.

"What do you mean?" Penelope halted.

Lady Elizabeth knit in silence for a few minutes, as if she didn't hear the question. "We can't let the poor boy hang for something he didn't do. Or worse."

"Worse? What could be worse than hanging?" Penelope's voice quivered.

"We must save him before he goes through with his plan." Lady Elizabeth paused to retrieve the ball of yarn that had tumbled to her feet. "Before he does something truly stupid and actually marries Daphne." Her eyes twinkled.

Both Lord William and Penelope froze until Lord William sputtered with laughter. Penelope and Lady Elizabeth joined him.

When they stopped, which took some time, Penelope wiped tears from her eyes. "That felt good. I don't think I've laughed in well over a week, not since this whole nightmare started."

"Right, right. How do we do it? How do we save Victor?" Lord William asked.

"First, I think we shall have to figure out who killed that poor man, don't you, dear?" Lady Elizabeth asked. "We shall have to find the real murderer."

Chapter 10

Realtors kept odd hours because potential buyers kept odd hours. They needed to be available to show houses at all times of day and night. My realtor, Chris Martinelli, had a lot of irons in the fire. Life as a real estate broker, single parent, and county commissioner would more than fill most people's days. Add in house flipper and author and his schedule was packed. I called early Wednesday morning. He, of course, had a full day planned but would be downtown around noon for a closing and promised to swing by the building.

Nana Jo was still recovering from her night of drinking and dancing. She appeared to be nursing a hangover, but by noon she was dressed and moving, albeit rather slowly. I spent the morning shelving the last of the books and magazines and dusting, tidying, and making sure everything was ready to go. I picked up chicken salad sandwiches and chips from Harbor Café for both of us, and Chris arrived as we finished eating.

A stocky, balding, and extremely nice man in his early fifties, Chris Martinelli was quiet, which surprised me considering all of the things he was involved in. He reminded me of my husband. Leon had joked he was only quiet because he couldn't get a word in edgewise around our family. Maybe Chris was the same way.

"This place is looking great. When are you going to be opening the doors?" Chris took in the shop.

"I'm hoping in a week," I said. "If everything goes okay."

"We'll be ready in a week." Nana Jo had more confidence than I did.

The closer I got to opening, the more nervous I became. What if it didn't work out?

Chris took a seat in the area that would one day be part of a fully functioning café. For the time being, there was a workbench that belonged in a garage and several bistro tables with chairs. I set out tea for all of us.

"Now, what can I do for you?" Chris took a sip of Earl Grey tea and grabbed a scone. He watched Nana Jo and I load ours with clotted cream and strawberry preserves and followed suit.

"I'm sure you know about Clayton Parker's death," I said between bites.

Chris nodded and shoved the rest of the scone into his mouth. I might not be the best cook in the world, but I enjoyed baking. I'd tested a variety of recipes for scones, trying to decide which to serve in my tea shop. The current batch was my favorite and destined to be one of the staples.

"I did hear about it." Chris took another scone and smothered it with clotted cream and preserves. "Honestly, I was surprised to hear he had the nerve to come here after everything that went down."

"That was my thought too. I couldn't believe he showed his face here. He certainly knew I couldn't stand him." Remembering everything Clayton Parker did to prevent me from closing on the building brought vigor to my voice.

"I filed a complaint with the board against him, and we were scheduled for a hearing next week." Chris wiped his mouth with a napkin and took a sip of tea. "This is delicious. What is this stuff anyway?" Chris eyed the last scone on the tray.

Nana Jo slid it onto his plate.

"These are scones and the white stuff is clotted cream. It's popular in England," I said.

Chris finished off the last scone in no time. "What did Parker want?"

"I have no idea. I never talked to him. I refused to open the door," I said, with only a small amount of shame.

"Chris, I was wondering what you can tell me about him. If he treated everyone the way he treated me, I can only imagine the police have a long line of suspects."

"I can't say he treated everyone the same. If you were rich and a member of the country club or the yacht club, he could be really charming." Chris paused. He seldom spoke ill of anyone. "At least that's what I heard. I wasn't born on the right side of the harbor for Parker, so I never got a chance to see that side of him."

"So, you're saying this Parker person was a South Harbor snob?" Nana Jo's straight forwardness shocked many people, but Chris was accustomed to her.

"To put it simply, yeah, he was. Frankly, I'm surprised he even listed this building. I don't recall him listing any other North Harbor properties, but the downtown area is turning around and money is money. I talked to one of the other local realtors, and he thought the Parker family used to own this building."

"Really? That's hard to believe." I tried to imagine Clayton Parker appreciating this building. It wasn't huge as far as square footage, but it was just the right size for a cozy bookstore.

"You have to remember, back in the day, North Harbor was where all of the wealthy people lived," Nana Jo said. "That's why we have so many big old Victorian houses. South Harbor was where the servants and working-class people lived."

"True. After the race riots of the sixties, everything shifted. South Harbor became the preferred area, but North Harbor will turn around," Chris said. "At least I hope so."

"Especially now that we're going to have a new mystery bookstore and tea room." Nana Jo glowed with pride, and I couldn't help but glow at the faith she had in me, even while my stomach clenched with fear.

Chris promised to ask his realtor friends if they knew of anyone with a grudge against Parker and promised to share anything he found out. He was a busy man, and soon, Nana Jo and I were left alone.

Lady Elizabeth had planned to send her regrets to Lady Dallyripple and decline her invitation to tea. More than fifteen minutes in the presence of Lady Amelia Dallyripple and her annoying, yipping, ankle-biting corgis made her want headache powder and a tall glass of Sherry. If she was totally honest, she preferred the company of the dogs to that of Lady Amelia. However, Victor was in trouble and one had to do distasteful things from time to time to help one's family. She was comfortable with the thought of Victor Carlston as family. From the moment he took his first childhood steps in Wickfield Lodge, he was destined to unite the two families.

"Don't you agree, Lady Elizabeth?" Lady Amelia asked.

She shook herself out of her reveries and tried to focus. The constant barking and growling of the three dogs, attempting to herd Lady Amelia's grandson, made it nearly impossible to hear. One little beast intently nipped at the hem of Lady Elizabeth's dress and snagged the lace. Clearly, drastic measures were needed. A knock at the door provided the required distraction. All eyes turned toward the newest arrival, and Elizabeth leaned forward. The plate of biscuits in her lap slid onto the floor. The little terror abandoned his hold on her dress and devoured the treats.

"Oh, dear. I'm terribly sorry about the mess," Lady Elizabeth said.

"No problem." Lady Amelia's voice was strained and her smile forced.

The other two dogs abandoned their attempts to herd and joined their sibling in licking crumbs from the carpet. The room was considerably quieter.

Lady Honorah Exeter leaned close and whispered, "Thank you. I wish I'd thought of that."

"I've had some experience with these little ankle biters," Lady Elizabeth said.

"Oh, yes. The king has corgis, doesn't he? Have you seen them?"

Daughter of an American oil baron, the young and pleasantly plump Honorah Exeter sported delicate features. She married into an old and titled, but destitute, British family. Despite the arranged union, she and Lord Peter Exeter, 15th Viscount of Norwalk, had a comfortable relationship, which suited them both. For Lady Honorah, the only fly in the ointment was the Exeter's lack of intimate terms with the Royal Family. Like many Americans, Lady Honorah was unfamiliar with the British peerage. When she arrived in England, she clearly believed a title would provide daily invitations to tea at Buckingham Palace and shooting trips to Windsor and Balmoral Castles. While that might have been true in years past, King George VI was shy and rarely entertained, preferring small, quiet dinners with his immediate family.

As a much loved second cousin, Lady Elizabeth was on familiar enough terms to call the king "Bertie." The relationship brought her a large number of invitations to tea, in the hopes she'd share intimate details of the royal family. Lady Elizabeth remained tight-lipped and careful, ensuring her close relationship with her royal relations continued.

"Yes, I've seen the king's dogs. They are better behaved." Lady Elizabeth inclined her head toward the pack still sniffing for crumbs. "But then, the king does have a larger staff to look after and train them."

Lady Honorah seemed eager to hear any royal news, no matter how mundane. Could Lady Elizabeth use it to her advantage?

"Police running all over the house and grounds. It's a terrible shame." Mrs. Baker, the Vicar's wife, the slightest bit deaf in her right ear, had a tendency to speak louder than needed.

The Misses Marjorie and Octavia Wood had the decency to blush. Obviously, they were uncomfortable with gossip, especially with the object of the gossip present.

However, the Vicar's wife had provided the opening Lady Elizabeth needed and she took advantage of it. "Oh my, yes. You are so right, Mrs. Baker," she said loudly enough for Mrs. Baker to hear. "We were shocked and surprised to have such a horrible thing happen."

The Wood sisters looked relieved that Lady

Elizabeth took no offense and openly discussed the topic. Something as exciting as a murder—made more exciting having happened to an American—had to be on everyone's minds.

"What was he about, I asked myself," Miss Octavia Wood, the more talkative of the two spinster sisters, said.

"I'm sorry but I don't understand your question." Lady Elizabeth thought she must have missed part of the conversation.

"Getting himself killed like that. What was he about?" Miss Octavia looked from face to face. "Why travel all this way just to get stabbed?" She sipped her tea, and her sister nodded eagerly.

"I honestly don't know." Lady Elizabeth was indeed puzzled. "I don't suppose he expected to get killed."

"Rubbish." Lady Amelia warmed to the subject. "Men like that always end up getting themselves killed. You'd think he would have the decency to get himself killed in his own country and not let it happen in someone else's garden." Everyone murmured their agreement, everyone except Lady Elizabeth and Lady Honorah.

Lady Honorah flushed and fidgeted with her teacup.

Time to intervene. Lady Elizabeth cleared her throat. "I don't believe he intended to be killed, and I'm sure he didn't mean to be killed in my garden. Since he did, I wonder if any of you noticed anything unusual?"

"By unusual, do you mean like a vagrant?" Miss Marjorie Wood asked timidly.

"Well, yes. I suppose, but anything unusual or out of the ordinary," Lady Elizabeth said.

Everyone looked curious, but clueless. Everyone except Lady Honorah, who went from a pink flush to a deep red and dropped first her napkin, then her handbag, then a spoon, while avoiding eye contact with Lady Elizabeth.

"I didn't suppose any of you did, but I thought I'd ask." Lady Elizabeth skillfully turned the conversation in another direction. "Have any of you seen the latest collection by Norman Hartnell? Aren't his gowns just marvelous? And, didn't Princess Elizabeth look beautiful in that white concoction? Such a lovely girl."

As predicted, the general conversation shifted to the latest in haute couture. Lady Elizabeth turned her attention on Lady Honorah and used the same firm but motherly tone she used with Daphne and Penelope. "Now, dear, don't you think you should tell me what's on your mind?"

Chapter 11

The funeral services for Clayton Parker were held on Thursday at South Harbor Lutheran Church. Nana Jo, the girls, and I put in an appearance. Originally, the girls weren't included in my plans, but when they found out Nana Jo and I were going to a funeral, they were upset about being excluded. Personally, I would have preferred to skip the event. Under normal circumstances, nothing could have compelled me to go to the funeral service for a man I disliked as much as I disliked Clayton Parker. Circumstances being what they were, I needed to attend. However, I refused to wear black and feign mourning. Instead, I wore my navy-blue suit, purchased more than a decade ago and worn to interviews and the annual teachers' recognition dinner. Nana Jo also opted out of wearing black. She wore a bright, short, tight-fitting turquoise dress. Despite her age, she had a good figure, and the dress accentuated every bit of it. Nana Jo was stunning. Irma wore a black miniskirt, black lace camisole, a pillbox hat with a veil, and six-inch bright red hooker heels. Dorothy and Ruby Mae dressed more traditionally in dark suits with sensible shoes.

South Harbor Lutheran Church was the oldest, largest, and

stateliest church in town. Its massive white steeple and traditional brick façade had graced South Harbor for well over a hundred years. The church sat atop a large expanse of lush green grass on the bluffs that overlooked the lake shore, a real estate gold mine with well over two acres of land. A vacant lot with views of the Lake Michigan shoreline was worth close to a million dollars. I'd bet every time Clayton Parker drove to church and saw the adjacent cemetery full of graves with high dollar, prime real estate lake views, he wanted to bang his head against a wall. I should have been ashamed at the joy the visual brought me. I wasn't.

I dropped off Nana Jo and the girls at the front of the church and drove off in search of a parking space. The main lot was full, but the church had commandeered parking at a nearby bar. I supposed the arrangement suited both parties, since the bar didn't open until late in the day, but my Baptist sensibilities bristled at the situation. My ten-year-old Honda CRV looked old and cheap in the sea of German vehicles crammed into the bar's parking lot. I spotted a space between a Jaguar and a Mercedes and tried to avoid drooling.

By the time I'd parked and hiked back to the church, I was hot and sweaty. The seats in the main sanctuary were full, but the church had set up a video camera and huge screen in the basement. Wooden pews were uncomfortable, but foldaway metal chairs were worse. Nana Jo and the girls had saved me a seat. I flopped onto it and used the program I was handed when I entered to attempt to fan away my sweat and foul attitude.

Clayton Parker ran with the South Harbor elite, and they had all showed up to pay their respects. The mayor, a United States congressman, the chief of police, and a host of people I only saw during election season sat in positions of prominence at the front of the church, although I only saw them on the basement screen.

The service was long and dull. Each of the invited dignitaries stood and shared kind words about Clayton Parker. I tried to come up with nice things to say about him when I introduced myself to his widow. I didn't have much luck. I was hard-pressed to come up with more than five kind words to say, other than backhanded compliments. *His breath didn't smell like garlic. I never smelled his body odor. His fingernails were always clean.* I decided to ask Nana Jo for suggestions as soon as we were alone. She had more experience with that type of stuff.

It took almost the entire time for me to cool down from my hike from the bar parking lot. Just as the throbbing in my feet subsided and the kink in my neck relaxed, Nana Jo elbowed me in my side. Perhaps I was a bit too relaxed. I'd dozed off. I hoped I hadn't snored. Nana Jo passed me a handkerchief. I certainly wasn't crying. The dampness on my face must have meant I drooled in my sleep. How long had I been out?

"You better head out to get the car," Nana Jo whispered.

I looked at the screen. The minister got up to deliver the eulogy. Geez, this had to have been the longest funeral service I had ever attended. The service lasted almost two hours.

I left and made the long walk back to the bar. If it had been open, I would have gone inside and had a glass of wine. Instead, I sat in my car and allowed the air-conditioning to blow away my bad mood.

By the time I drove back to the church, the service was over and cars were lining up for the caravan to the grave site. I spotted Nana Jo and pulled around the hearse. She and the girls hurried to get into the car. Off we sped, barely avoiding an attendant when he tried to stick a funeral flag onto my car.

"Well, that was a waste of time." I headed toward the retirement village.

"What are you talking about?" Nana Jo looked at me as though I'd suddenly been taken over by aliens.

"We learned a lot in those two hours," Dorothy said from the back seat.

"You've got to be kidding me. Were we at the same funeral?" I looked at Dorothy, Ruby Mae, and Irma in my rearview mirror.

"Well, if you'd stayed awake, you might have learned as much as we did," Ruby Mae said.

They had to be pulling my leg. "Like what?"

"Well, for starters, we learned that despite his horrible personality, Clayton Parker was either very well respected or his family was. A United States congressman, the mayor, and the lieutenant governor don't come to just anybody's funeral service," Nana Jo said.

"We also learned Clayton Parker's wife doesn't appear to be the grieving widow," Dorothy said. "Did you see the way she strutted into the church?"

"No, it must have been when I was out parking the car," I said sarcastically.

Nana Jo and the girls tsked in sympathy.

"And that outfit," Ruby Mae said. "Can you believe she wore that bright red dress to her husband's funeral? The back was cut so low you could see the crack of her behind."

"And her tramp stamp. Although, I did love those shoes. Louboutin's. Eight hundred forty-five dollars at Chandlers." Irma broke into a coughing fit.

"For a pair of shoes?" She had to be joking. I glanced at the mirror.

Irma took a swig from her flask.

"Who was that walking beside her?" Nana Jo asked.

"I don't know, but did you see his hand around her waist? That was just plain tacky, if you ask me." Ruby Mae sounded like she'd just tasted something sour.

"Maybe it was a relative?" I got snorts and harrumphs in response.

I nearly ran a red light when Ruby Mae said, "Honey, don't no *relative* pat a woman's backside like that unless he's getting some."

The others cracked up.

"Wow! You saw all that on the television screen in the basement of the church?" Obviously, the funeral was a lot more exciting than I thought.

"Of course not. We saw it all when we arrived and went snooping. Why do you think we had you drop us at the door?" Nana Jo said.

"We took positions and went on reconnaissance," Irma croaked before she broke into another coughing fit. She really needed to see someone about that cough.

"Reconnaissance?" I couldn't believe my ears.

Nana Jo turned to face me. "Irma is great at ferreting out information from elderly men. She went in and attached herself to the old geezer working the door."

In the rearview mirror, Irma nodded.

Nana Jo continued, "Dorothy went to the ladies' room."

"You can find out a lot of information in the ladies' room," Dorothy said.

I thought Dorothy spent so much time in ladies' rooms because she had weak kidneys. Who knew a ladies' room was a newsroom?

"Ruby Mae knows so many people in this town, if she stands in one place more than thirty seconds, someone always comes up and starts talking. Even strangers talk to her." Nana Jo glanced back at Ruby Mae. "And I went to the sign-in book and pretended I was a distant relative who wanted to get a picture of all of the signatures." Nana Jo held up her cell phone.

"You guys couldn't have had more than five or ten minutes before the processional started." I was truly awed.

"Honey, this ain't our first rodeo," Ruby Mae said.

"Where are you going?" Nana Jo asked.

The drive to the retirement village was almost a straight shot from the church. Unless Nana Jo had suddenly gone senile, there was no way she didn't recognize the route.

"I'm going back to the retirement village."

"Why? We have to head to South Harbor Country Club. Didn't you hear? Family and close friends are going there for refreshments." Nana Jo spoke as if she was talking to a dim-witted child.

"But we aren't family or close friends." I answered Nana Jo like she was the one whose wits were less than bright.

"How do you suppose we're going to get more information? Besides, I'm getting hungry. Turn around."

She was right. If I wanted information, I needed to get over my dislike of Clayton Parker and start investigating. I hated it when she was right. I drove a few extra blocks before turning around in the parking lot of a nearby grocery store and heading back to South Harbor.

South Harbor Country Club represented the divide between South Harbor and North Harbor. Built in the 1960s, SHARC, as it was referred to by the locals, sat on the manicured lawn of an eighteen-hole golf course. The main building was white. Eight pillars supported a two-story porch that wrapped around the building and overlooked the greens in front and the St. Thomas River in back. It was an antebellum plantation house straight out of *Gone with the Wind,* and the country club symbolized the elitist, separatist attitude held by many of South Harbor's residents.

A long winding drive led the way to the main entrance, where valets in red livery from a bygone era waited to park my car. I pretended to not notice the disappointment on the young man's face when he took the keys to my CRV and handed me a ticket. His friend ran to attend to the Porsche that had pulled in behind me.

Nana Jo and the girls headed up the steps to the front door.

I took a few deep breaths. The ostentatious country club was a sore spot for me. Despite the fact we were in the twenty-first century, South Harbor Country Club continued to adhere to ancient rules of discrimination and separatism. Several legal battles had forced them to take their discriminatory practices under cover. SHARC's bylaws no longer specifically denied membership to African Americans, Jews, women, and all other minorities. However, the stringent rules for admittance, along with the exceptionally steep membership fees, ensured the club membership remained haughty and homogenous.

Leon and I had participated in several protests just outside the gates, despite the fact neither of us golfed. The protests died down a few years ago, when the Senior Professional Golf Association (SPGA) built a new course in North Harbor as a part of the North Harbor revitalization efforts. The professional quality course attracted golfers from all over the world. Many locals abandoned SHARC for the newer course.

Up close, SHARC looked ancient. I was surprised Nana Jo and the girls wanted to set foot in the place.

"Come on. Let's get this over with so we can get away from this racist mausoleum," Nana Jo said as I reached the front porch.

"Amen." Ruby Mae plastered a smile on her face and walked through the large double doors with her head held high.

A tuxedo-clad maître d' led us to a reception room filled with faces I remembered from the television screen, both at the funeral and in advertisements soliciting votes. There were more people at the reception than at the church. We stopped at the edge of the crowd. Dorothy flagged down a passing waiter, and we each grabbed a glass of champagne.

Nana Jo held up her glass and addressed the troops, "All right, ladies, time to divide and conquer."

We clinked our glasses in a toast and each took a sip. The girls spread out and left Nana Jo and me alone.

Nana Jo scanned the crowd. I gulped my champagne and snatched another from a passing waiter.

"You better ease up on that or you'll find yourself puking, especially with nothing in your stomach," Nana Jo said.

She was right. I never was much of a drinker, but standing in the crowd of hoity-toity bigwigs left me feeling like a fish out of water. My pulse raced, and I started to sweat. I needed a bit of courage, even if it came through artificial channels. But, I agreed and promised to grab some appetizers.

"See that really pathetic-looking man in the crumpled blue suit?" Nana Jo pointed to the front of the room. "If I'm not mistaken, that's David Parker, Clayton Parker's uncle."

"How do you know?"

"I looked him up on Facebook." Once again, Nana Jo sounded like she was talking to a child. "I'm going to see what I can get out of him." And away she went.

I stood by myself, unsure of my next move. I downed my second glass of bubbly and handed my glass to a waiter, who offered me another. I accepted. I would just hold this one. I wound my way around waiters and guests. Irma preened in the middle of a group of men admiring her . . . *assets*. Ruby Mae sat at a table talking to several people. A young man brought her a plate of food, which obviously hadn't come from the appetizer trays the waiters carried around the room. Real food. Maybe she knew someone who worked in the kitchen.

No sign of Dorothy. She was most likely in the ladies' room. I wandered aimlessly until I spotted a bright red dress. The Widow Parker. I made my way in her direction. I didn't realize I'd finished my glass of champagne until a waiter offered me another, my third. Or was it my fourth?

Up close, Clayton Parker's widow was stunning. Not what one would call skinny, although she was fit and toned. Her Louboutin heels made her well over six feet tall. Barefooted, she was probably five foot seven. Short dark hair and dark eyes, combined with a deep tan, gave her an exotic appearance. She turned from the elderly couple giving their condolences, and I was face-to-face with my former enemy's wife.

"Yes?" she asked.

Although I'd spent the seconds it took to make my way to Mrs. Parker formulating what I would say, my mind went blank and my mouth went dry. A waiter offered me another glass of champagne. I didn't even remember drinking the last one, but I gratefully accepted and downed it.

"I . . . uh . . . I wanted to give you my condolences on the loss of . . . your husband."

"Thank you. Thank you very much." Mrs. Parker extended her hand and we shook.

Someone approached. Mrs. Parker turned to greet them but stopped. I hadn't released her hand.

Her face held a frozen smile and a question.

A wave of guilt overtook me, and I had to say something. I pulled her close and whispered, "Your husband died in my backyard."

Her eyes, wide as silver dollars, darted from left to right. She was searching for something or someone. Her hand went cold and trembled in mine. She opened her mouth as if to speak but didn't. She swayed and would have fallen if not for the tall, handsome man who appeared and caught her.

"Diana? Dearest?" Mr. Amazing's whisper held a heavy Russian accent. He patted her cheeks and scowled at me. "What did you do to her?"

I didn't feel so hot myself and scowled back while I tried to figure out what I'd done to her. I grew hot. The room spun. *Maybe this is what overtook Mrs. Parker.* I leaned forward and puked on Mr. Gorgeous's leather shoes.

In one graceful movement, he scooped up Mrs. Parker and carried her away.

The next thing I remember, I was laying on my own sofa with a damp cloth on my forehead and a wastebasket on my chest. Nana Jo and a tall, stocky man dressed like a penguin hovered over me.

"Looks like you'll live," Nana Jo said, without the least bit of sympathy in her voice.

I groaned and made good use of the wastebasket. When I finished, she brought me another towel to wipe my face and replaced the liner in the wastebasket.

"What happened?" I asked.

"You made a spectacle of yourself." Nana Jo handed the bag to the Penguin. She went to the kitchen and banged cabinet doors.

My head was twice its normal size and throbbed as though someone was using it for a drum.

"Stop," I wanted to scream, but it came out as a whimper.

Nana Jo quit banging doors. When she turned on the faucet, it sounded like I was standing underneath Niagara Falls. She returned and handed me a glass of water and four aspirin. My head weighed a ton. Nana Jo helped me sit up. I swallowed the pills and enough water to get them down.

"What's with the Penguin?" I whispered in her ear.

I heard footsteps on the stairs and looked in that direction. When the Penguin appeared, Nana Jo waved him to the sofa.

"Sam, I believe you know Dawson Alexander."

Dawson Alexander? Why did the name sound familiar? I might have figured it out if my head hadn't been full of cotton. My confusion must have shown. His smile faded.

"Hello, Mrs. Washington," Dawson said. "I guess you don't remember me. I used to go to—"

"*Dawson.* Dawson Alexander. Of course I remember you. You were in my—" I moved too quickly. The room spun, and I needed my wastebasket. When I finished, Nana Jo swapped out the liner and helped to clean me up.

Dawson made another trip downstairs to dispose of my bag of shame.

"I think I have the plague," I said.

"Nope. You'll live, but you probably will wish you hadn't," Nana Jo said.

I fell asleep, and when I woke up, my loft was dark. The room was peaceful and quiet, except for the heavy weight on my chest and the snoring near my feet. Lifting my head was still painful, but pins no longer stabbed the backs of my eyes. My moment of panic at the weight on my chest vanished when I saw Snickers. Oreo was the buzz saw at my feet.

My head had shrunk two sizes during my nap and was still two sizes too big. The pounding had subsided, somewhat. I didn't want to move. I would have lain on that sofa until I drew my last breath if my kidneys had cooperated. No matter how much mental energy I expended, they refused to be silenced. I was forced to move. Moving dislodged the sleeping poodles, who barked and announced I was up and moving.

After taking care of necessities, I made the mistake of looking at myself in the bathroom mirror. The phrase death warmed over would have been a compliment. I stuck my tongue out at my reflection and went to bed.

I awoke to pitch black darkness, still feeling like I'd been run over by a truck. The bed sheets tied me down like a straitjacket. Oreo paced up and down on top of me—sadly, not an unfamiliar occurrence, but the growling was new.

"You've got to be kidding."

Hearing my voice seemed to agitate Oreo more. He leapt from my chest to the bed. The resulting wave of nausea was, in my confined condition, terrifying. I kicked and flopped until I freed myself enough to sit up and find the wastebasket by the side of my bed. Oreo growled and scratched at the door. Snickers was curled up in a ball, sound asleep on the pillow. I didn't remember letting the dogs out to do their business. There would be packages for me to clean up in the morning, but I couldn't deal with getting up and walking downstairs to let them out. I ignored Oreo and went back to sleep. I'd clean up later.

In the morning, I felt worse. My head pounded like Ricky Ricardo on the bongos. My eyelids were glued shut. The effort to wrench them free was taxing. Once I managed, yellow daggers of light squeezed between the blinds and stabbed my eyes. I immediately shut them.

A gust of wind hit the room and opened blinds, turned on lights, and sang, "Wake up, sleepyhead."

Nana Jo was an evil woman. I would have gladly strangled her if I could have convinced her to bring her neck down low enough for me to reach it.

"Shoot me," was all I managed to croak.

I'd never noticed how loudly Nana Jo laughed until that moment.

"Come on, sweetie. Drink this." Nana Jo pulled the pillow off my face and pried open one eyelid. "It'll make you feel better."

It was the lie I wanted to hear, the only thing that could induce me to endure the pain of opening both eyes.

"What is it?"

Nana Jo held a glass filled with a dark liquid that looked like something Oreo had hacked up after eating an entire bag of Doritos.

"This is my surefire hangover remover, guaranteed to get you feeling like a human being in no time."

"What's in it?" I narrowed my eyes.

"You don't want to know. Just hold your nose and chug it down as quickly as you can. Trust me." Nana Jo pushed the glass into my hand and helped me sit up.

I was suspicious but desperate. It couldn't be worse than the way I felt. I held my nose and downed the concoction as fast as

I could. The smell and taste were horrible, but the sliminess was worse.

I sputtered and gagged, sure I would puke.

"Swallow," Nana Jo said.

I squeezed my eyes shut and did as I was told.

"Why was it slimy?" I wiped my mouth and lay back on the pillow.

"Raw egg."

My stomach tensed, and I frantically hunted for my waste-basket. Nana Jo handed it to me. Just as I got my face to the basket, I belched. Loudly, but nothing came up. I waited. And waited. Nothing. I decided I wasn't going to puke and lay back down.

"See. You'll be back to your old self in no time." Nana Jo was way too perky. "Come on, you can't stay in bed all day. I'll let the dogs out. You better go and clean yourself. Your hair looks like a rat's nest." With that, Nana Jo got up and turned to go. "Come on, let's go get a treat." Nana Jo used the magic word. Both Snickers and Oreo followed her like she was the Pied Piper.

I stayed in bed a few more minutes before I managed to get up and drag myself into the bathroom. I leaned against the shower walls and let the heat and steam batter my skin. Even though the water felt like torture, I started to feel better. When I finished, the aroma of coffee and the distinct smell of bacon reached me. Rather than retching, my stomach growled. It took a while to remove the fur from my teeth, but after a thorough brush and a few extra-strong swills of mouthwash, I started to feel somewhat human.

In the kitchen, Nana Jo had a plate ready, but the strong cup of coffee was the first thing I addressed.

"Feeling better?" Nana Jo peered at me over her cup of coffee.

"Hmm," I said between shoveling in food and slogging down steaming hot coffee. Once I started, I realized I hadn't eaten anything the day before. I was starving.

"Did you hear anything last night?" Nana Jo asked.

"Anything like what?"

Nana Jo didn't answer right away. "I don't know. I thought I heard a noise. I almost went down with my gun, but I figured it was probably some drunk wandering home late from a bar." She grinned. "Sorry, present company excluded."

I ignored her last comment. "I didn't hear anything."

After we ate, Nana Jo, bless her soul, cleaned the kitchen. I was mobile but not speedy. I took things easy and drank a lot of water. By the end of the day, I was exhausted, but much better.

Friday night meant poker night for Nana Jo and the girls. I decided to skip that bit of fun. Instead, a quick excursion to the British countryside was in order.

Chapter 12

"Lady Honorah Exeter knew Charles Parker?" Penelope leapt from her seat and dislodged Cuddles, the napping Cavalier King Charles Spaniel using her lap as a pillow. "That's great."

Lady Elizabeth didn't share her niece's enthusiasm and continued to pour tea for her husband and niece. "Yes. She said she met him last year, on the Queen Mary when she returned from her sister's wedding." Lady Elizabeth calmly passed Lord William a cup.

Ignoring the tea, Penelope clumped across the wood floors and paced in front of the floor-to-ceiling bookshelves lining the library walls. Despite the room's size, a massive fireplace and comfortable, overstuffed furniture made it feel warm and cozy.

"Dear, do sit and drink your tea before it gets cold," Lady Elizabeth said. "All that noise is giving me a headache."

"Sorry." Penelope took her seat. "I wonder what happened to the carpet?"

"Thompkins must have sent it out to be cleaned. Now, where's Daphne?"

"She left for London early this morning." Penelope took the cup her aunt offered.

"London? Good Lord, whatever for?" Lord William blustered.

Penelope sipped her tea and hid a smile.

Lady Elizabeth gazed lovingly at her husband. "Dear, just because you hate going to town doesn't mean everyone does. I believe she went shopping."

"Shopping? Whatever for?" Lord William discretely passed a biscuit to Cuddles.

Penelope soberly put down her teacup. "She said she was going to look for items for her trousseau." Penelope once again rose and paced.

Lady Elizabeth shook her head, quietly signaling to her husband to change the subject.

"What else did Lady Exeter say?" he asked.

"Not much, really," Lady Elizabeth said. "She met Charles Parker on the boat. They were about the same age and both Americans, so it was natural for them to strike up an acquaintance. She said they dined together, and I believe he saw her once or twice after they landed in England."

"That sounds reasonable." Lord William helped himself to a scone.

"Yes, but why didn't she tell anyone she knew him?" Penelope stopped pacing.

"I asked her the same thing." Lady Elizabeth sipped her tea and carefully put the cup on the table.

Penelope searched her aunt's face. "Well? What did she say?"

"She said she didn't want anyone to know. She—"

"There must be something wrong. If it was just an innocent acquaintance, then why hide it?" Penelope resumed pacing.

"Do sit down, you're making me dizzy," Lady Elizabeth said.

"Sorry." Penelope returned to her seat.

Lord William sipped his tea in silence.

Both waited for Lady Elizabeth to continue.

She wiped her hands on her napkin. "You know that Lord Exeter's mother, the Dowager Countess, never really approved of Honorah."

Lord William harrumphed. "They certainly approved of her money."

"Yes, dear. The Exeters were in desperate need of money. Honorah's family wanted a title. No one is saying it was a love match. But, I do think, all things considered, it seems to have been suitable. They do appear genuinely fond of each other."

"What does that have to do with Charles Parker's murder?" Penelope's confusion showed on her face.

"The Dowager Countess barely acknowledges Honorah at social occasions." Lady Elizabeth glanced at her niece.

"She can be very rude," Penelope said. "I had the misfortune of sitting next to the Dowager Countess at the Westmorelands' dinner party. She spent thirty minutes criticizing the way Americans eat. She said it was uncivilized the way Americans cut their meat and then put down their knives. Poor Honorah couldn't help but hear her. Her face turned bright red and every time she reached for her knife, she dropped it."

"I know. The poor dear," Lady Elizabeth said. "Lady Honorah was afraid if the Dowager thought there was any connection between her and Charles Parker, she would treat her even worse."

"Dashed silly." Lord William shook his head and slipped another biscuit to Cuddles. The dog sat attentively by Lord William's side, a place food was likely to be deliberately dropped.

"Hard to imagine how she could be much worse than she is now," Penelope said.

"It's not hard for me to imagine. She was always a spiteful cat," Lady Elizabeth said with more venom than normal for her. "Anyway, that's why Lady Honorah didn't want anyone to find out she knew Charles Parker. While I don't believe Victor killed that man, I honestly don't believe Honorah killed him either. We'll just have to keep looking."

With that, Lady Elizabeth turned her attention to her tea.

Lord William didn't hide the sadness in his eyes. "I'm going to town tomorrow. I've got a friend in the home office. He might be able to help. I'll ask him to do some digging."

Penelope rushed to her uncle and gave him a hug. "That would be wonderful. Are you sure you feel up to it? What about your gout?"

Lord William patted his niece. "Yes, well, I'm doing much better, much better. I'll swing by the club and have a word around there too."

Lady Elizabeth hid a smile. Her husband might not be overly fond of traveling to the city, but he did enjoy his club. And, several members of the same gentleman's club were also present the night of the murder. He might find out something useful, something to help Victor.

"Now, now. You just go and enjoy your tea," Lord William said.

"I think I'll go have a word with Victor. We really haven't had a chance to talk much, not since the murder." Penelope avoided making eye contact with her aunt and uncle.

"Yes, dear. I think that's a good idea," Lady Elizabeth said. "You go have a word with Victor, and I'll go have a talk with the servants."

Penelope and Lord William both regarded her quizzically.

"Servants notice a lot more than one might think. Maybe one of them saw something they didn't know was important at the time," Lady Elizabeth explained.

"Aunt Elizabeth, you're brilliant. Thompkins notices everything. I don't know why I didn't think of that," Penelope said.

"Thank you, dear." Lady Elizabeth picked up the teapot. "More tea?"

Chapter 13

The low rumbling sounded distant and far away in the night. I tried to block it out, but when it turned into a deep growl, I couldn't. Ever the optimist, I hoped if I lay completely still maybe, just maybe, I could snatch fifteen more minutes of sleep. Surely, that was possible. Through the slits in my eyelids, I saw it was still dark. Other than the usual night noises, ones I was accustomed to, the house was quiet. The darkness around me crept inside my head and doused my thoughts. I drifted back to sleep—for perhaps two glorious minutes before ten pounds of poodle jumped on my chest and knocked the breath out of me. I opened my eyes. Sure enough, Snickers stood on my chest, her muzzle inches from my eyes.

"What the—"

Snickers stuck her tongue in my mouth. After living with her all those years, I should have expected it. Where my dogs are concerned, I'm a slow learner. I rolled over, ungraciously sliding Snickers off my chest, and used my pillow to wipe her doggie kiss off my tongue.

"You have to go outside?"

Snickers jumped off the bed and went to stand next to

Oreo, who growled and scratched at my bedroom door. If you've lived with animals for any period of time, you learn their moods. Humans and dogs might not speak the same language, but they manage to communicate. The poodles' behavior was a repeat from the day before, but not their normal, prancing, *wake up and let us out wench* dance. It was more like their *a small rodent is on our turf and we must pounce and let them know who's boss* dance. Either way, I wouldn't get a moment of sleep unless I complied with their demands. Best get it over with quickly. I got out of bed and slipped my feet into a pair of sneakers. When I opened the door, Oreo took off for the stairs. Snickers followed closely, while I plodded along and hoped we wouldn't wake up Nana Jo.

I almost ran into her in the hallway. She held her gun.

"What are you doing?" I stared at the gun.

She shushed me and whispered, "I heard a noise. I bet the dogs heard it too." She waved her gun toward the lower level. "Someone's down there."

I hadn't heard anything but decided to play it safe. I ran to my bedroom and grabbed the Louisville slugger I kept next to my bed.

Nana Jo and I tiptoed down the stairs. At the bottom, we paused and listened. Oreo growled. I heard his nails as they scratched the door that separated the apartment from the store. When we reached the bottom, we unlocked it and the dogs sped toward the back of the building. We rounded a corner and found the dogs scratching at the door to the bathroom. Snickers, normally pretty meek, snarled and sounded poised to pounce. Nana Jo put her finger to her lips and motioned for me to get behind her.

My heart raced. The blood pounded in my ears. I took a few steps back, gripped my bat, and got in my stance. On my high school fast-pitch softball team, I hit .654. Nana Jo looked back. I nodded and readjusted my stance. Feet planted, I was ready. Nana Jo aimed her gun at the bathroom. Perhaps sensing that something was about to go down, Oreo stopped scratching and stood ready to pounce on whatever came through the door.

I reminded myself to swing from the hips.

"Whoever you are, we've got you covered. The police are on their way. Come out slowly with your hands up or I'll plug you full of holes," Nana Jo shouted.

A whimper came from the bathroom. "Please don't shoot me. I'm coming out."

Nana Jo and I stepped back. The doorknob turned, and the door slowly swung open. Nana Jo and I held our positions, but Oreo did not. As soon as the door opened wide enough for him to squeeze in, in he went.

Oreo snarled. I assumed the yelling and banging and thrashing that followed came from the intruder.

Poodles aren't known to be violent. In the twelve years I'd owned him, I had never seen Oreo attack anything bigger than a stuffed toy. Despite the screams and pleas from the bathroom, I had to admit to a certain amount of pride that my otherwise tame fluff-ball not only could, but would, defend me. Snickers, on the other hand, stood back, barked, and attempted to look fierce. My shock at Oreo's attack slowed me, but I quickly recovered. I flipped on the lights, and Nana Jo opened the bathroom door.

Dawson Alexander backed up against the toilet. Oreo gripped his pants leg in his teeth.

"Please get him off of me. Please."

I reached down to grab Oreo. He didn't want to let go of Dawson's pant leg, but I eventually managed to get the fabric out of his mouth. I still held my bat, so my grasp on Oreo wasn't tight and he escaped.

Dawson crouched on the toilet and pulled his knees up to his chest in an effort to keep his limbs out of biting range. I grabbed Oreo, stuck him under one arm, and backed out of the bathroom.

Nana Jo pointed her gun at Dawson's chest. "Give me one good reason why I shouldn't blow your head off."

"Nana Jo, please, let's just let the police take care of him." The adrenaline that had me ready to crack someone's skull just moments before seeped out of my body and left me weary. Whether at the thought a former student had broken into my store to rob me or worse, or at the thought a young man with talent and potential had thrown it all away, I was drained and close to tears.

"Please, Mrs. Washington. I didn't mean any harm. Please, let me explain." Dawson's pleas were pathetic.

"Really? You have words to explain why you broke into my store and hid in my bathroom? I'd like to hear them." I stood in the hallway with one dog under each arm. Oreo had stopped snarling but kept his eyes on his prey. One false move and he'd be all over Dawson faster than a tick on a deer. "Now, come out of there."

Dawson stayed as far away from Oreo as he could and inched into the hallway.

Nana Jo kept her gun leveled at his chest. "Don't get any ideas. I'm a darned good shot and, at this range, you'll be easy pickings."

"Please. I didn't break in to hurt you or to steal from you. I just . . . I just needed a place to sleep." Tears ran down his face.

"What are you talking about? Why aren't you on campus?" His answer shocked me.

Dawson Alexander was one of the best high school football players in the state. He went to Michigan Southwest University on a football scholarship.

He swallowed a few times. "Football was good, but I couldn't keep up with my classes. I got put on academic probation after the season."

My heart started to thaw, but a few slivers of ice still held fast. "Why didn't you go home?"

"Home is . . . not a good place." He stepped away from the wall and out of the shadow and stood beneath the bright fluorescent overhead light. The colors of his swollen and bruised face went from red to dark purple. His lip was cut and puffy, and his clothes were more torn than could be blamed on a ten-pound poodle.

I stared. "Oh my God" was all I could say.

"I look pretty bad, huh?"

My heart melted. The young man had been used as a punching bag.

Nana Jo lowered her gun and took charge. "Come with me." Her voice left no room for argument. She cast one look in my direction, and I nodded agreement.

Dawson hung his head and meekly followed Nana Jo up the stairs.

I took a moment to let Oreo and Snickers out to take care of their business—and to clear my head—before I followed them. While I waited for Oreo to sniff every leaf, I couldn't help but think back to the classes I'd had with Dawson. He was bright but focused on one thing and one thing only. Football. I remembered bruises and broken bones, all attributed to football injuries. Now, I wondered. There was never anything as bad as this. He could have come by his current injuries only one way.

I said a prayer and locked the door. In the morning, I'd look into an alarm system.

Upstairs, at the breakfast bar, Dawson drank hot chocolate while Nana Jo poured tea into two mugs. I hopped on the other barstool and drank my tea in silence. For the life of me, I couldn't figure out how to initiate the conversation.

Nana Jo kept busy. In addition to the tea and hot chocolate, she opened a bag of Oreos and dropped a few dog biscuits on the floor. Dawson ate an entire row of cookies in less than a minute. On a bad day, I'd been known to do the same thing, but Nana Jo must have noticed the hungry look in his eyes. She silently took out a skillet, butter, bread, and cheese and made grilled cheese sandwiches.

She put two in front of him. "Eat. We'll talk later." With that, she went into the bathroom and came back with a towel. I kept an ice pack in the freezer for emergencies, which, in my case, usually meant twisted ankles or wrenched knees following bouts of exercise.

Nana Jo wrapped the ice pack in the towel and handed it to Dawson. He held it to his eye with one hand and shoved sandwiches into his mouth with the other.

When his eating slowed to a crawl, I thought it was time for some answers. "Dawson, who did this to you?"

I thought he wasn't going to answer, but he must have decided he owed us an explanation.

"When my old man found out I might lose my scholarship, he went crazy. He was drunk. Well, he's always drunk, but he was really lit last night. He called me a lot of names and laid into me." He paused. "I thought he was going to ki . . . I just grabbed my backpack and ran."

Nana Jo and I looked at each other. It was obvious what Dawson thought his father was going to do. "You need to go to the police." I had a feeling he wouldn't.

Dawson jumped off his stool before the words were out of my mouth. "No. No. I'm not going to the police." He backed away from the counter, about to bolt for the stairs.

"Sit down." Nana Jo's tone meant business anywhere in the world.

Dawson hesitated but sat down.

"Why did you come here?" I asked.

"I like how nice and quiet the bookstore is. I was going to ask if you needed any help, unloading or shelving books, anything. I thought maybe I could work here during the summer. You wouldn't even have to pay me."

"How did you get in?" After a murder in the backyard and an intruder, I was seriously questioning my safety.

"Last time I was here, I noticed the lock on the storm cellar was broken. I came in through there. I didn't think about the dogs. They seemed pretty friendly the other day. Who knew this little guy had the heart of *Cujo*?"

Oreo was prostrate in Dawon's lap, having his belly rubbed. Obviously, all was forgiven and forgotten.

"I still think you should go to the police, but I won't force you."

Dawson absentmindedly stroked Oreo and avoided looking at me with the one eye not covered by ice. After a few moments, he asked, "What are you going to do?"

"Tonight, I'm going to sleep. Tomorrow, I'm going to call a locksmith to fix the storm cellar."

"No. I mean what are you going to do about me? Are you going to call the police?"

I'd been wondering what I was going to do and hadn't come up with a good solution. I made up my mind. "No."

"Thank you. I'm really sorry, Mrs. Washington. I promise I won't do anything like that again. I'll just grab my backpack and . . ." He stood and dislodged Oreo, who wasn't pleased.

Oreo barked, and Dawson headed toward the stairs.

He halted at the sight of Nana Jo with her hands on her hips.

"Where do you think you're going?"

"I was just—"

"Just what? I cooked. Your job is to load the dishes into the dishwasher."

"Yes, ma'am." He hurried to the kitchen and gathered the dirty dishes.

Nana Jo went to the linen closet and came back with

sheets, a blanket, and a pillow. She plopped them on the sofa. "When you're done loading the dishes, make up the sofa bed and turn out the lights. I'm going to bed. I'm tired." She took her gun from the counter, went to her room, and shut the door.

Dawson stood in the middle of the kitchen with his mouth open.

"You heard her." I walked to my bedroom, followed by Oreo and Snickers, and closed the door.

Chapter 14

I didn't expect to sleep well, given the night's events. However, I slept like a baby and awoke to the glorious smell of coffee and bacon. After a luxuriously hot shower, I found Dawson and Nana Jo encamped at the bar, already eating bacon and French toast. The kitchen smelled of maple syrup and vanilla. I was ravenous, and the French toast tasted divine. I ate more than I should have.

"Dawson, why don't you take the dogs outside while Sam and I load the dishwasher," Nana Jo said.

"Sure. You think they'll come with me?" Dawson looked skeptical.

Oreo and Snickers scavenged for crumbs at his feet.

I handed him two dog biscuits from the jar on the counter. "They'll follow food anywhere." Biscuits in hand, Dawson led Oreo and Snickers downstairs.

The moment Dawson and the dogs were out of earshot, Nana Joe asked, "What are you going to do with him?"

"I'm sure I could use his help in the bookstore. We're supposed to have our grand opening in a couple of days. I should be able to afford one more worker for a few months."

Nana Jo headed toward the stairs and beckoned for me to follow.

Dawson had found a stuffed toy and was playing tug-of-war and keep-away with the poodles in the back courtyard. They barely noticed when we passed.

In the garage, Nana Jo skirted around my car to the door at the other side of the wall. She opened it and led me up the stairs. At the top was a large open area covered in dust and cobwebs. The previous owners must have planned to use the area for extra rental income. They'd squeezed in a toilet and shower. In the corner were the beginnings of a small kitchenette with a base sink cabinet and upper shelves.

"Jenna has been storing a set of twin beds in my attic since the twins outgrew them. Dawson's stocky, but he's not as tall as the twins. Besides, beggars can't be choosers." Nana Jo walked around the small studio. "If you got a dorm-sized refrigerator, microwave, a hot plate, and a small table with a couple of chairs, the kitchen would be done. He'll need a desk and a dresser. I saw a small desk in that little antique store across the street. I'll bet if you flirt with the owner, we can get it for a reasonable price. Maybe you better let me handle that. Then you'll need paint and rugs." Nana Jo had it all worked out.

I went and gave her a big hug.

Although I used the garage to park, I hadn't been upstairs since I'd closed on the building. "I think that would be great." I was overwhelmed at how fast she'd worked out a plan. I gave her another squeeze and wiped away a couple of tears.

"He can work in exchange for room and board. You know he made the French toast this morning. I think that young man has a career as a chef. He said he loves to bake," Nana Jo said with a wink. "Besides, I'll feel better knowing there's a man around the house."

"It'll be wonderful. Plus, it will be convenient. I was going to offer to tutor him at night."

"Great. You can tutor him in English, and I'll tackle math."

"Sounds like a great plan, but maybe we should ask Dawson."

Nana Jo went to the window and pried it open and yelled to him to come join us.

Thrilled didn't begin to describe Dawson's reaction, and we got started making the garage apartment habitable right away. Nana Jo's plans were good, but a few other modifications were needed for it to qualify as a legal apartment. After a quick call to Chris, Andrew, the Amish contractor and builder of bookshelves, was on the job. By sundown, Andrew had repaired the plumbing, attached stairs for an external fire escape, added a small skylight to allow more light into the space, and installed a microwave convection oven and the tiny two-burner stove Nana Jo got from the antique dealer when she purchased the desk. Chris and Zaq helped, and many hands made light work. Dawson found a couple of gargoyles in the basement of the bookstore and put them on his desk for inspiration.

Sunday morning, we moved in the bunk beds. Jenna suggested they be taken apart, pushed against the wall, and made up with extra-large pillows to look like a sofa during the day. When all was said and done, the space was cozy and functional. I had new locks and dead bolts put on the outside door and on the cellar door. The security company would be out Monday to install a new alarm system. Even Oreo and Snickers seemed happy with the new arrangement. After days of working on the garage apartment and the last minute details for the store opening, I needed an escape.

❧

"Victor, don't be such a bloody fool." Penelope shook with anger. She turned her back to Victor and folded her arms across her chest. She had found him sitting in his garden after her three-mile walk from Wickfield Lodge.

Victor's home, Bidwell Cottage, wasn't the humble dwelling the name implied. The summer home to the Earl of Lochloren was a large estate used by the Scottish lord for hunting and shooting parties in centuries past. Considerably smaller than the castle, Bidwell Cottage had been the full-time residence of the family. Over time, the drafty Scottish castle fell into disrepair. Although still owned by Victor's family, it was uninhabitable and derelict. Unlike the manicured gardens on most British estates, Bidwell Cottage's gardens were untamed, natural woodlands full of rolling wildflowers and undulating hills. Lady Penelope wasn't in a mood to admire gardens. She'd pleaded with Victor to tell the police everything he knew. He'd refused. Victor wouldn't say or do anything to cast suspicion onto Daphne, even though his silence meant he might be arrested and hung for murder.

Victor stepped toward her. Even with her back to him, she sensed his presence, so close she felt his breath on the back of her neck. The heat from his body sent a tingle up her spine. She trembled. If she turned around, would she find anguish on his face? She didn't turn. After an eternity, Victor stepped away. A chill crawled up her spine. Penelope shivered.

Victor removed his jacket and placed it around her shoulders. "Penelope, please. Surely you have to understand?"

In a flash, her anger returned. She spun to face him. "No. I don't. I do not understand how you can toss your life away like that." She snapped her fingers.

"A gentleman doesn't abandon a lady in distress."

His shoulders slumped. "Besides, she's your sister." His voice was weary.

"Yes. She's my sister and because she is, I know there's no way she killed Charles Parker. Daphne is too shallow to be a murderer. She wouldn't risk ruining her dress for the likes of him. Can't you see that? Can't you see she doesn't need a knight in shining armor to come and save her? She's innocent. What she needs is a good spanking."

Victor searched Penelope's eyes.

She looked into his eyes and saw the logic of her pleas hit home, but years of training in the chivalrous ways of a gentleman wouldn't go down without a fight. Victor dropped his gaze and turned away.

"I gave my word. I—" Victor's attention seemed to be captured by a movement in the azalea bushes bordering the garden. He gently moved Penelope aside and peered into the shrubs.

The azaleas shook and out stepped an Adonis of a man.

He was shorter and stockier than Victor, but his broad shoulders and overall build suggested his familiarity with rugby was more than a passing fancy. Clad in country tweeds, fair-haired and freckled, sporting a broad smile and a pipe, he was the picture of a country squire.

"James?" Victor asked.

The newcomer nodded, and the two men embraced.

"Sorry about that mate. I took the back way from the train station and found myself in the middle of a private conversation." James had the decency to blush but not explain why he didn't make his presence known sooner.

"You took the train?"

"No. I drove down but by the time I got to town, it was clear something decisive would need to be done to the innards of the car or I'd be left stranded. I left it with a chap near the train station and walked the rest of the way."

Straight and proper, Victor bowed to Penelope. "Lady Penelope Marsh, may I present one of my oldest mates, His Grace James Fitzandrew Browning, the 15th Duke of Kingsfordshire." He bowed stiffly to his friend. "Lady Penelope Marsh."

Penelope performed a brief curtsy and extended her hand. "Your Grace."

The duke clasped Penelope's hand in both of his. "Please, call me James. I don't go in for all that bobbing and curtsying. I was just plain James until my uncle decided to go and kick the bucket." He held Penelope's hand long enough to bring heat to her face and a furrow to Victor's brow.

"What brings you to the countryside, your grace— I mean James?" Penelope gently extracted her hand from the duke's grasp.

"Yes. What brings you out this way? The last I heard you were fighting in the African desert," Victor said.

"Were you in the military together?" Penelope asked.

James took Penelope's arm, and the three of them walked toward the house. "Victor and I go back a lot further than the military. We were mates at Winchester."

The prestigious boarding school had, for centuries, educated Britain's greatest captains of industry and peers of the realm.

Although the walk to the house was short, the men filled it with *remember when we* stories. Penelope made her excuses and left them to their reminisces, but not before extending an invitation to Victor and James for dinner.

In the Gothic inspired study, Victor poured drinks. Beverages in hand, the gentlemen seated themselves in the comfortable overstuffed chairs.

"Now, what really brings you out here?" Victor's politeness softened his blunt question.

James took a long drink before responding. "I heard from one of my contacts at the home office that you've gotten yourself into a bit of trouble. There's a bloke at The Yard who wants to see your neck in a noose. I thought I'd better come down and see what you've gotten yourself into."

Victor took a drink.

Almost a full minute passed before James broke the silence. "I take it from the conversation I over-heard there's a lady involved."

Victor stared into his glass.

"Don't be a bloody fool man. Can't you see I'm trying to help?" James took a swig of his drink, placed his glass on the table, and stood. "Okay then, if that's how you want it. How about a game of billiards be-fore we have to change and head over to dinner with the lovely Lady Penelope Marsh."

Dinner at Wickfield Lodge went well. Victor re-mained noticeably silent, but James was lively and engaging and kept the conversation flowing. He re-galed the Marshes with humorous tales of his ex-ploits in Egypt with the 7th Queen's Own Hussars.

Good food, good wine, and good conversation provided the lift the group needed. After dinner, the party moved to the parlor for cards and drinks. Lady Elizabeth and Lord William retired for the evening, and the young crowd played games. Their laughter continued until the early morning.

The next day Penelope walked into town and ran into James on her way home. "Your Grace."

"I thought we'd already agreed you would call me James and I shall call you the beautiful Penelope Marsh."

Penelope smiled. "James, it flatters my vanity to think you'd be interested in me, but something tells me there's more to you than meets the eye."

"While I do find you enchanting, I suspect your heart lies elsewhere." He looked pointedly at Penelope.

Warmth rose up her neck and into her cheeks. "If I'm that obvious, I shall have to adjust my mask." She stopped walking. "I love my sister. She's superficial and self-centered, but she's also kind and gentle. I would never do anything to hurt her. If I thought she cared two figs for Victor . . ." She hung her head. "I'd make sure that nothing stood in her way." A tear trailed down her cheek.

James handed her a handkerchief.

Penelope gathered herself, and they continued to walk.

"I meant no disrespect," James said. "In fact, if the daggers my friend Victor shot my way last night are any indication, I suspect your feelings are reciprocated."

Penelope searched James's face, looking for the truth behind his words. What she found there filled her with joy. Half crying, half laughing, she dabbed at her eyes. Without speaking, she resumed walking.

"So, what are we going to do about this mess?" James said. "My friend is determined to marry a woman he doesn't love, a woman whom I don't believe loves him. For this, he is willing to risk his life."

"Surely you can talk to him. Convince him to talk to the police."

"Unfortunately, no. Victor is a chivalrous fool where women are concerned. He will do the gentlemanly thing. No, it will be up to us to save him."

"Perhaps you would like to come to tea this afternoon with my aunt and uncle," Penelope said. "I'm sure Daphne will be in town shopping, but I think you'll find the conversation very enlightening."

As expected, Daphne went shopping and was unavailable for tea. Without her presence, Lady Elizabeth, Lord William, James, and Lady Penelope could speak openly. Lady Elizabeth poured the tea, and they brought James up to speed on what they'd learned so far.

With his leg propped on a footrest, Lord William reported on his excursion to London. "I stopped at the home office first thing this morning and had a word with my old friend, Freddy Montgomery. Freddy promised to send a cable to an American he knows in the secret service over there—said he'd send word as soon as he found anything out."

Penelope leaned forward. "Is that all?" She'd hoped for more.

"Hold on to your horses. I'm not finished. I ran into Lord Exeter at my club. Nice man Peter Exeter. We had brandy, and he eventually owned up to the fact he was glad Charles Parker was out of the picture. Poor fellow suspected Honorah had gotten herself entangled with Parker on the Queen Mary. Seems the rascal got her gambling and who knows what else. Peter found out about the gambling when a chap had the nerve to approach him outside of the club. He had his solicitor discretely settle her debts."

"How did he manage? I mean, I didn't think the Viscount had very much money."

Lord William frowned. He found talking about money distasteful. "I gather the poor fellow sold some property. Estate is dwindling. Sale was a rush job. He got quite a bit less than it's worth, but he needed the money and was determined to not ask his American relations."

"Despite what the Dowager Lady Exeter thinks about Americans, I have always heard Lady Honorah's relations were very generous. I find it hard to believe they wouldn't help their daughter out of a mess." Lady Elizabeth was always sensible.

"I don't doubt that they would, but a man has his pride. If a man can't help his wife out of a bind, then, well . . ." Lord William sipped his tea.

Penelope rose and began her usual pacing. "So, Honorah Exeter had a gambling problem, and Lord Peter knew about it. And, both of them were at the party. Maybe Charles Parker approached Honorah at the party to get money from her? That would give her a motive. What if Lord Peter overheard him? Anger might have driven him into a murderous frenzy."

Lady Elizabeth pulled her knitting from her basket. "It's possible, although, for the life of me, I can't imagine Lord Peter Exeter in a frenzy of any kind, let alone a murderous one. He's a nice old man, but he's not exactly the passionate type, is he? What do you think, Your Grace . . . ah, James?"

"I have to say I agree with Lady Elizabeth. Peter Exeter is a nice man but certainly isn't known for his passions."

"At least it means someone other than Victor had a reason for wanting Charles Parker gone," Penelope said.

James went to the fireplace. "I have a friend who was able to share a little bit of information I think you might find interesting."

Penelope halted. "Please, I could use interesting right now."

James cleared his throat. "Apparently, when word of Parker's death hit America, a policeman from Chicago reached out to Scotland Yard. It seems they'd been looking for Parker for quite some time."

"Well, that's odd. There was a police officer who followed him from America," Penelope said.

"That's just it. The Chicago police didn't know anything about this police officer. My friend said Charles Parker is wanted by the Chicago Police."

Penelope plopped onto the sofa.

Lord William sputtered.

Lady Elizabeth dropped several stitches, and her knitting fell from her hands to the floor.

Lord William broke into a coughing fit. "Wanted by the police?" he croaked between coughs.

"Yes. According to this chap." James pulled a notebook from his breast pocket and flipped through the pages. "Fellow named Patrick O'Hara said Charles Parker was a, and I quote, Juice Lender."

"What on earth is a Juice Lender?" Penelope asked.

"According to O'Hara, a Juice Lender loans money at abominably high rates of interest. If the borrower fails to repay the money, let's just say they're known to apply physical pressure."

Penelope was truly shocked. From the look on Lady Elizabeth's face, she was too.

"Why the devil, I can't believe he was in this house and exposed to my nieces. Why, I . . ." Lord William's face reddened.

"You weren't to know, dear." Lady Elizabeth collected her knitting from the floor.

"Of course not," James said. "I assure you Charles Parker deceived a great many people. By falsifying his connections, he gained admittance to a good many homes in England. You were not to know. You are to be commended that he wasn't able to directly damage anyone in your family."

Lord William didn't appear reassured.

"A criminal. Well, that must mean there were tons of people with a reason to kill Charles Parker," Penelope said.

Lady Elizabeth unraveled a row of knitting. "Well, that's true, darling, but it's unlikely they were at the party."

"Exactly, Lady Elizabeth," James said, respect evident in his voice. "But, it does give us something to work with. O'Hara is trying to get permission to travel here to collect Parker's body. I've offered to pay for his trip."

"What about the other policeman or whoever he is, the cellist?" Lord William asked.

"No idea. No one seems to know anything about him."

"What do you hope to accomplish by bringing another police officer here?" Penelope picked up her teacup and set it back down.

"O'Hara is familiar with Parker and many of his underworld connections. He might recognize someone or something to help to solve this murder."

Penelope hoped so too, but was skeptical. "Surely we would have noticed someone unknown to us? The only people invited to the party were people familiar to us, friends."

"Not everyone at the party was an invited guest, dear." Lady Elizabeth didn't look up from her knitting. "There were the waiters and the orchestra, plus some of our invited guests brought guests unfamiliar to us. If I remember correctly, that's how we became acquainted with Mr. Parker in the first place."

"Very true, Lady Elizabeth," James said.

"James has a wonderful plan. And, I'm going to have that conversation with the servants. I meant to do it yesterday but got busy. They see and hear a lot more than anyone ever realizes. Isn't that right, Thompkins?" Lady Elizabeth turned to face the butler.

Thompkins had silently entered the room and refilled the teapot while they talked. He bowed and, with a "Yes, m'lady," left the room as quietly as he'd entered.

Chapter 15

The remainder of the week went by in a blur. The grand opening of Market Street Mysteries was a huge success. People filled the shop, and sales figures were promising. I was happy I'd hired my nephews, along with Dawson. Chris was amazing at setting up displays, customer service, overall organization, and marketing. He worked on a website and suggested I could build a lucrative online business with little to no overhead. He was studying business at the university and quite good at it. Zaq's skills lay with all things technology. He was a genius when it came to figuring out the quirks to my POS system. I called him the POS Whisperer.

Dawson didn't know much about mysteries, but he was incredibly strong and lugged boxes and boxes of books. Also a gifted cook, he mastered the complicated Espresso machine Jenna bought for the grand opening. At night, he baked cookies, brownies, and some delicious concoction he called Chess bars in my kitchen. We gave them away, along with the goodies we bought at the neighborhood bakery. Dawson's treats were hands down the crowd favorite. I considered opening the bistro side of the business ahead of plan. It could be a big moneymaker, and Dawson genuinely enjoyed cooking.

Nana Jo provided recommendations for new mystery readers and excelled at it. She asked a few general questions. *What's your favorite television show? Who's your favorite actor or favorite singer?* Based on the responses, she steered readers toward British cozies or hard-boiled PI or True Crime books. Only time would tell if her system was successful, but I thought she was onto something. Jenna came by for a few hours and helped with decorations. Even my mom stopped by and took Oreo and Snickers outside so I could focus on customers.

We were so busy I didn't have time to think about Clayton Parker. Once the thrill died down and the crowds became manageable, it was time to get back to sleuthing.

First things first, I owed Mrs. Parker an apology. Nana Jo and the boys had everything under control, so I wrapped up a cake Dawson and I had made the previous night. We'd made two, one for the store and one for a peace offering to Mrs. Parker. Cake in hand, I slipped out.

Clayton Parker's house was a newer construction modern beach house, what Nana Jo called a South Harbor McMansion, on the beautiful Southwest Michigan shoreline.

Up through the early part of the twentieth century, Lake Michigan was used for shipping goods to auto manufacturers. When the auto manufacturers shut their local facilities and moved across the border, they left behind equipment and polluted beaches. Later, Chicago's city dwellers, priced out of lakefront property in Illinois, came in search of less expensive vacation homes. They bought up the waterfront and campaigned with environmentalists for the city to clean up the beaches, which they did. The beachfront filled with a cacophony of structures. The Parkers' large glass and steel structure was wedged between a bright yellow New England–style cottage and a pink stilted coastal beach home.

I pulled into the driveway and took in the beauty of the Lake Michigan coastline, or what I could see of it around the glass box, and mustered my courage. Finally, I grabbed my cake and got out of the car. Best to get horrible things over with quickly. I walked around a large black BMW and a bright red Bentley convertible. I'd never been close to a car that cost more than my house and couldn't help gawking. A quick sniff confirmed the car still had the new car smell. Mrs. Parker had a new toy. The yard held a small and discrete sign with a telephone number and the words FOR SALE. I made a note to ask Chris Martinelli when the house went on the market. I suspected the listing was recent.

I waited for someone to respond to my ring. I was just about to ring the bell again when the door opened. Mrs. Parker took one look at me and rolled her eyes. Before she could slam the door in my face, I held up my peace offering.

"Mrs. Parker, I am so sorry for the other day. Please, may I come in?"

She hesitated so long I seriously thought she wasn't going to admit me. She huffed and walked away, leaving the door open. I took it as an invitation and entered. Hands full with my purse and cake, I closed the door with my foot. Inside, the décor was sleek and modern. The main living area had white walls, high ceilings, and a wall of windows overlooking the beach. A black leather sectional and glass and steel tables dominated the room. My heels clacked like a Clydesdale's with each cautious step I took across the slippery surface of the white polished marble floor.

Mrs. Parker's outfit, yoga pants, sneakers, and a sports bra, showed off her six-pack. She stood in front of the fireplace, her arms folded across her chest, and looked down her nose at me.

I searched for a place to set the cake. None of the surfaces looked like they had ever seen a cake, let alone held one. Mrs. Parker took mercy on me. She took the cake and walked around the corner to the kitchen. I followed and tried to not make too much noise, although I was trying harder to not slip. I rounded the corner in time to see Mrs. Parker place the cake on a granite bar top. I hoisted myself up onto a barstool, mostly to avoid falling on the marble floors, and smiled as big as I could. "It's carrot cake, and it's delicious with coffee."

She took the hint and pulled two coffee mugs from a white cabinet and put them on the black granite counter. She grabbed a couple of single-brew coffee packs, stuck them in a machine, and pressed one button. Instantly, the smell of coffee filled the room, and the sleek black and white kitchen felt welcoming. When both cups were full, she placed one in front of me, along with a spoon and sugar bowl.

"Cream?" She held up a bottle of Baileys liqueur.

"Oh, yeah." I had a silly grin on my face, but I couldn't stop myself.

I liked the way she cut big slices.

We ate in silence, both of us absorbed in raisin and nut-filled delight. The cream cheese icing held everything together. I forgot where I was. I think I moaned.

"This is delicious. Did you make it?" Mrs. Parker licked her fork.

Behold the power of cake.

I shook my head. "I wish. My new assistant at my bookstore made it. He's a fantastic baker."

She scraped the last bits of cake and nuts into her mouth and placed her plate into the sink. With a final lick of her fork, she faced me. "Okay, you've tamed the savage beast. Now, what do you want?" Her tone was much nicer than her words.

"I came to offer my condolences and to apologize for my

behavior at the reception. I'm not a big drinker, and I had four or five glasses of champagne on an empty stomach. It's no excuse, but—"

She held up her hand. "It's all right. Forget it."

"Thank you." I'd rehearsed my apology many times in my head, and none of my scenarios involved being forgiven. Definitely not this fast.

"Was there anything else you wanted?"

If I didn't do something quickly, I'd be escorted out without answers. Without thinking, I blurted out, "Mrs. Parker, why did you faint when I mentioned your husband died in my backyard?"

She grabbed a paper towel and wiped the already spotless countertop. Her silence lingered like a bad odor, but I did nothing to alleviate it. If there was anything I'd learned in my years as a teacher, it was the power of silence.

Eventually, she turned toward me. "I don't know what you're talking about."

"Really? All that time and that's the best you came up with?"

She appeared shocked at my boldness.

I gave her my *surely you can do better* expression.

She smiled. The smile turned into a laugh, and we both laughed.

"Honestly, I don't know. I guess it was the shock."

I started to interrupt.

She held up a hand to stop me. "I know it sounds lame, but it's the truth. Ever since the police told me Clay was murdered, I've been on edge."

Understandable, but I could see the wheels turning inside her head.

She stared at my face, as if she was searching for something. Whatever it was, she must have found it. "Clay had been acting strange for months. Don't ask me why. He never shared his personal business with me. I was just his trophy wife, an adornment he wore like a badge to the yacht club or the country club. I think it had something to do with that building you bought. At first, he was happy to find a buyer, but then he got really scared."

"Scared? How do you mean?"

She was silent for a moment. "It's hard to explain. He drank more. He didn't sleep. He got angry at the drop of a hat. He started gambling."

"Did he gamble a lot?" I took a sip of my coffee. It was cold, but the Baileys still tasted pretty darned good.

Mrs. Parker looked out the window at the waves lapping the sand. She shook herself. "I didn't think so, but he must have. He didn't share any details of his business, his finances, or anything personal with me. It's been a long time since we've been married in anything other than name."

Her openness about their relationship gave me the courage to delve deeper. "I couldn't help but notice the handsome, godlike hunk who accompanied you to the reception." I raised an eyebrow.

She giggled like a schoolgirl. "Hans. Hans Ritter. He's my personal trainer."

"Hmm, yes, I see. Your *very* personal trainer."

She laughed. "Hans is sweet. He treats me well." She paused. "I don't know why I'm telling you this. I don't even know you."

"Sometimes it's easier talking to a stranger. By the way, my name is Samantha Washington, but you can call me Sam." I scooted around on my stool.

"Diana."

"Great, now that that's over, tell me about Hans." I lingered on the name.

"What the heck difference does it make?" She grabbed a couple more coffee pods from the cabinet and refilled our mugs. She sat next to me, and we sipped our coffee.

"Hans and I have been close for over a year now. He wanted me to leave Clay. He knew I wasn't happy."

"Why didn't you leave?"

She stared into her mug.

That's when it hit me. "You couldn't leave because you signed a prenup right?"

A spark lit up her eyes and went out quickly. "How did you know that?"

"It sounds like something Clayton Parker would do." I wasn't anxious to destroy the female bonding moment so I tried to look sympathetic and waited for her to continue.

"I did sign a prenuptial agreement. If I left, I got nothing. This is going to sound mercenary, but I'd invested too much time and effort into my marriage." As she spoke, she picked up speed and volume. "I put up with all of his moods, his women, and his condescending behavior. I couldn't walk away after ten years with nothing." She practically shouted the last words but took a sip of coffee and regained her composure. "I guess that makes me sound like a gold digger."

"Not really. I had the misfortune of meeting Clayton Parker. He was a first-class jerk." As soon as the words left my mouth, I panicked. It was one thing for a woman to complain about her husband's flaws, it was another for someone else to do it.

Diana Parker didn't seem bothered by my boldness. "He wasn't always that way." She tilted her head and looked into her mug as if she was seeing into the past. "He could be very charming when he wanted to." She smiled at a memory and then the smile faded. "He could also be cruel."

"Do you know anyone who would want your husband dead?"

"Other than Hans and me, you mean?"

I didn't mean to imply I suspected her of murdering her husband, but Diana was no fool.

"The more successful he got, the crueler he became. Clay had a way of rubbing people the wrong way. The list of people who wanted to murder him was probably a mile long, but I did not kill my husband and neither did Hans."

I must have looked skeptical.

"We were together that night. The police have already checked. I'm sure the manager at the South Harbor Inn will confirm what time we checked in and what time we checked out."

I stayed another fifteen minutes. Diana Parker was a very lonely woman who obviously needed a friend, but I'd been gone from the bookstore a lot longer than I'd intended. I reluctantly left.

During the drive back to the store, I sifted through the information I'd picked up. I wasn't sure how it fit together, but something told me it was important.

The remainder of the afternoon I worked in the store and tackled the paperwork that had piled up during the week. Christopher had run reports I needed to analyze. The POS system book said the reports would help determine future inventory. My brain wouldn't focus. Between getting Dawson settled into the garage apartment, seeing the fulfillment of a lifelong dream with the bookstore, writing a novel, and trying to solve a murder, I was exhausted.

Miss Marple made investigating seem so easy, but it was a lot of work. Nana Jo and the girls had accumulated a lot of data, certainly more information than I could have collected on my own. Sitting in my office, I looked out the glass door onto the courtyard. Snickers slept in a sunny corner. Oreo stared at an impudent robin strutting around the courtyard. My mind wandered.

Thoughts of Leon were ever present. He would have loved the bookstore. I stocked a lot of hard-boiled mysteries because of him.

Since we had decided to make life easy for ourselves and shelved the books alphabetically by author rather than by sub-genres, Zaq recommended setting up displays of books recommended by staff. The Hard-Boiled Mystery Table, with a foam board placard identifying Leon's favorites, brought tears to my eyes. He would have loved it.

The crowds dwindled after the opening, but that was to be expected. My job was to create ideas to inspire people to continue to come. I'd received a couple of requests from book clubs who wanted space for their meetings.

Even though neither of my nephews shared my love of mysteries, I was thankful they were willing and able to help me in so many ways. Dawson was great too. He was strong and dependable and his treats were becoming one of the main attractions. I overheard him and Christopher discussing the possibility of converting a storage room at the back of the building into a commercial kitchen.

I wanted to be financially responsible and was reluctant to sink too much money into the bookstore until I knew it was successful. But, I'd gotten the building at a really good price. There had been some structural damage, which had frightened away two local banks and forced two previous offers to fall apart. However, Chris Martinelli and the ever-handy Amish Craftsman, Andrew, didn't frighten easily. Between the insurance money left over from Leon's death and the money from selling my home, I was in a strong financial position. Initially, I was going to finance the building, but thanks to Clayton Parker's antics, my banker got cold feet. Finally, my attorney offered the sellers a cash deal in exchange for a quick closing and that had cooked Clayton Parker's goose. Looking out at the courtyard, I was filled with warmth and satisfaction. This building belonged to me. I still had my pension from years of teaching. If I didn't live too extravagantly, I should be able to live comfortably.

It was Friday night. Poker night for the girls and Nana Jo. Both Christopher and Zaq had dates. Dawson agreed to stay to help me close up. The sun was setting, and I looked at my watch. Seven forty-five, almost closing time.

I started to get up. A shadow moved across the back fence. Oreo's growl and erect stance told me he saw it too. Snickers, aroused by Oreo's growls, got up and looked. At one time, I might have shrugged off the intruder as teens looking for a place to relieve themselves, but those were the days before a man was murdered in my courtyard. I reached for my cell phone and dialed the police.

The wait for the police was interminable. I peered into the darkness and considered opening the door and letting the dogs take care of the intruder. Oreo had proven he was a fierce protector, but I saw no sense risking his safety. I tried to not attract attention by moving and mentally willed Oreo and Snickers to not bark or move. It didn't work. Whether due to the dogs barking and lunging at the window or the sound of the police sirens, the shadow disappeared.

The police officer checked the courtyard but didn't find anything worth reporting. He promised to request the officers patrolling the downtown area to make a couple of extra checks of the alley and to notify Detective Pitt in case my "alleged intruder" had any bearing on the murder investigation. The prospect of another visit from Stinky Pitt left a bad taste in my mouth.

I needed a drink. I warned Dawson, who promised to be watchful without doing anything stupid. Football had made him a big guy, but he was still no match for an armed intruder.

I needed to go upstairs and relax. "*Alleged intruder* indeed."

Chapter 16

I thought writing would help me unwind, but my mind refused to focus on Great Britain in 1938. I decided to start revisions. With a stack of printed manuscript pages, a glass of wine, and a red pen, I curled up on the sofa. Within a minute, I was transported to the British countryside.

It felt like a minute later when I woke to my favorite smells, bacon and coffee. The pillow under my head and the blanket over me meant not only had I slept through Nana Jo's arrival last night or this morning, but I'd slept while she'd made me comfortable. I grunted at her cheery good morning and hurried to the bathroom to take care of pressing business and to brush my teeth.

Refreshed, I joined Nana Jo at the breakfast bar. I downed almost an entire mug of coffee before I noticed she was reading while she ate.

My manuscript. "Where did you get that?"

"Off the floor when I put the blanket over you. Why didn't you tell me you're writing a book?"

"You had no right." I grabbed the pages and clutched them

to my chest. The sudden rush of blood to my head made me a little dizzy.

I wasn't being reasonable. She didn't know about my book. She certainly didn't realize how protective, or perhaps the better word was fearful, I was. The novel was my baby. I'd dreamed of writing a book for more years than I could remember. Leon was the first person with whom I'd shared my secret. Jenna happened to overhear us talking about it and was brought into my dream.

"I'm sorry. I didn't realize," Nana Jo said. "Please forgive my intrusion."

I felt like a total and complete idiot. "I'm sorry, Nana Jo. I didn't mean to be rude." I put the pages on the counter. "It's just, I didn't want anyone to know. It's sort of personal."

"I understand, honey. No need to apologize. I should have asked. I'm really sorry." She patted my hand and returned to her breakfast.

"I was only doing some editing. I must have fallen asleep."

She nodded and continued to eat. Her body language said she wasn't angry, but I felt guilty and a little curious. I smoothed the pages I'd creased when I grabbed them and started to eat.

Those one hundred or so pages turned into the eight-hundred-pound gorilla. I couldn't keep my eyes off them. Curiosity got the better of me. "What did you think?"

Nana Jo beamed. "I thought it was wonderful. I really did, honey. I liked the characters, and I was amazed how you transported me to England."

"You aren't just saying that because you're my grandmother, are you?"

"You know me well enough to know that if I didn't think it was good, I'd tell you, granddaughter or not. God knows there are enough bad books out there. No point adding any more. A good cozy mystery is a rare thing."

I basked in the glow of my nana's praise and slid the pages to her. "I guess it would be okay if you read it, but please, don't tell anyone. I'm not ready to talk about it yet."

"Are you sure?"

I nodded. Nana Jo thanked me, found her place in the pages, and read. I studied her facial expressions and body language. She smiled a lot and laughed out loud a couple of times.

After a particularly funny bit, she said, "I can read a lot faster without you watching me. Don't you have work to do?"

She was right. It was almost nine thirty, and the store opened in less than thirty minutes. I heard Dawson downstairs getting things ready. Oreo and Snickers barked and did their Lassie-trying-to-lead-me-to-Timmy-down-the-well act.

"You get dressed. I'll take the dogs." Nana Jo scooped up the pages, grabbed a couple of dog biscuits, and headed downstairs.

I took a quick shower, got my wet hair under control, put on jeans and a T-shirt, and rushed downstairs. From the moment I hit the bookstore, traffic was nonstop.

Despite the economic depression hanging like a moldy blanket over the rest of North Harbor, the downtown area thrived. Small business owners had turned the vacant, abandoned, and derelict buildings into an eclectic mixture of antique shops, bakeries, art shops, and cafés. On weekends, artists brought their paint, photography, glass, ceramics, and ironwork onto the sidewalk. Christopher suggested we move some books outside and take advantage of the foot traffic. The experiment paid off. Inside, Nana Jo and I tended to customers while Zaq and Dawson took care of the cash register and the baked goods and espressos. Despite a few glitches, we were turning into a well-oiled machine.

At almost two, Stinky Pitt walked into the store. I was helping a customer decide between Rex Stout's Nero Wolfe and Raymond Chandler's Phillip Marlowe when Nana Jo let me know the detective was waiting in my office. I had a hard time getting away. My confused customer wanted my personal opinion about the books, and I'd never been shy about sharing my personal opinion when it came to mysteries. Just when I thought she'd made a decision, she launched into more questions.

Nana Jo intervened. "Personally, I don't see what the big deal is. The only logical solution is to buy them both."

That's exactly what she did.

Happy, I walked back to the office. My good mood died as soon as I got there. Detective Pitt sat behind my desk, reading my manuscript.

"What do you think you're doing?" I was furious.

Detective Pitt waved his hand. "Interesting reading you have here."

"You have no right! That's mine!" I grabbed the pages on the desk and tried to snatch the other pages out of his hand.

He was too fast for me. He held the pages in the air, playing keep away.

Nana Jo appeared. "What's going on here, Sam? We can hear you yelling all over the store." Seeing the papers I clutched to my chest and the ones Detective Pitt held away from me, she halted and, in her best schoolmarm voice, said "Put those down right now!"

Detective Pitt began to lower his arm but shook himself free of the trance. "No."

For the second time in one day someone had read my story without my permission. Tears filled my eyes, and I shook.

"What is this about?" Nana Jo confronted Detective Pitt. "You give Samantha back those pages. You have no right to take things that don't belong to you."

Detective Pitt looked abashed but pulled his shoulders back. "I have to take this as evidence."

"Evidence? Evidence of what?" Nana Jo and I said at the same time.

"Murder."

"Look, Detective. I think you have the wrong idea here. That's just a story I wrote. It's fiction. I made the whole thing up."

"Of course she did. Anyone with half of a brain can see that. It's a historical British Cozy. Only an idiot would think this is true." Nana Jo wasn't helping my case by insulting him.

Detective Pitt smirked and rattled the pages he held. "Mrs. Thomas, I may not be that bright. I'm just a dumb cop, but I can read." He held up one finger. "Murder victim, Clayton Parker. That sure sounds mighty close to Charles Parker." He held up a second finger. "Cause of death, stabbed." He stood and walked from behind the desk. "Only thing missing is motive. I figure if I keep reading, you'll provide that too."

My knees gave way, and I sank into the chair in front of my desk.

I had deliberately used a name similar to Clayton Parker's name for the murder victim. He was the most odious person I knew. I found it cathartic to murder him on paper. I intended to go back and change the name before anyone read it.

"What are you talking about? You can't possibly be implying my granddaughter killed that man?" Nana Jo was indignant.

"She had the opportunity and was known to dislike the victim."

"I didn't kill anyone." I couldn't believe what was happening.

"Well, I'm going to need to take this, ah, book as evidence," He pried the rest of the pages away from me. "We'll look it over down at the station. I'll give you a receipt."

"Don't you need a search warrant?" Nana Jo asked.

"Nope. I didn't search. It was in plain sight. You invited me to come back here to wait for Mrs. Washington." Detective

Pitt was confident as he smoothed the pages. "Although, I take it this was written on a computer. I may need that."

That was the last straw. I cracked. "Then you can ask my attorney to bring it to you." I pulled out my cell phone and dialed my sister's number. "Jenna, I need you at the bookstore. It's an emergency."

To my sister's credit, she asked very few questions. The well-being of her sons was her first and foremost priority. I outlined the situation and she made it to the bookstore in less than fifteen minutes.

If Detective Pitt thought Nana Jo was tough, he hadn't seen anything until he saw my sister in full-blown lawyer mode. Both she and her husband were lawyers. They met in law school. Tony was a corporate attorney, and Jenna was a criminal defense attorney.

In the end, Detective Pitt took my manuscript but not my laptop.

Nana Jo was jittery. Jenna paced.

It wasn't until that moment I realized the similarities between the people in my book and the people in my life. Lady Penelope Marsh paced, just like my sister. Victor was a chivalrous gentleman, just like my brother-in-law. Clayton Parker was a no-good lowlife who went to someone else's house and got himself killed, just like the Charles Parker in my book. I'd unconsciously taken bits and pieces of people I knew and turned them into characters in my fiction.

Jenna promised to call a friend at the police station and see what she could find out. I left Dawson and Nana Jo to take care of the bookstore and went upstairs. Curled up in my bed, I was a basket case. I missed Leon. Oreo was my tough protector, but Snickers sensed my need for a cuddle. I tried to ignore the loneliness where Leon's soul once resided. When my tears fell, Snickers licked them away.

It was dark when Nana Jo flipped on the light and sat on the side of my bed. I'd dozed.

"Honey, I'm so sorry. I feel awful. You trusted me with your manuscript, and I let it fall into the hands of that no-good weasel. Can you forgive me?"

Nana Jo's face was filled with sincerity and hurt. My normally vibrant grandmother had aged. Maybe my nap helped to put things back into perspective, a job Leon had excelled at. Maybe he hadn't vacated that place in my soul after all. It had to be a piece of his practical common sense that made me understand the manuscript was just a story. Detective Pitt read my book, but it wasn't the end of the world. I didn't kill Clayton Parker. My family loved me, and they would be with me no matter what happened. I was blessed.

Nana Jo and I hugged. Snickers wiggled her way in between us.

"I think you need a bit of fun." Nana Jo said. "Why don't you wash your face and put on some makeup? I'm going to call the girls. You need to kick up your heels."

"What do you have in mind?" I should have known better.

At the Four Feathers Casino, I tossed back shots with Nana Jo and the girls. I'd learned my lesson and made sure to eat something before drinking. Even so, I limited myself to two shots and drank diet soda the rest of the evening. Dorothy was friends with one of the managers, who promised to get us rooms if we drank too much, but I planned on sleeping in my own bed. I had no plans to get wasted.

The Four Feathers, owned by a recently recognized Native American Tribe of the Pontolomas Indians, was located in the middle of nowhere. A winding road led guests through two acres of picturesque woodland and around a man-made lake to a 150,000-square-foot casino with a five-hundred-room luxury hotel and resort. The casino sported three bars, seven restaurants, retail shops, and an event center that drew big name entertainers from all over the world.

I wasn't much of a gambler and was uncomfortable at first. Nana Jo and the girls were seasoned veterans and anxious to show me the ropes. Dorothy's friend got me a member card with fifty dollars of casino bucks. After dinner and drinks, Irma strutted to the bar and joined a couple of gray-haired gentlemen wearing cowboy hats and boots. One of Ruby Mae's grandsons worked at the buffet. He got us comps for the buffet. She pulled out her knitting and sat and talked. Dorothy went to the high-limit room, where she seemed well-known, to play blackjack. Nana Jo and I strolled to the poker table. She sat down and quickly raked in lots of chips. I didn't fully grasp the game but didn't have to be a pro to see Nana Jo was doing well. I watched her for a while and then wandered on and discovered the penny slot room. I sat at a machine with a huge picture of the Clue board game. After watching the people around me, I put my member card in the machine. I wasn't sure how the machine worked, but understanding wasn't required. Once I selected the number of lines I wanted to play and the amount of money I wanted to bet on each line, the machine did the rest. People around me bet five dollars per spin, but I played a conservative fifty cents. My wins weren't huge, but I played for a long time. Women in short brown skirts periodically served drinks.

I met some very nice people, playing penny slots. The woman sitting next to me smoked like a chimney but kept me laughing. My new friend hit the bonus multiple times. Each time she won a significant amount, she asked me to watch her machine while she cashed out her ticket. When she returned, she stuck her winnings in her bra and twenty dollars in the machine. She had to have at least two grand in her bra by the time her husband came to get her. He said he was broke and ready to go home.

The smoke in the penny slot room got to be too much, and I moved on. I found Ruby Mae sitting in the lobby in front of a massive fireplace. Young men and women, all grand- or great-grandchildren, surrounded her. I enjoyed sitting with Ruby Mae and her family. Irma divested herself of silver-haired cowboys and joined us. The girls always met in the lobby at midnight to catch the bus to the North Harbor train station, just a short taxi ride from the retirement village. Nana Jo and Dorothy arrived last, which didn't surprise any of us.

"I don't see why we have to leave so early." Dorothy was argumentative. "We don't have to worry about the bus. Sam can drive us back. I was on a winning streak." She flashed several tickets at us.

Nana Jo whistled.

"I'm tired. It's been a long day. Plus, we have to get up early for church tomorrow," Nana Jo said.

They all looked shocked, except Ruby Mae.

"I go to church every Sunday," she said, "but I don't know the last time some of you saw the inside of a church, except for Clayton Parker's funeral."

"Church? Why do we have to go to church?" Dorothy asked.

"Because Clayton Parker went to church, and we need to get back on the case and figure out who killed him so that idiot Stinky Pitt will leave my granddaughter alone," Nana Jo said.

I grew warm and misty eyed. "I love you, Nana."

She hugged me.

"Of course you do," Dorothy said, "but not all of us were idle in our time here." She lowered her voice. "Listen, when I was in the back, I saw the manager talking to an older man whom I saw at the funeral. George Parker."

My mouth wasn't the only one open. "George Parker? He's Robert Parker's brother, right? The accountant?"

"Yes. I kept an eye on him. We were at different tables, but when a seat opened at his table, I moved and introduced myself."

"Well, well, well," Nana Jo said.

"Well done," Ruby Mae chimed in.

We all praised Dorothy's skills.

She preened. "Apparently, George Parker is a frequent visitor at the Four Feathers. Marty says he's a whale."

I must have looked as confused as I felt.

"A whale is someone who spends a *lot* of money at the casino. Casinos provide lots of comps. Perks. Free rooms, free food, jets, whatever they want to attract whales."

"But why?" I couldn't wrap my mind around the idea. "That seems backward to me. You'd think the casinos would want to attract people who don't already spend lots of money at the casino so they will? I mean, wouldn't a whale spend money anyway, whether they got perks or not? Why lavish them with gifts?"

Dorothy looked at me like I was dim-witted. "Whales can spend their money anywhere. They want to attract them to their casino, instead of Vegas or Atlantic City. Sometimes, whales win and take the casino's money. More often than not, they lose, and the casinos clean up."

I shook my head in amazement. "What else did you find out?"

"Marty said George has been coming a lot and losing a lot."

Dorothy reminded me of something Diana Parker said. "Did Marty say anything about Clayton Parker coming here? Was he a whale?"

Dorothy shrugged, but Ruby Mae answered. "I mentioned

Clayton Parker to my niece, Savannah. She works in the hotel. She looked him up, and he did come to the casino. She didn't say he was a whale, but he came with many different women, none of them Mrs. Parker."

"Is George Parker still here?" Nana Jo asked.

"He was when you dragged me out of the high roller room."

We trooped back to the high roller room, but George Parker was nowhere in sight.

"Darn it." Dorothy left to find a cash machine to cash out her tickets.

The girls had an agreement. If one of them won, they all won. At the end of the night, when everyone's tickets were cashed out, each of us left with six hundred dollars. Most of the money came from Nana Jo and Dorothy. I contributed a hundred to the pot. Irma and Ruby Mae contributed the least, fifty dollars each, the same amount they started the night with. Nana Jo won close to a thousand dollars and Dorothy won the rest. I tried to protest and return the money, but the girls were adamant. It was their system, and they were sticking to it. It made the casino more fun for all of them. Rarely did everyone have a bad night. Sometimes, one person was lucky. The next time, it was someone else. By splitting the winnings, they all shared in the fun.

By the time I'd dropped the girls off and drove Nana Jo and me home, it was almost two a.m. I hated entering the garage at that time of morning and waking up Dawson and the poodles. He was looking after them while I was gone. When I pulled in to the alley, his light was still on. Once I parked in the garage, his door opened, and two barking poodles rushed down to greet me.

My hair and clothes reeked of smoke. I felt the need to shower and wash my hair. I made quick work of it and didn't bother to dry my hair. I climbed into bed after a crazy day, full of highs and lows, and tried to sort through my emotions. Nothing made sense.

I fell asleep and dreamed of Indians harpooning whales in the British countryside.

Chapter 17

After three hours of sleep, I was rudely awakened. Nana Jo flipped on the lights and ordered me to get up so we could grab a bite to eat before getting to the early service. That moment was probably the closest I'd ever come to murder. Church was fine, but why did we need to go to the early service?

"You have got to be kidding." If I ignored her, maybe she'd go away.

Not my nana. She pulled the pillow off my head, leaned close to my ear, and screamed, "Get up." She followed up with a slap to my derriere and marched out of the room.

Oreo leapt over me, not bothering to notice either my limbs or Snickers. She growled and moved to the other end of the bed, as far away from Oreo as possible, without leaving the bed. I rolled onto my back, stared at the ceiling, and tried to figure how long I could delay getting up. Oreo sat on my chest, facing my feet, and wagged his tail in my face.

Nana Jo stuck her head into my room. "Grace called. She has a migraine, so she's not going to church. Are you still in bed?"

I dislodged Oreo and got up. I was grateful I'd taken a

shower last night, or rather this morning. Normally I blew my hair dry and beat the curls into submission. Without a firm hand, they were unruly, with a mind of their own. Letting them air-dry overnight was a mistake. One look in the mirror told me a hat was required.

Hat secured, coffee in hand, and Nana Jo by my side, I headed to South Harbor Lutheran Church. A church van collected people from the retirement village, and Irma and Ruby Mae waited for us in the lobby.

"Where's Dorothy?" I asked before I spotted her coming out of the ladies' room, chatting with a middle-aged woman.

We took seats near the back of the sanctuary. South Harbor Lutheran was a large church and had two services. The early service was conservative. Most of the attendees were older.

After the service, they served coffee, cookies, and punch in the basement. We each grabbed a cup of coffee and dispersed. Irma batted her eyelashes at a gray-haired usher. She'd winked at him earlier. Ruby Mae sat at a table and talked with a woman who sang in the choir. Nana talked to the pastor, and Dorothy talked to a man I recognized from the funeral service, George Parker. I tried to muster up the energy to strike up a conversation with someone.

"Samantha, is that you?"

I turned and saw Diana Parker. "Diana, it's really good to see you. How are you doing?" I was grateful to see a familiar face.

"You attend South Harbor Lutheran?"

"Oh, no. My grandmother and some of her friends wanted to come, so I tagged along."

She relaxed and leaned in. "I usually don't come to the early service," she whispered. "Too many old people, but Clayton's uncle likes this service. I came with him." I looked in the direction she pointed. George Parker still chatted with Dorothy.

Whatever she was saying, he looked fascinated. "Looks like he's found a friend."

"Is your uncle married?"

Diana sipped her coffee and shook her head. "No. He's a widower. His wife died a long time ago. It would be nice if he met someone, though."

"It must be very lonely for him. When my husband died, I didn't know what to do with myself."

"I'm sorry. I didn't know."

I waved her off. "Of course not. There's no reason to apologize. You're a widow too."

"Well, my situation isn't exactly the same." She was quiet for several seconds.

I waited.

"You probably loved your husband," she said.

"Yes. I loved Leon very much. But, I'm sure you must have—"

"I did love Clay once, but I don't know if he ever loved me. There were so many affairs."

I tried to think of something to say. The next service would start soon, and I didn't have much time. "Was there one person in particular?" I might not have been so blunt were I not feeling so rushed.

Diana either didn't notice or was accustomed to my bluntness. "I don't think so. I used to think he was having an affair with someone from his office. He spent so much time there. But, he fired his receptionist about a week before he was killed. If there had been anything going on, it was certainly over."

I wasn't exactly thrilled at the prospect of sitting through another service and thankful George Parker attended the early service. We left before the second service. With my mom out with a migraine, my Sunday was free.

Nana Jo, the girls, and I went to Riverside Grille. Housed in a converted warehouse, the restaurant was popular with the

Saturday and Sunday brunch crowd. Without reservations, the wait for a table could be hours. Ruby Mae's great-niece was one of the hostesses. Within five minutes, we had a first-floor table with a great view of Lake Michigan. The girls took full advantage of the one dollar Mimosas and Bloody Marys, a big attraction of Riverside's brunch. Their shrimp and grits was one of my favorites, but I decided on the banana bread French toast with bacon and fruit.

While we ate, we shared the information collected during church. I reported my conversation with Diana Parker.

Irma didn't get anything helpful to our investigation out of the cute usher, but she did get his phone number.

According to Nana Jo, the pastor had nothing but glowing things to say about the Parkers. Most of them. He wasn't overly fond of the youngest Parker brother. The pastor didn't like to speak ill of anyone but found it hard to find anything kind to say about David.

George remembered Dorothy from the casino. She had a date with him the next night.

"Do you think that's wise?"

The murmur that went around the table told me I wasn't the only one who questioned the rationality of Dorothy dating one of our suspects.

"We're going to meet at the casino. We'll have dinner in the Gold Room and then play for a bit. I'll make sure I leave by midnight. I'll be fine. The casino is always packed. Plus, I know too many people there for him to try anything."

We tried to dissuade Dorothy, but she was determined. I dropped the girls off at the retirement village, and Nana Jo and I went home.

"Sam. What's the matter with you? You've been sweeping that same spot for the past fifteen minutes." Nana Jo took the broom out of my hand.

"I'm sorry." I'd opted to not open the bookstore on Sundays. I might change my mind and offer Sunday hours in the future, but right then, I was thankful for the peace and solitude and the opportunity to set up for the coming week. Nana Jo and I cleaned the store. Upstairs, Dawson tried out a new scone recipe he found on the Internet.

"What's bothering you?" Nana Jo made short work of the sweeping and moved on to dusting.

"I'm worried about Dorothy going out with George Parker. What do we really know about him?"

Nana Jo's guffaws weren't the answer I expected.

She pulled herself together. "We know the man is almost eighty-five. He's as old as dirt. Sam, did you see him at the church? Dorothy is a strong woman. She just earned her green belt in Aikido. She's spry. I suspect it's the yoga. She's well-known at the casino. She has more boyfriends than Irma, and that's saying a lot. If you're really concerned, there's one thing you can do."

"What's that?"

"Go to the casino. Monday nights aren't busy, but they do serve fried chicken on the buffet. I'll bet Ruby Mae can use her connections to get us free buffet tickets."

I was the one with reservations about Dorothy's date, but something in the way Nana Jo's eyes twinkled and the twitch at the corners of her mouth made me wonder if I was being manipulated. I agreed to the excursion anyway.

"Good. I told the girls you'd pick them up at seven thirty," Nana Jo said.

I'd been played.

Monday morning Jenna called. She'd talked to her friend at the police station. The general consensus was Detective Pitt was a lazy blowhard who couldn't detect his way out of a brown paper bag. He was promoted when his uncle was the chief of police. After his uncle's retirement, Detective Pitt's career stalled. He was assigned the Parker case because he was the only detective available. Budget cuts had significantly affected the police numbers. Many of the detectives knew me from parent-teacher conferences and were inclined to believe Detective Pitt was way off base in suspecting me. Jenna said I didn't need to worry about my laptop being confiscated, which was a big relief. My nephew Zaq had set up my laptop when I bought it and set it to back up everything on the hard drive. So, I knew my files were safe, but I didn't realize how much the situation had worried me until the weight lifted. With a spring to my step, and a smile on my face, I opened the bookstore and worked with a joy I hadn't felt for days.

Later, I drove Nana Jo and the girls to the casino. Dorothy, confident either of my protective instincts or Nana Jo's manipulative skills, had informed George Parker she would ride to the casino with friends. Dressed in khakis, a polo shirt, and a jacket, he met Dorothy in front of the lobby fireplace. She introduced us. He was tall and gangly, with a slight hunched back, and appeared soft-spoken and timid. My concerns for Dorothy's safety vanished. Even without her green belt in Aikido, she was clearly the dominant of the two. After the introductions, she led him toward the restaurant. George Parker was a follower, not a leader.

Ruby Mae's niece came through with free buffet passes. Dorothy and her date headed off to the VIP Gold Club Dining Room, and the rest of us headed to the main buffet. The casino wasn't as crowded on Monday as Saturday, but the buffet was still packed. In the middle of the floor stood a circular table and the customary salad bar. Throughout the dining area, buffet tables were piled high with everything from lo mein and Peking duck on the Chinese buffet to lasagna and chicken parmesan on the Italian buffet. The fried chicken, very popular, according to the girls, was on the American buffet, along with hamburgers, roast beef, and meatloaf. There was truly something for everyone and every taste. We stuffed ourselves so much we didn't have room for dessert. Ruby Mae's great-niece and a cousin several times removed brought each of us takeout bags stuffed full of fried chicken, slices of cakes, cookies, and tarts. We couldn't walk around the casino smelling of chicken, so I was nominated to take the bags to the car. I was glad to do it. After that meal, I needed the exercise.

When I returned, I made my way back to the Clue slot machine and played on twenty dollars until it was time to meet the girls. Ruby Mae and Nana Jo were already in the lobby when I arrived.

"Where's Irma?" I asked.

Nana Jo rolled her eyes. "Making goo-goo eyes at a bartender young enough to be her grandson last time I saw her. She'll be here soon."

Sure enough, I spotted her making her way across the marble floor, not an easy feat in four-inch heels. When I saw Dorothy and George approaching the lobby, I hurried off to the parking garage to get the car and bring it around. I kicked myself for not listening to Nana Jo and using the valet parking. I told myself the walk was good for me. By the time I got the car to the front door, George and Dorothy had finished their good-byes, and the girls and I were off.

Dorothy declared George Parker the dullest man she'd ever had the misfortune of dating. "I'd believe that man murdered someone only if it was possible to bore them to death. Halfway through dinner I could fully understand why wild animals gnawed off their foot to free themselves from traps. I was sorely tempted."

I laughed so hard I almost missed my freeway exit.

"That man talked about obscure tax codes for nearly an hour."

"Did you learn anything helpful?" Nana Jo asked.

"Not much. He and Clayton weren't close. I got the impression Clayton didn't particularly care much for his uncle either."

"I don't suppose he mentioned where he was the night his nephew was murdered?" I tried to sound optimistic but didn't hold out much hope.

"Said he comes to the casino almost every night."

"That's a bit odd, isn't it? Don't accountants tend to be conservative with their money? 'Almost every night' seems excessive."

From the back seat, Ruby Mae said, "Not as odd as you'd think. Unfortunately, a lot of older people don't have anything else to do."

I felt Nana Jo look at me even before she spoke. "Did you notice all of the wheelchairs?"

I had noticed quite a few people in wheelchairs, carrying oxygen tanks and shuffling along with walkers. Saturday night, the casino crowd was mostly younger people. Monday was definitely an older crowd.

Dorothy explained, "Younger people work during the week and go to the casino on the weekend. The casino attracts older people during the week. They run a van service to and from the retirement village on weekdays, but not on weekends. On weekends, we take the casino shuttle to the bus stop and then a taxi from the bus to the village."

"Plus, they offer seniors a half-priced buffet on Mondays and Tuesdays," Ruby Mae said.

"It's a good place to meet people." Irma coughed.

"There are a lot of lonely people out there," Nana Jo said. "For some, the casino is the only entertainment they get."

Thinking about those lonely seniors in the smoke-filled casino made me sad. They put their hard-earned pensions into slot machines in the hope—what? Maybe being able to spend their golden years in a warmer climate surrounded by friends and family. I was thankful my nana was surrounded by good friends and family who loved her. I felt truly blessed to be able to spend time with these amazing women.

I dropped the girls at the door.

Dorothy got out. "Sam, I did manage to put in a plug for your bookstore. Sir George the Dull said he likes to read, so I suggested Market Street Mysteries. He promised to stop by. Don't let yourself get trapped into talking to him. You've been warned."

The girls made their way inside with their bags of chicken and desserts. No one had been particularly lucky tonight, and we left the casino with a little less than fifty dollars each. Considering I only put twenty in the slot machine, I was still on the positive. The extra funds covered the cost of the gas. Not bad, all things considered.

I parked in the garage, collected the poodles, and went upstairs with Nana Jo with a sense of déjà vu. Despite the late hour, I was too keyed up to sleep. After forty-five minutes of tossing and turning, I gave up on sleep, went to the kitchen, made myself a cup of chamomile tea, and sat at my laptop. I'd missed it over the past few days when I thought the police would confiscate it. I reread the last few pages, to remind myself where I'd left off, and returned to the twentieth century British countryside.

"Raised in a barn. That's what I say. Naked as a jaybird he was. No home trainin'." Lady Elizabeth stopped. If she went into the servants' area, all conversation would cease, and she'd never find out to whom Mrs. McDuffie referred. The housekeeper didn't elaborate, and Lady Elizabeth continued into the servants' area. Two footmen dragged a sopping carpet out the back door. The mystery of the missing carpet was solved.

At the sight of Lady Elizabeth, the servants halted what they were doing.

"Oh, dear. I didn't mean to interrupt. Please carry on. Is that the carpet from the library? What happened?"

Thompkins signaled for the footmen to proceed and stepped forward. "I'm sorry, m'lady. When Gladys was cleaning, she found the carpet soaking wet. Not wanting to ruin the floors or the rug, I authorized the removal of the rug. The men are taking it outside to dry. I hope that's okay?"

"Of course. Thank you, Thompkins." Lady Elizabeth turned to Mrs. McDuffie. "How on earth did it get so wet?"

"That's just what we was discussin' when your ladyship came in," said the stout, middle-aged woman. "It must 'ave been done the night of the party, when that young man was done in is my guess." Her freckled complexion flushed to match her thin, curly red hair.

"That's why I've come down here, actually. Did anyone see anything unusual the night of the party? I know you all spoke to the police, but sometimes . . ." Lady Elizabeth searched for a tactful way to continue without outright stating the police might not ask the right questions.

Mrs. McDuffie seemed to have no qualms about such things. "Sometimes the bloomin' police don't know what the ruddy 'ell they're doin'."

"*Mrs. McDuffie.*" Although it hardly seemed possible, Thompkins's back became stiffer, and he stood straighter and taller than usual. His eyes flashed. Times had changed, but Thompkins had not. He'd been in service with the Marsh family for over thirty years, and his father and grandfather served before him. His great sadness was that he had no sons to follow in his footsteps. He'd fathered three daughters, who married and moved into their own homes, none within a reasonable distance to serve the family.

Turning to Lady Elizabeth, he said, "I apologize, your ladyship. Please forgive the coarse manner in which you were addressed. I assure you—"

Lady Elizabeth halted his assurances. "Please, Thompkins, it's quite all right. I am not offended, and Mrs. McDuffie is not to be reprimanded. She only spoke her mind with frankness, which I appreciate."

Lady Elizabeth followed the two servants into the small office.

Thompkins pulled chairs out for the women and stood by expectantly.

Lady Elizabeth sat and clasped her hands in her lap. "You both know about the poor man who was killed here, and I'm sure you've heard the police suspect Victor might have been involved."

Mrs. McDuffie snorted. "Poppycock. That's what that is. I've known that boy since 'e was born. Born and raised right 'ere in the village, 'e was. 'E's a gentleman if ever I saw one. No gentleman would 'ave put the knife to 'im. Not Mr. Victor." Mrs. McDuffie leaned back and folded her arms.

Thompkins coughed. "I have to say, m'lady, Mrs. McDuffie and I agree Mr. Victor is a gentleman. I don't believe he had anything to do with that man's death."

The faith the two trusted servants had in Victor

touched Lady Elizabeth, but she needed information. "Agreed. Lord William and I don't believe Victor had anything to do with the murder either. However, did you or any of the others notice anything or anyone suspicious that night?"

Mrs. McDuffie and Thompkins looked at each other for a few minutes.

Mrs. McDuffie spoke first. "There's the rug."

Thompkins cleared his throat. "As I said earlier, one of the maids noticed the rug was wet. We have no idea when it happened."

"Could it have happened on the night of the murder?"

Thompkins shifted from foot to foot. "I hesitate to say that's when it happened, but given the amount of water and the state of the floor underneath, it seems likely."

Thompkins never jumped to conclusions and only went out on a limb if he was thoroughly sure of himself.

Mrs. McDuffie didn't possess the same compunction for caution. She snorted again. "Well, I'm *not* 'es-itatin'. If not the night of the party, when?" She looked at Thompkins. "We cleaned this entire 'ouse from top to bottom before the party. And none of my girls are dumb enough to pour buckets of water on a two-'undred-year-old wool carpet." Mrs. McDuffie's chest heaved in anger.

Thompkins added, "I wasn't implying that you or any of the staff were negligent in your duties."

"I should 'ope not," Mrs. McDuffie huffed. "And, none of the family would 'ave done somethin' like that without tellin' us."

"Of course not," Lady Elizabeth said.

Thompkins scrunched his forehead. "Well, of course not, m'lady. The weather has been nice so we haven't had a fire in the library. The maid was polishing the fireplace grate when she noticed it."

"Where do you suppose all that water came from?" Lady Elizabeth asked.

Before Thompkins could answer, Mrs. McDuffie said, "The killer must 'ave jumped in the pond."

Thompkins coughed delicately.

"Why would anyone jump into the pond? It wasn't warm enough for a swim," Lady Elizabeth said.

"There's only one reason a body would go in that pond at night. They must 'ave wanted to wash." She raised her eyebrows. "All kinds of crazy thin's goin' on that night it was."

"Mrs. McDuffie, I believe you must be right." Lady Elizabeth asked a few more questions, but neither Mrs. McDuffie nor Thompkins had anything to add. Both promised to question the other servants and report back. With nothing further to do downstairs, Lady Elizabeth returned upstairs to think about what she'd learned.

Chapter 18

Traffic at the store settled down, and we all fell into an easy, comfortable routine. When I hired my nephews to work in the store, Christopher created a logo with a deerstalker cap and a magnifying glass, and we ordered T-shirts and aprons emblazoned with the logo and "Market Street Mysteries." They arrived a few days after we opened and were a huge hit with the customers. Dawson baked cookies and decorated them with the same logo. I would miss the boys when the summer ended and they returned to university. Nana Jo would continue to help out, but I'd grown to rely on my nephews, and they genuinely enjoyed working in the store. I'd deal with their departure when the time arrived. Until then, I was determined to enjoy each and every minute.

Around noon, David Parker showed up. I wouldn't have known him, but Nana Jo spotted him immediately. She went to say hello and pulled me along with her.

"Sam, this is David Parker. Clayton Parker's uncle."

"I'm pleased to meet you, Mr. Parker." I reached out and shook his hand.

"Call me David."

"I'm very sorry for your loss. Please accept my condolences." The customary expression of sorrow sounded trite, but I didn't know what else to say.

David seemed uncomfortable. He avoided looking at me as much as possible. He darted his eyes from side to side and poised like a trapped rat expecting a cat to leap out at any moment.

David was the youngest of the three Parker brothers, and in his mid-seventies, he wasn't exactly a spring chicken. Something about him said he had once been handsome, but those days were long gone. He hadn't aged well. His pale skin was almost transparent, his hair thin, and his eyes, surrounded by dark rings, sunk into his head. His clothes hung loosely, like excess skin on an elephant. He smiled, but the coldness in his eyes made my skin crawl.

We made a point of greeting people when they entered the store but then backed off and left them to explore on their own. After our greeting, we left, allowing David to wander through the store alone. A customer looking for an out-of-print book distracted me, and I promptly forgot about him.

The book in question wasn't valuable, but it was first printed in 1948. It also happened to be one I owned two copies of. Possessing multiple copies of books wasn't unusual for me. I often bought boxes of used books at garage sales. Plus, after decades of reading mysteries, there were books I'd read so long ago I forgot I'd read them until I bought another copy and started reading. This particular book happened to be one of those. Market Street Mysteries wasn't a used bookstore, but I would gladly give away a book to someone who would read it.

I let Nana Jo know I needed to run upstairs. When I hit the back stairs, the hair on the back of my neck stood up and my skin tingled. Something wasn't right. I hesitated and tried to picture what was in the shop. I'd left Nana Jo helping a customer find a Nancy Drew book for her granddaughter.

Christopher was running the cash register, and Zaq was in the back room working on inventory. I wasn't sure about Dawson. It must have been him upstairs. I released the breath I held and continued upstairs.

Something scraped across the floor. "Dawson, is that you?"

It wasn't Dawson. David Parker stood in my living room and stared at the ceiling.

"Mr. Parker. What are you doing here?" My emotions swung from pleasant shopkeeper to *what the heck are you doing in my home* in less than five seconds.

"I am so sorry. I must have gotten lost. I was looking for the restroom and must have taken a wrong turn."

The explanation was logical but off. I usually locked the door to the back stairs that lead up to my living area. I tried to remember if I'd locked it that morning. Nana Jo and Dawson both had keys and might have run upstairs, but both were good at locking up afterward. If either left it unlocked, it would be a first. And, David had passed right by the door clearly marked RESTROOM on his way to the stairs. I made a mental note to check the lock when I went downstairs.

"I also have to admit I was curious about the building. You know, I used to own it." David Parker must have known I didn't believe his story.

"No. I hadn't realized that." I waited for him to expound.

"It was a long time ago. When my brothers and I returned from the war, we came into a little money. We bought several pieces of property. This was one of them."

"I see." It didn't explain why he was in my living room.

After an awkward moment, he continued, "Of course, it looked nothing like this when we owned it. Back then, it was just an old warehouse. You've really done a wonderful job renovating. It's a beautiful home."

I had done a lot of work. The building had been abandoned for years. The upstairs had been a big open loft area, with water-stained floors and exposed brick walls. A leaky roof had caused a great deal of water damage and a hole in the ceiling. I was proud of my building and my home. Finding David Parker in it was still bizarre.

"Thank you. I've done a lot of work to the place. But, the upstairs is my personal space. You'll understand if I ask you to leave." I motioned toward the staircase.

David had the decency to look contrite before hurrying downstairs.

I surveyed my space. Nothing appeared to be moved, other than one chair. He'd moved it away from the living room area, close to the wall.

I'd kept the exposed brick. Elaborate plasterwork detail, including gargoyles and angels, topped the walls. Initially I'd considered having the gargoyles removed. They weren't exactly my design aesthetic, but they were unique and quite the conversation piece. I left them.

"Sam!" Nana Jo pulled me out of my reveries.

I grabbed the book and ran downstairs. I checked the door. It looked okay, but there were small scratches around the lock that I didn't recall being there before. I made sure I locked the door behind me.

The store didn't slow down until close to closing. I was about to lock the door when George Parker walked in.

Nana Jo greeted him just as she had his brother. "Well, isn't this amazing, we've had visits from both Parker brothers in one day."

I knew Nana Jo well enough to see she saw their visits as anything but a coincidence.

"My brother, David, was here?"

"Why yes. David did pay us a visit, didn't he, Sam?"

"Yes. I had an opportunity to give him my condolences." I wasn't sure whether I should tell George about finding David in my living room. Maybe he was in on whatever weird thing led David upstairs.

"Did my brother say anything . . . unusual?" He fidgeted.

"What do you mean by unusual?" Nana Jo was all sweetness and innocence.

George blustered. "I don't know. He is a bit odd."

"How do you mean?" I was curious about what constituted odd to George Parker.

"Is there someplace where we can sit down?" he said.

We escorted George Parker to a bistro table at the back of the store. Nana Jo grabbed us each a cup of tea and a scone, and we sat. Nana Jo and I sipped our tea and waited for George to explain.

He finished his scone and most of his tea before starting. "I suppose you know David spent many years in prison?"

I wondered how to tactfully ask what David's crime was.

Nana Jo jumped right in. "What crime did he commit?"

Nothing like the direct approach.

George squirmed. "Armed robbery." He swallowed. "And murder. David was always getting into trouble, ever since we were boys. Initially it wasn't bad, but after we came back from the war, he was different." He gazed out of the window. "I guess we were all different after the war. We'd seen so much evil. Friends and enemies killed, brutally killed. It was horrible."

"Who did he kill?" Nana Jo said quietly.

"He robbed a bank. One of the security guards tried to stop him. David swears it was his friend who fired the shot, but the witnesses all said it was David. He was sentenced to life in prison."

"Then why is he here?" I shuddered at the thought of the time I spent upstairs chatting with a convicted murderer.

"David is dying. He was released under the compassionate release policy. Doctors say he has maybe three months."

That certainly gave me a lot to think about. David Parker was in town before Clayton was murdered. Just because he'd killed once didn't mean he'd kill again, especially if the victim was his flesh and blood. Even if that person was an annoying jerk.

"How did Clayton and David get on?" I hoped I wasn't being rude.

George stared into his tea. "David and Clay never did get along very well. I think they were too much alike. David was angry at Clay. He felt . . ." George seemed reluctant to share what David felt.

I needed to know. David might very well have murdered his nephew. David could be my chance to get Detective Pitt looking at someone other than me as Clayton Parker's murderer.

Nana Jo placed her hand on George's. "Please. This is very important. I know this has to be difficult for you, but we need to know."

Boy, was she good.

"David was unhappy about a number of things. One of them was that he felt Clay was taking advantage of him."

"How? What did Clayton do?" I asked.

"When my brothers and I came back from the war, we inherited some money and bought properties. My brother Robert started his real estate business. We never drew up any papers specifically stating we were all equal partners. We were brothers. There wasn't a need for legal documents. Then Robert died, and Clay took over. He started selling off the properties." He waved his hand. "Like this one. He even sold the real estate business before my brother was cold in the ground."

"Why? Wasn't the business doing well?"

"The local economy went through some tough times. We took out several loans, and things were a bit tight. Clay liked to live well. Mostly, I think he wanted to get involved in a risky business deal and needed cash, a lot of cash."

"Okay, so Robert dies and all of the businesses are in his

name. Clayton starts selling the properties and the family business. Then David comes back."

He nodded.

"Did David talk to Clayton about this?" In David's place, I would have been furious.

"Talk? David came back looking for his share. He wanted to go to Bermuda and spend the remainder of his days on a beach. Clay claimed David wasn't entitled to anything and refused to part with a dime. David was furious and threatened to kill—" Crimson rushed up his neck, and he attempted damage control. "I didn't mean he did anything. David was always a hothead, but he would never hurt anyone, especially Clay."

Nana Jo apparently had less scruples about hurting George's feelings than me. "He did hurt someone. He's killed before. What's to say he wouldn't kill again?"

George's eyes got as large as half-dollars and he squirmed. "I should be going." He left.

Nana Jo looked at me, "What do you think?"

I waffled between excitement and fear. The thought of giving Detective Pitt another suspect and getting him off my back thrilled me, but the fact I'd found a murderer in my loft terrified me. As many murder mysteries as I'd read, those murders and murderers weren't real. David Parker was real.

Nana Jo wanted to call Stinky Pitt on the telephone immediately and tell him we'd found the killer. Well, maybe not the killer, but definitely a strong suspect. After my last encounter with Detective Pitt, I wasn't thrilled about seeing him again, even if it meant getting him off my back and rubbing his nose in it a bit. We decided on a compromise. We called Jenna and passed along the information. She promised to relay it to Detective Pitt.

The next day's headline story in the local newspaper, *The Harbor Town Post,* said David Parker had been taken in for questioning for the murder of his nephew. Jenna stopped by and told us David had been arrested. Part of me was relieved a murderer was off the street. I'd be able to sleep easy, and Nana Jo would be able to move home, although I'd grown quite accustomed to having her around. The other part of me was sad at the thought of David Parker killing his nephew over something as trivial as money. How did a family recover from something like that?

The girls and I went to Randy's Steak House to celebrate the conclusion of our successful sleuthing. The girls were disappointed they weren't there to hear the final bit of information that led to the arrest, but I assured them they all played a major role in solving the case. The North Harbor Billiard Club had one dollar beers and half-priced margaritas on special, so we decided to kick up our heels. As the designated driver, I restricted my drinking to diet cola, but the girls made up for my lack of alcohol. We closed the place down at three a.m. It took the owner and a nice bartender to help get Dorothy and Irma in the car.

When I arrived home after dropping the girls off at the retirement village, it was almost five a.m. My cell phone battery had died hours ago, and I was too tired to bother checking my voice mail. I plugged my cell in to charge and fell asleep the instant my head hit the pillow.

Two hours later, my phone rang. I was inclined to ignore it, but I checked the caller ID. It was Jenna, and she wouldn't stop until I answered. After a muffled "hello," I put the phone on my pillow and listened. Within seconds, I was wide awake.

David Parker had bonded out of jail overnight. By morning, he was dead.

I hung up and lay in bed, unable to move. The air was thick and dense. When I forced myself to get up, it was like trying to push my way through an invisible wall of pudding.

My mind couldn't wrap itself around the reality of David's death. Was it only two days ago I talked to him? I showered and dressed on autopilot and found myself sitting at the kitchen bar drinking coffee, or rather, staring into the cup. I don't know how long I had sat there.

"What's wrong?" Nana Jo interrupted my stupor.

"Jenna called. David Parker's dead."

"We knew he was sick, but that was really fast."

She must have thought he died from the cancer.

"No. He hung himself. We killed him."

Nana Jo put down her coffee and hugged me. I needed to feel her arms around me. I cried like a baby. When I'd cried myself out, she handed me a wet dishcloth and told me to wipe my face. The cool cloth felt good. I didn't know if I'd cried for David Parker, Clayton Parker, Leon, or myself. Everything had welled up in me. Tears felt good. I was empty inside, and even that was good. I went to the bathroom and splashed cold water on my face. My eyes were red and swollen, but I didn't care. All of the pent-up emotions of the past few months were gone, and I felt like a real person, instead of a robot. When I returned to the kitchen, Nana Jo set a plate of bacon and toast on the counter. I was ravenous.

"Thank you," I said between bites.

"You needed that. Feeling better?"

I nodded and kept eating.

"You realize David Parker's death had nothing to do with you, right?"

"I do know that. It's just the loss." I struggled to put my emotions into words. I wanted Nana Jo to understand. "Leon fought so hard. He fought for every second he could, for every breath he could. David Parker took his life. He just gave up and killed himself. He treated life like a dirty tissue and tossed it away. It doesn't seem fair."

Nana Jo nodded. I did feel some responsibility for David Parker's death. I didn't blame myself for his actions, but I mourned the loss nonetheless. We ate quietly.

"You going to be okay to work?" Nana Jo loaded our dishes into the dishwasher.

"Yeah. I'm going to be fine."

We went downstairs and lost ourselves in books. Store traffic wasn't heavy, but it was steady. I stayed busy. By the end of the day, I was physically tired, but my mind was restless. We ordered pizza for dinner. Afterward, Nana Jo and Dawson went back downstairs for a tutoring session. She'd tutored him for the past week, and I would take over the next. He'd come to an arrangement with his college counselor. If he took online courses over the summer and passed with a B average, he would be eligible to play football in the fall.

I tried to watch television and then to read. Nothing settled my thoughts. Something wasn't right, and I couldn't place my finger on it. I decided to write in the hope it would, if not help me figure out what was wrong, at least distract me.

⁓

"Victor, don't be such a bore," Daphne said, not for the first time.

As had become the custom since the duke's arrival, James and Victor dined at Wickfield Lodge. It rained all day so James and Victor drove the three miles this evening. After dinner, Lord William and Lady Elizabeth declared themselves exhausted far too early for the statement to be true. The younger group nonetheless accepted it, and Lord William and Lady Elizabeth retired.

James entertained the ladies with stories of his

days in the military, his days at Cambridge, and his days at Winchester school with Victor. Victor declined cards, music, and any other entertainment Daphne suggested. After his refusal to drive into town for dancing at a new club, which was, according to Daphne, all the rage, she had an outburst of temper.

"I'm sorry, but it seems bad form to go dancing at a time like this," Victor said stiffly.

"I don't see why." Daphne pouted. "Why should we be stuck inside as though we've done something wrong? We didn't have anything to do with Charles's death. I don't see why we can't go out and have fun."

Victor went to a corner and smoked.

"I want to go out," Daphne said to James. "I say we leave Victor here and go enjoy ourselves."

"I don't know." James joined his friend in the corner.

"By all means, don't let me keep you all from your fun." Victor's chin was set.

If Daphne heard the cynicism in Victor's voice, she chose to ignore it. "Good. Let's go." She rang the buzzer to summon Thompkins.

The butler arrived, and Daphne gave him his orders. "Thompkins, see that the duke's car is brought around. We're going out."

Thompkins nodded and backed out of the room. Daphne left to grab her shawl and switch handbags.

James watched his friend.

"Perhaps you should go," Penelope said. "It would be good for Daphne to get out. I'm rather tired. I'll sit this one out."

Victor gazed into his drink.

"Cheers. No worries, mate. I'll be sure to take good care of your betrothed." James hurried out to the hallway.

Daphne's voice floated in from the hallway. The front door closed. A finely tuned engine revved and sped away. In the parlor, Victor continued to gaze into his drink.

Penelope wasn't sure he'd even heard Daphne and James leave. "Are you just planning to sit there smoking all evening?"

Victor stood. "I'm terribly sorry. I'll head home."

"Don't be such a bloody fool. Sit down." Penelope stamped her foot and glared at Victor. She didn't know if the shock on his face came from her choice of words or her tone, but he sat back down.

"Are you angry?" he asked.

Her temper flared. "Angry? Am I angry? Are you joking? You're the one who should be angry. You just let your fiancée leave the house and go out dancing. The question isn't whether or not I'm angry. The question is why aren't you angry?"

"I'm not angry because, frankly, I don't care what Daphne does. And I think you know it."

"You don't care?" she whispered.

Victor shook his head.

She searched his face and summoned the courage to ask the question she'd dared not ask before. "Why don't you care?"

With a strength that sent a shiver up her spine, he pulled her to his chest, bent down, and kissed her. Tenderly, softly he kissed her.

She responded to him, and what started as an ember quickly grew into white hot passion. Hungrily she clung to him as if she were drowning and clinging to a life raft.

Victor finally broke the embrace. He looked into Penelope's eyes. "What a fine mess this is."

Penelope clung to him and murmured, "What do you mean?"

"My whole life, all I wanted was Daphne. Now that I'm engaged to her, I realize I'm in love with her sister."

"You're in love with me?" Penelope snuggled closer.

Victor pulled away and looked into her eyes. "Yes. I love you." He kissed her again.

When he was finished, Penelope smiled at him. "Well, it's about time."

Chapter 19

I spent the next few days taking care of the store and tutoring Dawson. The boys were a godsend and I had just about mastered the POS system. My comfortable routine left me so tired at night I didn't have time to think about Clayton or David Parker—well, not much time. I tried to block the entire Parker family and all of their problems out of my mind, but David's death nagged at me.

Nana Jo scoured the local newspaper for David Parker's obituary and the announcement of the funeral service but found nothing more than a brief death notice.

The girls missed playing detective, so they started a mystery book club. The Sleuthing Seniors planned to meet once a month in the back of the bookstore. Irma campaigned to name the group the Sleuthing Madams and get T-shirts made that read S&M, but wiser heads prevailed. Their first meeting was spent eating the brownies provided by Dawson and arguing over what book to read first. Dorothy wanted a suspenseful, dark book with lots of gore. Irma wanted a mystery with plenty of sex, while Ruby Mae and Nana Jo were open to anything. I suggested they start with a cozy mystery, and they settled on Dorothy Gilman's *The Unexpected Mrs. Pollifax*. The Mrs. Pollifax series was one of my favorites, although I questioned the wisdom of exposing the girls to a senior citizen who becomes a CIA spy. I was anxious to hear their thoughts after reading the book and hoped they didn't find Emily Pollifax too inspiring.

With the book question resolved, they went back to chatting and eating brownies.

"Dorothy, have you heard from George?" Nana Jo asked.

Dorothy swallowed and took a swig of coffee to wash the brownie down. "I haven't seen him."

Ruby Mae, as usual, had her knitting. She worked a few stitches and muttered to herself, "I expected there'd be something in the paper 'bout the funeral, but I ain't seen nothing."

"I was sort of looking forward to another funeral service. There were some really hot men at the last one," Irma said.

"Maybe you could call George and ask about the funeral service," Nana Jo addressed Dorothy. "David was his brother. He might be in need of consoling."

Dorothy didn't seem to be in a mood for Nana Jo's jokes. "I don't care how much consoling he needs. That man is a bore. Besides, I thought the case was over."

I stared at my brownie. No one spoke.

Eventually, I couldn't take it anymore. "I don't know if the case is over or not. Something doesn't feel right."

"What's wrong? The police must have had a reason to believe David Parker killed his nephew or they wouldn't have arrested him," Nana Jo said.

Nana Jo made sense, but I couldn't shake my qualms. "I don't know. The police get things wrong. They could be wrong about David Parker. I mean, they almost arrested me."

"But they didn't arrest you. Stinky Pitt is a jack—"

"Irma," we all yelled. She stopped, although the coughing fit that followed probably would have prevented her from swearing anyway.

"I can't explain it. It just doesn't feel right," I said.

Dorothy got up and left the room.

Ruby Mae put away her knitting and patted me on the knee. "Honey, we've all lived long enough to know you have to trust your gut."

I was touched by their faith in me. Nana Jo handed me a handkerchief, and I wiped my eyes and blew my nose.

Dorothy came back. "Okay. I'm meeting George at the casino for dinner at eight. We better go home so I can freshen up." The girls collected their things. Ruby Mae asked if I'd drive or if they should take the shuttle. Driving was the least I could do.

George said the family decided not to have a public funeral service for David. He'd been away in prison so long he didn't have friends in the area. His past was so shady the few people who still remembered him didn't do so fondly. Diana hadn't met David prior to his release from prison and was anxious to start a new life as quickly as she could—a new life that didn't include any Parkers. As soon as the coroner released the body, George would have David cremated.

Ruby Mae's great-niece was a blackjack dealer in the high limit room. According to her, George Parker's whale status was in jeopardy before Clayton's death. He'd been on a losing streak, normally a good thing for the casino. However, they'd extended him a large amount of credit, and he was struggling to pay it off. I wasn't sure what George Parker's gambling debts had to do with the murder, but I filed the information away.

Irma cozied up to a blue-suited banker at the bar. Plied with enough alcohol, he revealed Parker & Parker Real Estate was in financial difficulty. His ethical compass didn't allow him to spill why, but he'd given us a place to start digging. Ruby Mae promised to pump her goddaughter, a teller at the same bank, for information.

Nana Jo arranged to meet her boyfriend, Freddie, at the casino. Freddie's son, Mark, the state trooper, confirmed Clayton Parker was involved in suspicious real estate transactions. Someone had filed a complaint accusing Parker of fraud.

I managed to ferret out some information. A former employee of Parker & Parker Real Estate sat at the slot machine next to mine. Maggie Johnson was once secretary to Robert Parker, the founder of the company. I'd met Maggie during the ordeal when I was trying to purchase my building. To say Maggie didn't care for Clayton Parker would be the understatement of the century. She loathed and detested her former boss's son. According to Maggie, it wasn't just that he was a spoiled, selfish, self-centered prick. Oh, no, his sins were numerous. Clayton Parker was a shady, deceitful, dishonest swindler who skirted the law. Maggie had volunteered to testify against Clayton Parker in two impending lawsuits.

"The thing that really bites my butt," Maggie said, not missing a beat with the one-armed bandit, "is now that Mr. Robert is dead, whatever comes out may blacken his good name too."

If Maggie was to be believed, Robert Parker was a saint, the only honest one of the whole bunch. She was probably in love with him, but that didn't concern me.

"What specifically did Clayton Parker do?"

Maggie pushed her replay button, leaned close to me, and whispered, "He lied."

Not the great reveal I'd hoped for. My disappointment must have shown.

Maggie quickly continued, "He lied and cheated his clients. He charged 7 percent commission to his clients when the going rate is six. He worked little fees into contracts, administrative processing, document reading, and a host of other charges that could amount to tens of thousands of dollars. When he got an offer on a property, he told the buyer's lawyer he had other offers when he didn't but he really liked *these* buyers, and if they came up with an extra thousand dollars, he'd talk his seller into accepting their offer."

"The dirty rat." That was exactly what Clayton Parker had done to me, and it made my blood boil.

Maggie hit a bonus round, and I let her concentrate on the slot machine. The bonus played out, and she smacked the replay button.

"How was he able to get away with this?" I asked.

Maggie played on, losing her bonus winnings. Finally, she answered, "He threatened and intimidated people. The Parker name still carries weight in this town. He knew the right people. He played golf with bankers and lawyers. He sailed with politicians and businessmen. One bad word from him and suddenly you're unemployed, living on social security, and coming to the casino in the hopes of free gifts and a payout that will pay your medical bills."

A tear ran down her cheek. Her machine was silent. Her hand rested on the replay button, and I reached over and gave it a squeeze. Maggie sniffed. I found a packet of tissues in my purse, and both of us made use of them. The mood was broken by a scantily clad waitress with a drink tray. Maggie requested a beer. I offered to pay, but she had her pride and handed a few dollars to the server.

After a swig, she turned to me. "I may be down, but I'm not out. I will dance on that prick's grave as soon as they get the marker in place."

"I just might join you."

I knew Clayton Parker was dishonest. My dealings with him proved he was a dirty scumbag. I didn't want to think about any extra money he cost me in fictitious fees. Our dealings were so bad I'd hired my own attorney. Ultimately, I'd closed on the building. Given what I'd learned, I easily believed there were complaints against him. I wondered how he stayed in business as long as he did, but none of it explained why David killed him. David had been in prison, but it was suspicious that Clayton Parker died not long after his uncle was released and was overheard threatening his nephew.

Another late night at the casino left my clothes smelling of smoke and my pockets fifty dollars richer. After a shower, I drifted off to sleep with Maggie's words swimming in my head. *Clayton Parker lied and cheated his clients. Robert Parker was the only honest one of the bunch.*

Chapter 20

James pulled his 1938 Rolls-Royce convertible onto Victoria Embankment, parked in front of New Scotland Yard, and decided it was safe to leave the roof down. Within fifteen minutes, he sat in the office of Chief Inspector Albert Buddington.

"James, it's good to see you. I was very sorry to hear about your uncle's death. The duke was a good man." Everything about Budgy, for that was what James had called him since he was a small boy, was large. A large mustache, a large nose, and large ears graced a larger than average-sized head, and the man was large both horizontally and vertically.

"Thank you, sir." James tried not to fidget. The size of the guest chair was out of proportion to the rest of the room's large furniture. He felt like a small boy summoned to the headmaster's office.

"Now, how can I help you?" Budgy's voice was as large as the rest of him.

James leaned forward. "Well, sir, one of my mates is . . ." He cleared his throat. "He's involved in the murder of that American fellow, Charles Parker."

The chief inspector scowled and leaned back. "Bad business that. You must be careful whom you hang around with, now that you're a duke."

"I quite agree, but Victor's okay. He didn't kill the man. Comes from a good family and all. There is a lady, and Victor is protecting her."

The chief inspector nodded approvingly. "Yes. Chivalry and all that."

"Exactly." James was relieved at the chief inspector's easy acceptance of his explanation. "I don't know that your detective shares our feelings on chivalry."

Chief Inspector Buddington's grin exposed his big teeth. "Giving your mate a hard time, is he? Let me see what I can find out." He pushed a button on his desk. A crackly voice answered. He requested the file on the Charles Parker murder investigation and tea.

The tea arrived, followed shortly by a man with a case file in hand. Tall, lean, and gangly with thick curly hair, he stood awkwardly waiting for an invitation to sit or join with tea. He was not invited to do either.

James set his cup down, stood, extended his hand, and introduced himself.

The chief inspector was forced to acknowledge Detective Covington's presence. "Yes. Covington. Now that all of the introductions are over, let's get down to business. What have you got on the murder of that American Charles Parker?"

Detective Covington shifted his weight from one foot to the other.

"Well?" The chief inspector glared.

"Sir. Yes. Was there anything particular you wanted to know about the case? I have the file here, with all of my notes. Sir."

"If I wanted to read the case file, I would have had

you bring it and leave. I want to know if you have a suspect. You might as well sit and stop twitching."

If Detective Covington looked uncomfortable standing, he was even more so sitting. He balanced on the edge of his chair and clutched the file. "We have questioned several members of the Marsh family." He spoke too fast.

"Marsh? That wouldn't be Lord William Marsh, would it?"

"Yes, sir."

"Well, you can forget about him. Lord William Marsh is a member of the House of Lords—belongs to my club. He wouldn't have anything to do with murder."

"Sir, I'm just doing my job." Covington tapped his foot.

"Yes. Yes. I understand there was a lady involved."

"Lady Daphne Marsh, Lord William's niece, but I've eliminated her as a suspect."

James started at the news that Daphne was no longer a suspect. "Really? I was given to understand you were quite suspicious of Lady Daphne Marsh."

Covington visibly relaxed. "Now I understand. You can rest easy. I do not believe that Lady Daphne Marsh is a killer."

James's ears warmed at Covington's implication that his interest in Lady Daphne was more than casual friendship. Daphne was a beautiful woman, but he wasn't interested in finding a wife. His reaction to Covington's words angered him. "May I inquire why?"

"The coroner determined the nature of the wounds were such it would be extremely unlikely a woman delivered them. In fact, they appear to have been delivered by someone with military training."

James's heart raced, but his voice stayed steady. "Really? Modern medicine is amazing. How exactly were they able to determine that?"

"It's actually very simple." Detective Covington stood. "If you wouldn't mind standing, I'll be happy to demonstrate."

James stood and faced the detective.

"If you'd just turn around, Your Grace."

James turned his back to the detective. Covington put his arm around the duke's neck. "We believe the killer came up behind the victim and grabbed him, like this."

James stood still while the detective applied pressure to his neck.

"Once he immobilized his victim, he stabbed him." Detective Covington raised his free arm above his head and brought it down several times in a stabbing motion. After several enthusiastic thrusts, he ended his demonstration.

James stumbled slightly, returning to his seat. "I see."

"We have photos showing the angle of the stab wounds." Detective Covington opened the file, pulled out the photos, and eagerly pointed out various wounds.

James became lightheaded and was unable to look at the gruesome photos. Detective Covington didn't appear to notice.

"All right. All right. Enough of that," Chief Inspector Buddington said. "What about that other fellow? Carlston. What do you have on him?"

"He served in the Royal Tank Corps, sir." Covington put the photos away.

"Serving in His Majesty's army doesn't automatically make someone a killer." James bristled. Things weren't going the way he'd hoped. "I served."

"I understand there was an American detective at the party." Chief Inspector Buddington took out a handkerchief and wiped his hands.

"Claims he followed Parker to England to catch him." Covington opened the file and shuffled through the papers. "Putting the squeeze on people."

"Isn't that unusual?" James asked.

"Usually police from visiting areas will identify themselves. It's a matter of common courtesy to notify the local coppers before coming on someone else's patch," Detective Covington said.

"The American didn't?" James grasped at straws.

"Darned unsporting to put your foot in another man's wagon." Chief Inspector Buddington pursed his lips in distaste. "But, he is an American."

Clearly allowances had to be made for Americans.

"Darned nice chap, actually. I've talked to him several times already," Detective Covington said. "He had no motive to kill Parker. Others did."

Lady Elizabeth walked into the servants' hall with purpose and determination. Surprised maids and footmen scrambled to stop what they were doing and stand at attention but were unable to complete the maneuver without causing calamity.

Lady Elizabeth marched through the kitchen until she collided with Mrs. McDuffie. "So very sorry."

Mrs. McDuffie juggled an armload of linens but managed to avoid dropping them. "Oh my, Lady Elizabeth. I'm so very sorry. I didn't see you." She put the linens on the large farm table and faced her mistress. "May I 'elp you?"

"I believe you can. Would it be possible for us to go in the office?" Lady Elizabeth motioned toward the room.

Once they were inside, Lady Elizabeth closed the door, indicated the housekeeper should be seated, and sat. "Mrs. McDuffie. When I was last here, I overheard you mention you saw a naked man the night of the party. Is that true?"

Mrs. McDuffie bristled. "Well, I'm certainly not in the 'abit of telling lies."

"I know you're a very truthful woman, and I truly did not mean any offense." Lady Elizabeth touched Mrs. McDuffie's hand.

The housekeeper relaxed. "Sure enough, that's what I saw."

"Wasn't it dark?"

"Not so dark I couldn't see a naked man in the moonlight. My dad always said strange things happened during the full moon."

"I don't suppose you saw who he was?" Lady Elizabeth was unaccustomed to, and uncomfortable with, discussing naked men with servants, but she soldiered on.

"No, m'lady." Mrs. McDuffie folded her hands in her lap. Rather than being embarrassed, she appeared to have more to say.

When she didn't speak, Lady Elizabeth prompted her. "Do you remember anything else?"

"Not about that night, but you asked about anything unusual."

"Yes. If there's anything, I'd like to hear it."

Mrs. McDuffie hesitated a moment. "I don't know that it 'as anything to do with the murder of that American." She shifted in her seat. "But, one of the tablecloths came up missing right after the party."

Lady Elizabeth had hoped for more than missing linen. "Is that all?"

Mrs. McDuffie stiffened. "If your ladyship is finished, I should be getting back to my work."

"Oh, no. I want to know about the tablecloth, please." Lady Elizabeth feigned interest. A tablecloth might not be important, but she didn't want to shut down communication with the housekeeper.

"It was there before the party, but the next day we couldn't find it. I thought the new 'ousemaid, Gladys, might have taken it. She's an impertinent minx, that one."

"What could she possibly want with a tablecloth?"

"It's a fine linen tablecloth that is, 'andmade. Worth a pretty penny."

"Did she take it?"

"I questioned 'er, and she denied knowing anything about it. If she took it, she would do, wouldn't she? I put no stock in what she said. She got quite uppity, I tell you. Downright rude, she was." Mrs. McDuffie scowled. "I would 'ave fired the little minx, but Thompkins stopped me. We've 'ad such a 'ard time finding 'elp."

Lady Elizabeth didn't see how the tale of the housemaid and the missing tablecloth related to murder but listened as attentively as she could.

"It's a good thing I didn't fire the girl because one of the footmen found the tablecloth just this morning. Wait." Mrs. McDuffie hurried from the office. She returned with a neatly folded tablecloth. "'Ere it is." She handed the freshly laundered linen to Lady Elizabeth.

"How wonderful it was found." Lady Elizabeth held the bundle in her lap and continued to fake interest. The housekeeper obviously thought the tablecloth was important. "Where was it?"

"That's just it. The footman found it stuffed in the bottom of that old chest in Lord William's office." She leaned close and whispered, "Stained with blood, it was."

Lady Elizabeth no longer had to feign interest. She unfolded the tablecloth and examined it. "It looks fine now."

Mrs. McDuffie preened. "Of course. It took several soaks in vinegar and then baking soda. My grandmother's recipe for removing stains."

"Good work. Thank you so much." Lady Elizabeth didn't have the heart to tell the proud housekeeper she had destroyed evidence that might have helped the police catch the killer.

Chapter 21

Each day I discovered something new in the store. When I retired from teaching, I was full of doubt as to whether I could do this, especially without Leon. I'd learned I was a lot stronger than I'd ever thought I was. Watching my nephews, my grandmother, and Dawson, who was now practically one of the family, filled me with pride. These were my kin and they were all here to help make my and Leon's dream a reality.

We were all busy at our respective jobs when I heard a commotion in the café area of the store. I excused myself from the customer who couldn't decide if she'd like a historical mystery or not and went to check it out.

Dawson's face was red and he looked like a frightened rabbit cornered by a pack of hungry dogs. A thin, greasy, scruffy-looking man in grease-splattered jeans and a greasy T-shirt, with greasy hair and greasy fingernails, grabbed him by the collar.

"Let him go immediately." I pushed myself in between Dawson and his attacker.

"You stay out of this, lady." The man shoved me.

I stumbled backward. I would have fallen if it hadn't been

for Nana Jo coming up behind me. Before I knew what was happening, my nephews, Christopher and Zaq, appeared and presented an intimidating wall of protection between me and my attacker.

"Touch my aunt again and it will be the last person you ever lay a hand on," Christopher said with a soft, quiet certainty that sent a chill up my spine. My nephews were well over six feet each, and I've never known them to be violent. Both stared unblinkingly at this stranger.

I knew with assurance if he tried anything, they would intervene.

The stranger seemed to contemplate my nephews. Reason must have told him he didn't stand a chance against all of us. He sneered. Hands in the air, he backed away. My nephews didn't budge from their positions.

He turned his eyes away from them and onto Dawson. "You think you can get away from me, boy. But I'll be back when you don't have your bodyguards." He grinned and walked out of the store, stopping long enough to push a few books off a table onto the floor.

I breathed a sigh of relief and heard applause coming from the people sitting at the bistro tables. In all of the confusion, I'd forgotten about the customers enjoying the complimentary tea and scones. The noise broke the spell. Christopher and Zaq turned to look at me.

"You okay, Aunt Sammy?" Zaq asked.

"Yes. I'm fine. Thank you." I hugged them both. "Thanks. Now, we better get back to work."

Nana Jo's eyes held a question as they darted in Dawson's direction.

I shook my head.

She gave me a hug and a squeeze and went back to the front of the store.

Dawson refused to make eye contact and hurried out of the back.

I followed him to the courtyard. "You okay?"

"Yeah. I'm fine. I'm really sorry about that."

"Who was that man?"

He waited so long before answering I was just about to repeat the question. I felt certain he knew the answer.

"That was my dad."

"Your dad?" I should have known, but I don't think I'd actually ever met Dawson's family. They never showed up for parent-teacher conferences. When conferences were required, a neighbor attended.

"Yeah. Great, isn't he?"

"Do you want to talk about it?"

"I'm really sorry, Mrs. Washington. I don't know how he found me. I certainly didn't expect him to come here, causing trouble for you."

"It's okay. No harm done." He looked in need of a hug so I gave him one. "Now, let's get back to work."

The rest of the day was business as usual. The bookstore was doing quite nicely and seemed to be making a profit and filling a need. Each day I saw old and new friends who were sharing in my love for mysteries. The nights were full with hanging out with Nana Jo and the girls and tutoring Dawson. Helping him with his academic work provided the link that had been missing from teaching.

That night I helped Dawson with a paper for English literature. We were comparing Shakespeare's *The Taming of the Shrew* and Jane Austen's *Pride and Prejudice,* two of my favorite books. In fact, Jane Austen was my favorite author.

Nana Jo had a date with Freddie. She didn't want to leave, but I insisted.

"So, what exactly is a shrew? I Googled it and I doubt

Shakespeare was comparing Katherina to a small, rat-like animal," said Dawson.

I laughed. "Well, he might have been, but a shrew is also a person with a really bad temper and foul attitude."

"Okay. I get it. So, who is the shrew in *Pride and Prejudice*? Mrs. Bennett? Lydia or the Bingley sisters?"

"Good question. What do you think?"

We didn't get much further when we heard a noise downstairs. We both stopped and sat quietly, listening and waiting. Snickers slept near my feet, but Oreo was up and on alert. I held my finger to my lips and tiptoed to my bedroom and grabbed my bat and cell phone. Dawson, Oreo, and I crept downstairs. At the bottom of the stairs, Dawson placed a hand on my shoulder. I halted. He slid in front of me. I was touched by his desire to protect me, but I was the one with the bat. I offered it to him.

He shook his head and whispered, "Stay behind me."

At the bottom of the stairs, the broken glass from the back door lay on the floor. The red light on the security system blinked. The police would be here soon.

Dawson walked quietly down the hall with me. I picked up the dogs and carried them a safe distance away from the broken glass and then put them down. Snickers and Oreo followed closely behind, growling softly like predators prepared to pounce.

A huge crash came from my office. Dawson lunged into the room. I hurried behind, with Oreo and Snickers barking and charging ahead.

Dawson ran headfirst at the intruder and tackled him like a linebacker sacking a quarterback. They both fell flat onto the floor and a tussle ensued.

I stood by, bat in hand, ready to swing. My back to the door, I was shocked when the lights flipped on.

Nana Jo stood in the doorway, gun in hand. She shoved me aside, walked up to the fray of bodies on the floor, and fired a shot into the exposed brick wall. "Freeze or my next shot will blow your brains out."

Both men froze and I saw the face of the intruder.

It was Dawson's father. From his bloodshot eyes and the smell of liquor, it was obvious he was drunk.

Oreo snarled and lunged to get a piece of the action. Dawson grabbed him and backed away from his father.

"Call the police." Nana Jo never once lowered her gun or took her eyes off her target.

"I don't think I'll have to. He broke in. They should be on their way."

Right on cue, sirens blared, and police cars pulled up alongside the shop.

"You okay?" I looked at my grandmother.

She didn't even blink. "Yep."

I hurried to the back door and directed the police to the back room.

Two police officers, weapons drawn, entered the back office. "Down. Down on the floor. Hands up." They shouted. "Weapons down. Hands in the air. Everybody. Now." Just inside the door, they stopped, bottlenecking the doorway.

Nana Jo dropped her arm, placed her weapon on a nearby shelf, and held up both hands.

I had to stand on tiptoe to see around them.

"That's my grandmother. She's okay."

They accessed the situation. After what felt like an hour, they put away their weapons. The officers moved forward and unblocked my view.

"Well, if it isn't A-squared." One of the officers handcuffed the man lying prostrate on the floor of my office. Dawson, still holding Oreo, stood and backed against the wall.

"A-squared?" I asked.

"Alex Alexander," the officer who cuffed Dawson's father said.

His partner radioed the situation was under control and pulled out his notepad.

"Ah . . . Alex Alexander, A-squared. I get it," I said.

A red-faced Dawson paced. He was still holding Oreo and looked at everything, except his father, prostrate on the ground with his hands handcuffed behind his back.

"Okay if I take the dogs outside?" he asked.

One of the officers nodded. "Okay, but don't leave."

Dawson opened the glass door and stepped into the back courtyard without a backward glance.

The police had questions and paperwork and then more questions. Eventually, they left with their prisoner.

Dawson and the poodles were still outside. I felt sure he hadn't wanted to see his father being driven away. Outside, I let him pace.

"I'm really sorry." He now held Snickers rather than Oreo, who was much better at cuddling.

Oreo searched for a blade of grass he hadn't previously watered.

"For what? You're not responsible for your father's actions."

Dawson turned away.

"You want to talk?"

"He doesn't care about me. All he cares about is money."

"Money? What money?"

"Football. He wants me to try out for the NFL. Skip college and play pro ball before I get injured and ruin my chances. That's why he got upset before, when I left."

"Dawson, I'm so sorry." I walked over and gave him a hug. Snickers took the opportunity to plant a kiss on my nose. "What do you want to do?"

He gently pulled away. "I love football and I want to play. I want to play pro ball one day too. But . . . this season taught me I need an education too. I know I won't be able to play ball forever, and then what?"

I was pleased and impressed he'd actually thought about life after football. "I don't know. What do you want to do after football?"

"I know this sounds crazy, but I really like baking."

"That doesn't sound crazy to me."

"Whoever heard of a football player being a chef?"

I chuckled. "It sounds like a reality television show. If you enjoy baking, then I think you should follow your dream. You're an excellent baker."

We talked about what it would mean to be a chef. Mostly, we decided some research was in order.

He looked exhausted, and I was pretty tired myself. "I think we've had enough excitement. Let's call it a night. We can finish Shakespeare tomorrow. Why don't you keep the dogs tonight? Snickers can be a big comfort."

Dawson nodded. He patted the side of his leg and Oreo followed him to his apartment.

I found Nana duct-taping cardboard over the broken window.

"Good thing you got that alarm system, although nothing seems to deter criminals faster than my peacemaker."

"What made you come back? I thought you had a date with Freddie tonight?"

"I went but I couldn't enjoy myself. I guess I just had a feeling."

I gave her a hug. "Well, I'm glad you did."

We finished sweeping up the broken glass and rearming the alarm system and went upstairs to bed. I was so tired I hoped I would fall asleep quickly, but I tossed and turned for hours until I gave up and fired up my computer.

Lady Elizabeth watched as her niece hopped up from her seat and paced.

"What do you mean? He can't possibly believe Victor killed Charles Parker? He can't be that daft."

She, Lord William, and Penelope were in the study having tea and discussing the information they'd uncovered, such as it was. Lady Elizabeth's information about the bloody tablecloth received a lukewarm reception. Penelope wanted to call the police immediately as this new information would be sure to clear Victor. He knew where to find a towel. But, even she must have realized that it was a weak defense and wasn't able to maintain a convincing pretense of enthusiasm.

James sat quietly by the fire. It was only after some prompting by Lady Elizabeth that he had been convinced to relay his meeting at Scotland Yard and Detective Covington's theories.

Lady Elizabeth sipped her tea. "Well, I'm sure Victor isn't the only one with military training."

James shrugged. "True, but how many of the guests had military training and a reason to kill Charles Parker?"

Lord William refilled his pipe, careful not to drop too much onto the floor. "The military training eliminates the women from consideration. Not that anyone with an ounce of sense would have considered them suspects in the first place."

"I'm not so sure we can eliminate all of the women, dear, but it does seem rather unlikely." Lady Elizabeth poured more tea.

Lord William nearly choked. "What do you mean?"

He wiped tobacco from his shirt. "No women in the military."

Lady Elizabeth smiled vaguely at her husband before saying, "True, but that doesn't mean she couldn't have gotten someone else to do it. Or that someone in the military couldn't have shown her how."

Lord William stared wide-eyed at his wife.

James stared also, but there was something else in his eyes, something that resembled respect. The corners of his mouth twitched and he quickly took a drink of his tea.

"Well I'll be . . ." was all Lord William managed to say, but he said it several times.

"Yes, dear. Now who else at the party, other than Victor, had military training?" Lady Elizabeth returned to the heart of the problem.

"Just about all of the men there. We've all served in his majesty's service in one capacity or another, including myself." Lord William puffed out his chest with pride. "The Boer War, Mafeking—"

"Yes, dear." Lady Elizabeth cut off what promised to be a long-winded reliving of the glory days of war. "But you weren't really at the party. I mean, you were in the house, but you weren't downstairs with the guests."

Penelope smiled at her uncle. "Plus, we know you didn't stab Charles Parker."

"Darned right I didn't stab him. Horrible mess that would have made. If I'd wanted him dead, I would have shot him," Lord William said.

Lady Elizabeth froze, cup midair, and stared at her husband.

He promptly apologized. "I'm sorry, dear. Guess I got carried away. Hardly appropriate conversation for a lady. Please forgive me." He looked at his wife.

Lady Elizabeth was quiet for quite some time.

Finally, Penelope broke the silence. "What is it? You've remembered something."

Lady Elizabeth put down her coffee cup and pulled her needles and a mound of fluffy wool out of the bag at her feet. She found her place and knit a few stitches.

"You've thought of something haven't you?" Penelope rushed to sit next to her aunt.

Lady Elizabeth kept her eyes on her knitting. "Well, something did occur to me. Something Mrs. McDuffie and Thompkins mentioned." She stopped to count stitches.

"When I went down to the servants' hall, they were removing a carpet."

James looked at Penelope. She merely shook her head and waited.

"The carpet was wet. No one knew how."

"I'm afraid I don't see . . ." James stammered.

Gathering steam, Lady Elizabeth continued, "Well, I didn't see either at first. But then I remembered Mrs. McDuffie mentioned seeing a . . . uh . . . well, a naked man the night of the party."

"I don't really see how that can have anything to do with this business. Probably had too much to drink and fell into the pond. Bad manners that. Nothing worse than a man who can't hold his liquor," Lord William said firmly.

"I thought so at first too," Lady Elizabeth said. "But then I remembered Mrs. McDuffie's comments about the missing tablecloth."

James and Penelope looked at each other and

both looked at Lady Elizabeth as though a light had been turned on behind their eyes.

"That must be it," James said. "I wondered how someone could have managed to stab him and not get any blood on his clothes. I thought he must have left the party."

"Everyone was present and accounted for when the police arrived," Penelope added.

"That explains it then," James said.

"Will someone tell me what the devil you're talking about?" Lord William said.

"Can't you see, Uncle? The killer must have removed his clothes and then stabbed Charles Parker in the garden."

James picked up the tale. "Then he washed off the blood in the pond."

Lady Elizabeth shook her head. "No. I don't think he washed in the pond, at least not entirely. Or the carpet wouldn't have been soaked through."

James nodded. "I see what you mean."

"He must have gone into the library and gotten a container and washed in the library."

"Pouring the water on the floor and soaking the carpet," James added.

"There were several large vases in that room," Penelope said.

"Then he dried himself with the tablecloth and put his clothes back on. That's who Mrs. McDuffie saw running naked in the moonlight," Lady Elizabeth finished the story.

Lord William stared for several moments before illumination came and he smiled. "That's how the carpet got wet."

Lady Elizabeth nodded. "Yes. And he hid the table-cloth in the chest because it was wet and stained with Charles Parker's blood."

"But why?"

They turned to stare at Lord William.

"Why bother taking off your clothes and washing? Why not leave?" Lord William asked.

"Because he couldn't leave. If he left, it would draw attention to him. For whatever reason, he couldn't just walk away. He had to stay until the end," Lady Elizabeth said.

"That's why the police had such a hard time. Everyone was present and accounted for," James added.

Lady Elizabeth nodded.

Lord William pounded the arm of his chair. "Well, by Jove, I think you've figured it out."

Lady Elizabeth smiled vaguely and continued her knitting.

Penelope looked at her aunt and her smile faded. "What's wrong? We need to call Scotland Yard and tell them. You've figured it out."

Lady Elizabeth said, "I've figured out *how,* yes, but not *who.*"

Penelope's face dropped. "But surely it couldn't be Victor. I mean he would hardly have had time. We were dancing most of the evening. And, he certainly wasn't wet."

James nodded as he lit a cigarette. He smoked for a few seconds. "Your aunt is right. You'll need a lot more than a stained, wet tablecloth."

Penelope plopped down on the sofa.

Lady Elizabeth said, "We know how he did it. Now we just need to know who and why."

James suddenly reached into his pocket and pulled

out a telegram. "I almost forgot. This telegram came earlier from the policeman in America."

"What is it?" Penelope walked close by to get a better look at the telegram.

"The Chicago policeman, Patrick O'Hara, is coming to England. He should be here in a few days."

"How will that help?" Penelope looked puzzled.

James shrugged. "I hoped if the killer followed Parker from America, then maybe he might recognize him. At the time, it seemed so farfetched that anyone here would have killed him."

Lady Elizabeth stopped knitting and smiled brightly. "Perhaps you're right."

"All right, dear. What do you have in mind?" Lord William asked.

"I was thinking maybe we could re-create the scene of the crime."

"What?" Lord William and James exclaimed simultaneously.

"What do you have in mind?" Penelope asked.

"What if we have another party and invite all of the same people. The killer is bound to be there. Maybe this Detective O'Hara will recognize him."

"Absolutely not," Lord William said. "I will not have you inviting a killer into the house. He's killed once. What's to stop him from killing again?"

"We can make sure the police are present," James said slowly.

Penelope frowned. "But if the police are here, the killer will know it's a trap. He'll be on his guard. He might not even come."

"We'll have to make sure the police aren't obvious. If they're in disguise, they'll be like all the other invited guests."

"Invited guests? Who would believe that?" Lord William asked.

James stood and walked in front of the fireplace. "It might work if we're the only ones who know the truth. The killer might think he's been invited to another party."

"But why?" Lord William asked. "Why would we have another party?"

Lady Elizabeth resumed her knitting and smiled at Penelope. "Well, if we were to announce an engagement between Victor and Penelope . . ."

Penelope stood motionless as heat crept up her neck. "How did you know?"

Lady Elizabeth smiled, put down her knitting, and lifted the teapot. "More tea?"

Chapter 22

I would have slept late had it not been for biological constraints and the urgent allure of the smell of coffee. Nana Jo, Dawson, and the nephews kept things going until I made my way downstairs.

Dark circles and red eyes told the tale Dawson was too silent and sullen to tell. It was obvious he hadn't slept, but the delicious aroma of cinnamon indicated he hadn't been idle either. Dawson definitely had a talent for baking, and I was amazed at the delicacies he produced in his tiny kitchenette. He often tried out recipes in his apartment but was only able to cook on a small scale. When he baked complementary items for the bookstore, he needed more space so he used my oven. The last time I'd gone up to see him, he'd installed floating shelves which held an assortment of old cookbooks. Some were gifts from Nana Jo and the girls. Others were garage sale finds marked with price tags of one dollar or less. Today's treats were cinnamon and orange rolls with a sticky icing, and they were excellent.

His baked goods had gained a reputation among the nearby shop owners and vanished quickly. He'd taken to baking more batches to insure there were goodies for people who shopped later. I was thinking about moving ahead with the plans for the tea shop, but I didn't want to say anything to Dawson yet. It would be nice to sell the baked goods rather than give them away for free. Things were still in the early stages. He had school and football in the fall. I didn't want him to feel obligated. He'd be busy enough keeping up with his studies and football practice, training and travel and enjoying college. The last thing he needed was more pressure. No. The more I thought things through, the more I thought it better to wait. I'd given him a budget to buy supplies. He was free to bake as much as he wanted but providing a true *café* would be a bad idea right now.

One decision made, I grabbed another cinnamon roll and worked on inventory and store displays. A steady string of customers passed through, but at the end of the day, I wasn't tired, nor did I want to sit home alone. Dawson headed back to his studio. Nana Jo had a date. Even Snickers and Oreo abandoned me. I let them out to do their business, and they promptly went to the garage and barked and scratched at the door until Dawson came down and opened it. He glanced at me. I nodded and shrugged. He opened the door wide enough for them to enter, and I was alone.

Most nights the thought of eating alone in my apartment didn't bother me, but that night I didn't like it. I had friends and family I could call, but I wasn't in the mood for conversation. So, I grabbed a mystery by a new author that sounded promising. *Ghost in Glass Houses* by Kay Charles was a paranormal cozy mystery and if the blurb on the back cover was any indication, it promised to be an engagingly funny read. Since opening the bookstore, I'd had so little time to read. I guessed that came with the territory.

On the shores of Lake Michigan were many fine seafood restaurants. One of my favorites was a little place called The

Daily Catch. Locals called it The Catch. It wasn't fancy. The nautical décor reminded me more of *Gilligan's Island* than anything else. But the food was delicious. Leon and I treated ourselves there once a month. I hadn't been back since he passed away, thinking the memories would be too painful. However, as I sat on the wooden bench in a booth that extended out over the water and watched kids play on the beach, sailboats float across the lake, and the sky change from bluish purple to a vibrant orange as the sun set, memories of Leon and I enveloped me like a cozy, comfortable sweater and warmed my heart.

The rainbow trout was delicious, and after, I relaxed with a cup of coffee, a slice of cheesecake, and my memories. My book lay on the table, unopened. I never minded eating alone in restaurants. My mom said she always felt people stared at her, and she dropped food in her lap. That was one of the reasons we had started our Sunday dinner outings after my dad died. Mom was uncomfortable, and Jenna needed someone to talk to. When my sister found herself alone, she got out her cell phone and found someone to talk to. She often annoyed me by doing it, even when I was with her.

The high-back, hard wooden seats in the booths resembled church pews. Sitting in them made me feel I was in a cocoon. Nice for quiet, romantic dinners, but the high backs meant I couldn't see anyone in the booths around me. I heard an embarrassing story about a wife seated in a booth behind her husband and his girlfriend for close to an hour before she recognized his laugh, stood, and walked around and caught him in a compromising position. The story popped into my head when I recognized a laugh from the booth behind me.

The disembodied laugh belonged to a woman, and it was familiar, although it took me a few minutes to figure out who it belonged to. I leaned back, turned my head, and discretely tried to put my ear to the back of the bench and still present a somewhat natural-looking pose to onlookers. Snatches of conversation floated up and over the booth, not loud enough to make out more than every fifth word. If I could lie back and gaze out the window, maybe I could maneuver enough to justify having my ear plastered against the back of the bench. Unfortunately, grace was never my strong suit and when I turned, I hit my elbow against the back of the booth. It hit in just the right place and produced a booming thud, which caused me to jerk forward and then backward, hitting my head on the back of the pew with another thump. Tears came to my eyes. I must have cried out because two servers and the manager rushed over to make sure I was okay. Whether due to the thuds of my elbow and head hitting the bench, my cries of pain, or the concerned attention of the waitstaff surrounding my booth, the people behind me stopped talking and came to investigate the commotion. Through the tears I tried hard to keep from falling, I saw Diana Parker and her handsome hulk of a boyfriend, Hans Ritter.

"Oh my God. Are you okay?" Diana Parker seemed genuinely concerned. I guessed a clear conscience could make you sympathetic.

I forced a smile, which I suspected came out more like a grimace because she immediately asked her hunk to check my elbow and make sure nothing was broken.

"He's wonderful with identifying broken bones."

"Do you mind?" He smiled and firmly, but gently, checked for broken bones. "Nothing's broken." He gently massaged and exercised the joint, which functioned quite nicely. Satisfied my elbow worked, he lightly probed my head. "Yep, there'll be a bump." He suggested an ice pack and aspirin would be a good idea.

Diana watched the probing from the bench across from me. Once Hans had made his diagnosis, the restaurant staff left. The manager was so concerned for my comfort and well-being, he took care of my meal. Handsome Hans slid in beside Diana.

I knew an explanation was called for but, for the life of me, I couldn't come up with anything. "Lovely evening. Do you come here often?" was all I could manage.

Neither of them seemed the least bit suspicious.

"It's pretty close to the house, and we can walk over," Diana pointed out the window. The Parker home was probably less than three blocks from the restaurant.

"Wow. That is close." I stared out the window. The bump must have emptied out my brain cells because I couldn't think of anything to say.

The silence got awkward and I was just about to make an excuse and leave when Diana groaned. "I wonder what he wants now."

I turned and saw Detective Pitt heading straight for our booth.

"Hello, Detective Pitt. Can I help you?"

He barely looked at me. Maybe he was still upset about Jenna. My sister could be a real barracuda, and I suspected she had taken a few choice bites out of Stinky Pitt's tushy. He was probably still finding it painful.

Detective Pitt glanced at me and then turned all of his attention and focus onto Diana Parker and her hunk.

Diana was beautiful in a crimson red, sleeveless, curve-hugging dress. Her bright red lipstick and soft wavy hair made her look like a 1920s pinup model.

"We have some additional questions to ask you," he said.

"Now? You have questions now? Can't it wait until tomorrow?" Diana rolled her eyes.

Detective Pitt was stony faced. "It's a murder investigation. I'm sure you want us to catch your husband's killer." Detective Pitt turned his gaze to the hunk and then back to Diana. "Or, don't you?"

A flush rose from Diana Parker's sweetheart neckline straight up to her face. Her eyes flashed and a vein on the side of her forehead pulsed. She leaned toward Detective Pitt and spoke slowly and quietly. "Actually, I don't really care who killed him. He was a spoiled, arrogant prick, so unless you're prepared to arrest me, I'm not going anywhere with you. And, in the future, if you have questions for me, you can refer them to my attorney."

Surprise flashed across Detective Pitt's face before he returned to his normal, stony faced stare. He glared at Diana Parker in what looked like a misguided attempt at playing chicken. Whoever blinked first, lost. If that was his intention, he didn't know women. He certainly didn't know Diana Parker. After what felt like fifteen minutes, but was more like ten seconds, she lifted a hand and snapped her fingers.

The manager rushed to the table. "Is there a problem Mrs. Parker?"

"Would you please escort this gentleman away from our table? He's bothering us." Diana Parker was a modern woman and capable of multitasking. While she stared down a police detective and signaled for the manager with one hand, she pulled a cell phone from her clutch with the other. "Hello, Mr. Monteagle? This is Diana Parker. You told me to contact you if I had any more trouble with the police. . . ."

I guessed Mr. Monteagle was her attorney and she had him on speed dial.

Check and mate. Diana Parker accomplished all of this, and as far as I could tell, she still hadn't blinked.

Detective Pitt held up a hand to ward off the manager. With a sardonic smile, he turned and walked away.

I took a deep breath and watched Diana Parker in awe. She told Mr. Monteagle she'd be in touch and explain everything first thing tomorrow. She ended the call, reached for my glass of wine, and downed it. The only indication that the encounter rattled her was her shaking hand.

"You were amazing," I said.

"I can't believe I did that." She set the empty wineglass on the table.

Hunk Handsome grabbed her hand and squeezed it. Then he lifted it to his lips and kissed it. They gazed at each other like lovesick teenagers. Rather than gagging, a silly grin spread across my face and an "Aww . . ." escaped my lips.

Diana giggled. Hans smiled and slid out of the booth. He excused himself and mumbled something about getting some air.

When he was gone, I raised an eyebrow, and Diana giggled again.

Her face lit up and her eyes sparkled. "Oh my God. I just want to pinch myself. I can't believe how kind he is, especially after . . ." She shook her head as if to clear away any lingering thoughts of her husband. She leaned across the table. "I guess that's wrong, but I don't care. I was miserable with him for so long. It feels good to be free."

I didn't want to be a wet blanket, but time was short. "So, Detective Pitt has—"

"That crazy man thinks I killed Clay. He has been coming to the house and asking questions. He keeps asking the same questions over and over again. I thought he had eliminated me. I had an ironclad alibi, but now that David is dead, he's back at it."

"You have an alibi. You were at the hotel with Hans, right?"

"Well, yes. But now Pitt's implying we plotted together to kill Clay so we could get rid of him and take his money."

I hated to admit it, but it sounded like a possibility. I guess I didn't hide my feelings very well because Diana looked hurt.

"Not you too." She grabbed her clutch and started to leave the booth.

"I'm sorry." I reached out and touched her arm.

She stopped. "I suppose the spouse is always the best suspect. But it's not true. I didn't love Clay anymore, but I certainly didn't kill him."

"You could have divorced him." I tried to sound reassuring, but she shook her head.

"Remember I told you I signed a prenuptial agreement. That meant I got nothing if we divorced. Now . . ." The word lingered in the air.

"Now you get everything."

Diana snorted. "Yeah, everything. As if there's anything to get."

"What do you mean?"

"Clay had been scheming and siphoning money. There's basically nothing left. He never talked to me about business. Now I'm getting calls and subpoenas left and right. That attorney, Mr. Monteagle, I hired him to sort out this mess. Clay was in debt up to his eyeballs."

"Wow. And you had no idea?"

She shook her head.

"Lots of people are in debt, but they aren't killed for it. Who hated Clayton so much they wanted him dead?"

"Honey, everyone who got to know him. Clay was a lying, deceitful person. He sold the real estate firm the day after his father died. He and George had a big blow up about it."

"George?" My brain couldn't wrap itself around meek, boring George Parker arguing with anyone.

"Yeah. Clay had the nerve to blame him for the business going into the toilet, but I don't believe it. George wouldn't hurt a fly. Clay, on the other hand . . ." She smacked her hand on the table and demonstrated just what Clayton would do to a fly. Her movement was so sudden and unexpected I jumped.

★   ★   ★

Later, I lay in bed and thought about all that Diana Parker had said. I already knew Parker & Parker Real Estate was in financial difficulty. Ruby Mae told us that early on. We knew from Freddie's son that Clayton Parker had been involved in real estate schemes and was under investigation. Selling the company the day after his father's death was pretty cold-blooded. His father and his uncle George started the company. How could he have sold it without his uncle's approval?

Information tumbled in my head like a tennis shoe in a dryer. Parker & Parker was in financial trouble. Clayton Parker sold the real estate business. Diana Parker's prenuptial agreement prevented her from leaving her cheating husband and running off with Hunky Hans Ritter. Clayton argued with Uncle David. Uncle David, the ex-con had been in my living room. Why?

Clayton's money problems started six months ago. What happened six months ago? Robert Parker died. Clayton inherited his father's share of the business. Clayton sold the business. Uncle David was released from prison. Clayton argued with Uncle George. Uncle George was a whale. What was it Diana Parker had said? Clayton Parker's gambling problems started six months ago. David Parker arrived six months ago. Clayton had been fine with selling me the building until six months ago.

Suddenly, my eyes were open. I reached for the phone by my bed and dialed before I stopped to think.

"Hello?"

The groggy voice was my first indication I should have checked the clock before I dialed, but it was too late to hang up.

"Diana, this is Sam, ah . . . Samantha Washington. I'm so sorry to bother you. But I have a question."

"What time is it?"

I looked at the clock. "Uh . . . it's one thirty-seven. I'm so sorry. Since you're up, I wondered, how did Robert Parker die?"

The delay was so long I was afraid she'd fallen back asleep. I was just about to check when she mumbled, "He had a stroke."

That wasn't what I expected. "Oh . . . Really. Are you sure?"

The click was soft, but the dial tone that followed was pretty loud. I hung up. There went that theory. Robert Parker died from a stroke. I'd thought for sure Robert was murdered. Clayton Parker was murdered. David Parker was either murdered or committed suicide, or his murder was made to look like suicide. If David killed Clayton and then killed himself, why was Detective Pitt still questioning Diana?

There was no point in trying to go back to sleep. My brain was up. I might as well get up too.

I grabbed my laptop and turned it on. The glow from the screen was enough for typing. I didn't bother turning on a lamp. Writing might help me organize my thoughts.

⌒⌒⌒

Penelope knocked on Daphne's door.

"Come in."

She entered. Daphne sat on the window seat and leafed through a fashion magazine.

"Thompkins said you wanted to see me," Penelope said.

"Well, sit down."

Penelope perched on the edge of the bed and clasped her hands in front of her.

"You should know that I talked to Victor."

Penelope's cheeks burned. She promptly stood and began to pace, avoiding eye contact with her sister. "Oh . . ."

"Yes. I wanted you to know that I broke it off."

Penelope stopped. If Daphne had been looking, she would have seen her sister stood trembling in the middle of the room. She made her way back to the bed and sat. "Why?" Her voice cracked.

Daphne flipped through her magazine. "It's rather obvious, isn't it?"

Penelope leaned forward, on the verge of speaking, but no words came out.

"I don't love him. I never have," Daphne continued.

Penelope sat up straight. "You don't love—"

Daphne flung her magazine to the floor and jumped up. "Of course I don't love him. I never have." She looked her sister hard in the face. "Is it true?"

"Is what true?"

"Is it true what James said? That the police don't believe I had anything to do with the murder?"

Realization dawned on Penelope. Her lips twitched. "Yes. It's true."

Relief spread across Daphne's face and her eyes sparkled.

"Well, then, that's great. Everything is working out perfectly." Daphne picked up her magazine. "Now Victor's free, I suppose you'll be announcing your engagement soon."

Penelope stopped and stared. "You knew?"

Daphne laughed. "Of course. I've always known. You've been in love with him ever since we were children. For some reason, Victor believed himself to be in love with me."

Penelope narrowed her eyes. "But why did you? What about the engagement?"

Daphne flipped her hair. "Oh, that. I knew Victor and I weren't right for each other, but I needed him to see it. Sometimes, the worst thing that can happen is getting the thing you've always wanted. At least, that's what Aunt Elizabeth says. I guess she was right."

Penelope ran over and gave her sister a hug. "Plus, now you're free in case James decides he needs a duchess. . . ."

Color rose into Daphne's cheeks. "I don't know what you're talking about."

Penelope found Victor walking in the garden behind his home. She ran and flung herself into his arms. "I just heard the good news."

Victor held her. "I'm torn between feeling elated and feeling like a bit of a heel." He gently pushed her away.

"Why a heel?"

"Well, I promised I'd look after her. I can't help feeling I've abandoned my post."

Penelope turned away before Victor could see how his words had hurt her. "Well, you can just go back to your post then." She marched away.

Victor hurried to catch her. He grabbed her arm and spun her to face him. "Penny dearest, can you ever forgive me?"

Tears fell from her eyes. Penelope looked into his eyes and her doubts, insecurities, and fears melted away in the love and warmth that enveloped her. She laughed and cried and snuggled closely into his strong chest. Victor's arms enclosed around her.

A discrete cough and the smell of a cigarette brought Penelope back to the present.

"Looks like congratulations are in order," James said.

Penelope dabbed at her eyes with her handkerchief.

"I suppose this means the beautiful Lady Daphne is . . ."

Victor's brow creased and Penelope intervened, "Free and unencumbered."

"Ah . . . very good. Very good indeed." James tried to look stern, but Penelope was sure he hid a smile.

Victor walked over to his friend and patted him on the back. "Yes. Lady Daphne has tossed me aside in favor of someone more suitable."

The men shook hands.

James cleared his throat. "I have come out here with a purpose. Lady Elizabeth has asked me to fetch you both."

"Absolutely not." Victor was adamant.

"Obviously you're ashamed to announce your engagement to me." Penelope shot the words out like daggers.

Lady Elizabeth watched her niece work up a steam pacing around the room. Lord William sat with his leg elevated on an ottoman. Daphne and James hovered in the corner.

Victor set his chin and stood his ground. "That's not true and you know it. Be reasonable, Penny."

His determination gave his boyish good looks a manly charm.

"Personally, I think it's a wonderful idea, and about time too." Daphne's enthusiasm turned to impishness. "What do you think, James?"

"James, please help me. Surely you understand," Victor pleaded.

James lit a cigarette and winked at Daphne. "Actually, old boy, I have to disagree. I think an engagement party to announce your impending nuptials to the beautiful Lady Penelope Marsh would be a grand thing indeed."

Victor gaped in disbelief. "You can't be serious."

"Of course I'm serious. Why not?"

"Why not? After you've just told me Scotland Yard believes I killed Charles Parker? What if I'm arrested? Do you know what that will do to Penelope's reputation?"

"Is that your only reluctance? You're worried about my reputation?" Penelope asked breathlessly.

"Of course. What else?" Victor barely got the words out before Penelope flung herself into his arms. Caught off balance, he steadied himself.

Penelope hung on for dear life and nestled into his chest like a kitten. "You silly, wonderful man."

Victor pulled himself away. "I don't think you understand what this could mean. A trial would be in all the papers. It would be . . . scandalous. I can't . . . I won't do anything that would bring that type of attention to your name."

Victor's gallantry met with laughter. First it was Penelope, and then Daphne, Lady Elizabeth, and even James joined in.

Victor stood up very straight and tried to salvage his pride. "I don't understand what's so blasted funny."

Only Lord William didn't join in the laughter. Instead, he leaned on his cane, pulled himself upright, and limped over to Victor.

"I understand." He patted Victor on the shoulder. "Anyone who has that much concern for my niece and her reputation is exactly the type of man I'll be glad to welcome into the family." He offered his hand to Victor.

The men shook hands.

Penelope dabbed at her tears. "Thank you, Uncle." She kissed him on the cheek.

"But, don't you think it would better to wait until this murder investigation is settled?" Victor tried a final plea.

"Actually, I think unless we move forward with our plans, this whole thing may never get settled," Lord William said. "I think you better trust us."

Victor looked from Lord William to each of the other Marshes. Each one nodded in turn.

Finally, he turned to James, who said, "I think you better trust us."

Victor looked at Penelope. "Okay. What's the plan?"

Chapter 23

One of the stairs squeaked. I'd meant to have Andrew repair it, but there was so much to do with getting the bookstore and Dawson's studio ready, I'd forgotten.

After being here for months, I had just about blocked it out, but in the wee hours of the morning, that squeak sounded like a siren. Oreo and Snickers were with Dawson. I strained to listen but heard nothing. It must be Nana Jo coming back from her date. She was probably trying not to wake me. I was already awake, so maybe we could have a quick chat. I wanted to tell her about my conversation with Diana Parker. I got up, opened my bedroom door, and turned on the light.

"Nana Jo, I—"

Standing in the middle of the floor wasn't Nana Jo, but a man. I knew who he was before he turned around.

"This is unfortunate." George Parker pointed the largest gun I'd ever seen at me.

Unfortunate? That had to be the understatement of the century.

My mouth went dry and my tongue felt like it had expanded to twice its normal size. I couldn't take my eyes off the gun. My heart was beating so fast and so loud I barely heard what he said.

"What . . . what are you . . . Why are you here?" I asked.

"I've come to get what belongs to me." His eyes glanced at the ceiling.

I could barely tear my eyes away from the gun, but I managed to glance up. In the corner of the ceiling was a plaster gargoyle. There were gargoyles in each corner of the ceiling.

"So that's what you want? The gargoyles? Take them."

George sneered. "I intend to."

I kept my eyes focused on George and the gun. He had already killed his brother and his nephew. He wouldn't hesitate to kill me. I felt dizzy and lightheaded. I tried to think what to do, but my brain felt like I was walking through mashed potatoes. I thought I saw something from the corner of my eye, but I couldn't stop staring at the gun.

"Where's your ladder?"

I tried to get my brain to focus on something other than that gun. Ladder . . . ladder. I had one somewhere.

"Where is the *ladder?*" He spoke loudly and waved the gun.

"Basement. I only have a stepladder up here. The only ladder that will reach that high is in the basement."

George appeared to be thinking. I could almost see the wheels turning in his brain. He couldn't leave me upstairs alone while he went down to get the ladder. Nor would he send me down for the ladder while he stayed upstairs. He could tie me up, but if he brought rope or zip ties, I didn't see them. They might be in his pocket, but I suspected he thought the house was empty. I hoped he didn't decide to shoot me first and then get the ladder.

He stepped toward me. My heart raced.

His back was to the stairs. That's when I saw Nana Jo's

head. She was on the stairs. That knowledge allowed me to breath. Nana Jo would get help. I wasn't alone. I blinked back tears.

George stepped behind me and pushed the gun into my back. "Walk, and don't get any ideas." He shoved me forward.

I walked.

Downstairs the lights were out. I halted to give my eyes a chance to adjust to the darkness. When I stopped, George shoved the gun into my back harder. If I survived the night, I would have a muzzle-shaped bruise. I tried to not think of anything else other than that bruise. But I couldn't help picturing a bullet-sized hole to go along with it. All things considered, I'd take the bruise any day.

"Basement," George pushed forward with the gun.

"We have to go outside to access the storm cellar." My throat was dry, and my voice cracked. "I need to get the key from my office."

"Don't get any ideas or I'll shoot you."

I nodded. We slowly walked to my office. Where was Nana Jo? My eyes darted around but, for the life of me, I couldn't see her. I hoped she'd gone for help. I noticed the light blinking on the security system as I walked down the hall. The police would be here soon. With George's gun still in my back, I opened the office door and took a few steps into the room.

I sensed rather than saw the movement. Nana Jo stepped out from the shadows of the office. She had her gun pointed at George Parker.

"Drop your gun." Her voice was as deadly as her expression. I'd never seen my grandmother's eyes so hard.

"No. You drop your gun." George dug the muzzle of his gun into my back, and I gasped. "Unless you want to see your granddaughter's blood splattered all over this room, I suggest you put down your weapon and take a step back."

Nana Jo simply looked down the barrel of her gun at George Parker. I thought for sure she'd squeeze the trigger. I closed my eyes and waited. When I heard a thunk, I opened my eyes. Nana Jo's gun lay on the desk. She glared at George like a mama bear about to rip the throat out of someone messing with her cub.

George chuckled. "Good decision."

Nana Jo spat on the ground and continued her stare down. "You all right?"

Still unable to talk, I nodded.

Nana Jo never took her eyes off of George Parker, but she must have seen me. "Good. It's going to be okay."

I grabbed the basement key and George Parker motioned for us to leave the room. Nana Jo went first and then me. George and his gun followed us outside. We headed around the back of the building to the cellar door. The large metal doors to the basement angled and formed a triangle between the building and the ground. I unlocked the padlock and slid back the bolt. Concrete stairs led to the cellar. I hated dark basements, and this one was dark and damp and smelled of mold and earth. When I was considering purchasing the building, I had refused to go downstairs. Thankfully, my realtor, Chris Martinelli, had gone down and verified it was clean and empty of vermin. Only then did I descend. Now, here I was being forced at gunpoint. Nana Jo headed down first, then me with George following close behind. My fear of the gun at my back overcame my hatred of basements, and I followed Nana Jo down the stairs.

Nana Jo flipped on the light switch at the bottom of the stairs.

"What are you doing? Turn that out," George growled.

Nana Jo complied. "Okay, but I don't know how you're going to find anything with no light."

She was right. Without the light, the basement was pitch black.

George relented. "Okay, turn the light on. And get the ladder."

Nana Jo flipped the light switch. I spotted the ladder against the back wall and pointed.

"Get it," he said.

I crept toward the ladder, keeping an eye out for vermin and other creepy-crawlies. When I reached the back wall, I grabbed it and turned. Just as I turned, I saw a dark shape descend the stairs. George Parker must have heard or sensed movement because he turned around. As he began to turn, a shadow leaped down the last few steps and drop-kicked him. He fell onto his back. As it landed, I heard a loud shout of "*Tawanda.*"

From the stairs, Dorothy stood over George Parker. She had on a dress and pumps that made her look like an Amazon. She hiked up her dress and planted her feet wide and crouched low to the ground. George scrambled to his feet and charged toward Dorothy. As he lunged forward, she reached across and grabbed his arm that held the gun. Then she turned quickly, twisted his arm, and leaned her shoulder into his body. In two swift moves, she bent back his wrist and the gun fell out of his grip.

Nana Jo dived and grabbed the gun, while Dorothy used George's momentum to flip him over her shoulder. He came down with a thud and a series of screams and curses. Once George was on the floor, Dorothy placed her knee on his chest and held him down. Nana Jo stood over him with the gun pointed at his head. Down the stairs came a barefoot Irma with a red pump with a six-inch hooker-heel in her hand, which she promptly applied to the prostrate Parker with vehemence.

Ruby Mae stood on the stairs. "Them police better get here soon or there ain't going to be nothing left to lock up."

"I'm gonna knock your brains out if you make one move, you crazy mother—"

"Irma!" we all shouted.

"Sorry." Irma broke into a coughing fit. "I guess I got carried away."

"Put down that shoe and take this gun." Nana Jo handed Irma the gun. "Point it at his head. If he moves, blow his brains out."

George Parker looked like a caged rabbit, but he didn't move one muscle.

Nana Jo found a length of rope. Dorothy rolled Parker onto his front. Nana Jo used the rope to hog-tie George Parker. And I do mean hog-tie. Nana Jo wrapped the rope around his legs and tied them to his wrists. She worked fast. The whole thing took less than a minute. When she was done, Nana Jo raised both hands and stepped off of George. Cowboys roped cattle in seconds, but Nana Jo hog-tied a killer in less than sixty seconds.

Ruby Mae went up the stairs to wait for the police. The police cars arrived, sirens blaring.

I looked around in amazement. Irma hovered over the trussed-up George, holding a shoe in one hand and a gun in the other. Dorothy stood nearby, still in her Aikido stance, ready to pounce if the situation required.

Nana Jo ignored George and went to me. "You okay?"

I nodded. I was shaking and gripping that ladder like it was a lifeline.

"It's okay. You can let go now." Nana Jo pried my hands off the ladder and enveloped me in her warm embrace. With my nana's arms around me, I was safe. It was over.

After the police had removed George Parker from the cellar, Dawson and the poodles joined us in the café. Dawson made coffee and produced cookies to assuage his guilt at missing all of the action.

"Until I heard the sirens, I didn't know anything was happening," he said.

Detective Pitt showed up about forty minutes after the uniformed police. He wore sweatpants, loafers with no socks, and a T-shirt. He had bed hair, which stuck up defiantly in the back.

After a few cups of coffee, my hands had finally stopped shaking, but my insides were still on a slow quiver.

Detective Pitt had the decency to look sheepish. "So, George Parker killed his brother David and his nephew?"

I nodded. "Yes. I believe so."

"But why?"

"I believe it all started when Robert Parker died suddenly."

Detective Pitt shook his head. "Don't tell me he killed him too."

I shook my head. "No, I don't think so. I called Diana and she said Robert died from a stroke." I took a sip of coffee and tried to organize my thoughts. "But, when Robert died, Clayton inherited his father's share of the real estate company. And he sold it."

"That's what my son said," Dorothy said proudly.

"Yes. But how could Clayton sell the business without consulting George?" Nana Jo asked.

"I wondered that myself. But then I remembered you said when the Parker brothers came back from the war, they suddenly had all this money. You said Robert Parker bought a lot of buildings and opened a real estate company. George went to school to study accounting. Later he came and joined the company. That's when Robert changed the name to Parker & Parker. I'll bet George didn't own any of the business."

"That's right," Nana Jo said. "George told us that they never drew up any papers about ownership."

Detective Pitt scribbled on his notepad. "Okay, so Robert dies and Clayton wants to sell the business. Big deal. No reason to kill Clayton."

"That's not why he killed Clayton." I took another sip of coffee. "Irma found out that Parker & Parker had financial problems. George Parker was a gambler. He told Diana Clayton was the gambler, but no one at the casino remembered him gambling. George planted that lie with Diana because he owed the casino a lot of money. Then David came back. He was sick. He needed money. He wanted to go to a tropical island and live out his last days. But, there was no money and Robert was dead. Clayton sold the company. It was gone and there was no money. But David had money. He'd hidden this money for decades, waiting for just the right time."

"What money?" Detective Pitt looked up from his notes.

"Well, Nana Jo said when the Parker brothers were young, they were poor. But then they went off to fight in the war and when they came back, they had money. Obviously something happened during the war."

"What?" Detective Pitt asked.

I had been thinking about this. "Dawson, can you do me a favor, please. Will you bring me the gargoyles you found in the basement?"

Dawson looked surprised, but didn't ask questions. He turned and went outside. Oreo and Snickers looked up, unsure whether to follow him or not, but decided to stay with the cookies and wait for crumbs to fall their way. Dawson was only gone a few minutes. We munched cookies and drank coffee until he returned. He placed two gargoyles on the table in front of me.

"What's that?" Detective Pitt picked up one of the gargoyles and turned it around. He almost dropped it. "Heavy." He examined it and set it on the table.

"That, if I'm not mistaken, is the source of the Parker brothers' wealth," I said

"Ugly little booger." Irma broke into a coughing fit.

I picked up the gargoyle and looked at it. Everyone watched intently while I raised my hand and threw the plaster gargoyle to the floor.

They jumped at the crash. Bits of plaster flew all over the floor. As the plaster hit, the outer shell broke off. Amongst the pieces of plaster that littered the floor, were several bright, shiny coins. There were about forty coins on the floor. I picked a few of the coins out of the plaster and placed them on the table.

Detective Pitt's mouth hung open.

"Close your mouth, Stinky. You'll catch flies," Nana Jo said.

"Are those real?" Dawson asked.

"I think so. I think the Parker brothers must have come across either a hoard of Nazi gold or they confiscated the coins from a concentration camp. Remember Ruby Mae said their father used to plaster houses. He must have taught his sons the trade during a sober moment, and they used that knowledge to get the gold out of Europe."

Ruby Mae picked up a stray coin. She dropped it on the table and wiped her hands on her handkerchief.

"How did you know?" Nana Jo asked.

"I didn't, at first. It wasn't until I thought about the day I found David Parker upstairs. He was looking at the ceiling, but it's a loft, so there's nothing up there. George Parker did the same thing." I took a sip of coffee. "Clayton Parker was fine with selling this building until his father died. I don't think Clayton knew about the coins. After his father died, David came back. David must have told him there was something valuable here because, after that, Clayton did everything he could to prevent me from buying this building. I had to get an attorney and put a lien against the property to prevent him from selling to someone else. George told us he overheard David and Clayton arguing. That's when he found out where David had hidden his share of the loot."

"George didn't know about the gargoyles?" Detective Pitt was so intent on my story he'd quit taking notes.

"I checked the title for the building. David bought the building after the war. He must have hidden the money in the gargoyles, intending to return and get it. Then he was arrested for armed robbery and went to jail."

Ruby Mae shook her head. "He always was a bad seed."

I continued, "George was the accountant. He would have been responsible for paying the taxes. But as his gambling problem got worse, he started taking money from the business. The more in debt he got, the more he let things slide. I'm guessing the taxes on the Gargoyle building must have been one of the things he didn't pay. He probably intended to pay them at some point but got in over his head. Anyway, the building was foreclosed and bought by the previous owners. When they decided to retire, I bought it."

"But why did George kill Clayton?" Detective Pitt asked.

"I think Clayton found out George was embezzling from the business. Diana said Clayton and George had a big fight. Plus, George was under a lot of pressure to pay the money he owed to the casino."

"So, Clayton and George get into a fight and George stabs him and leaves him in the back courtyard. Why kill David?"

"I think David suspected George killed Clayton. When you arrested David, he must have argued with George. I can't imagine he wanted to go back to prison. He was dying. He planned to get his gold and leave. I think he threatened to tell the police it was George."

Dorothy said, "So, George killed him."

"That's what I think, but you'll have to ask him," I said to Detective Pitt.

Detective Pitt and the rest of us sat in the café until Chris and Zaq showed up for work.

The police showed up with a warrant and collected all of

the gargoyles. Seven total, including the one I broke. They provided a receipt, but I didn't think I'd see those gargoyles again. I didn't want to see them again.

My awesome nephews took over the store and sent Nana Jo and I upstairs to get some rest.

I tried to relax, but after the gallons of coffee I'd consumed, my mind was definitely overstimulated. I tossed and turned for what felt like hours, but was only about forty-five minutes based on the clock on my nightstand, until I gave up and got out my computer.

Chapter 24

Everyone who attended the first party seemed pleased to receive another invitation to Wickfield Lodge. If they suspected the party had anything to do with Charles Parker's death, no one let on. In fact, it seemed Charles Parker was all but forgotten. Lady Elizabeth had stressed she'd like to thank everyone who had been there during the unfortunate event.

All of the waiters, musicians, and guests were present and accounted for, and then some. The additional guests consisted of James, Sergeant Patrick O'Hara of the Chicago Police Department, and Detective Inspector Covington.

Lady Elizabeth had been tempted to invite additional ladies to balance out the party but decided against it. It was always good to have more men than women at a party, and she didn't believe Covington or Sergeant O'Hara would actually dance. They were technically on duty, although they were supposed to be undercover.

Detective Inspector Covington was wearing a shiny new tuxedo for the occasion. It looked new. It lacked the quality of Seville Row but fit him well, nevertheless. If only he would stop fidgeting with the collar, he might blend in. Few of the guests remembered him, despite the fact he'd questioned most of them. They probably hadn't paid him any more attention than they would a waiter.

Sergeant O'Hara was another matter. The American detective would stand out no matter where he went. He was short and stocky, with the build of a prize fighter. He hadn't packed a tuxedo and wore a brown suit that had seen better days. The fabric was cheap and the elbows were worn. His shirt might have once been white but was closer to ecru now and bore the signs of meals long ago consumed. He chomped on the end of a cigar. Ashes embedded into the fabric might make a casual observer believe the suit was made of tweed, were it not for the trails of ash he left behind like breadcrumbs.

Once the party was in full swing, Lady Elizabeth breathed easier. Her guests ate, danced, and drank. James took the place of Charles Parker and danced with Daphne. Penelope and Victor danced as an engaged couple in love should. If anyone thought the party suspicious, one look at Victor and Penelope wiped all doubt out of their mind. They were clearly in love and all who knew the two thought it about time.

Sergeant O'Hara lurked on the outskirts, smoking and watching. Detective Inspector Covington tried to mingle and danced with a few of the women.

James and Daphne were a topic of interest. Daphne wore a new dress from one of her excursions into London, and she looked even lovelier dancing with James than she had with Charles Parker. Her cheeks glowed, and her eyes sparkled. She appeared as deeply in love as her sister, and it appeared James was well on his way too.

The tricky thing for the small group of players in the dramatic reenactment was keeping as close as possible to the original timing. The two police officers had pre-arranged their movements as much as possible to provide coverage. When Daphne and James stepped out onto the terrace, Inspector Covington followed. Lady Elizabeth tried to remember where everyone was at the first party and note differences, but it was impossible, since the guests didn't know they were supposed to act a certain way. Thompkins was enlisted to watch for anything that differed significantly from the last time.

Lord William hadn't attended the last party. He sat by the fire with his leg propped up on an ottoman. He couldn't compare the movements from the last party, but he could note if anything seemed odd.

Lady Elizabeth joined, and Thompkins came by.

"Yes, Thompkins?"

"Your ladyship, you said you wanted to know if we noticed anything that was different from the last party, no matter how small."

"Yes, Thompkins."

"Well, the orchestra plays what are called sets. There are eight songs in a set. Then they take a break. The leader explained this to me last time. He wanted to make sure it was okay for the musicians to eat or drink or smoke here with the other guests or if it would be better if they went down to the servants' area."

Lady Elizabeth hadn't noticed any breaks. "Yes."

"And I know you asked the leader to make sure they played the exact same songs in the same order as they did on the last occasion."

"Yes." Lady Elizabeth and Lord William looked expectantly at Thompkins.

"Well, it's just that one of the housemaids noticed

one of the band members." Thompkins turned toward the orchestra. "That young man on the end with the cello."

Lady Elizabeth and Lord William glanced discretely at the orchestra. A very thin young man sat with his head bowed. Between the angle he held his cello, the hair obscuring his face, and the placement of his music stand, he was barely visible.

"Odd that he seems to be the only one with an instrument case," Lady Elizabeth said. "It's unsightly and takes up so much room."

"Yes, m'lady," Thompkins said.

"What did the housemaid notice?" Lord William asked.

"He has spent a lot more time downstairs this time than he did before. In fact, none of the staff remember him. Of course, this may not be important. Mrs. McDuffie is inclined to believe the silly girl has a crush on the young man."

"We should notify Sergeant O'Hara." Lady Elizabeth spotted the sergeant standing alone. With a regal inclination of her head, she signaled him to join her. "Sergeant. This may be nothing but—"

"Everything is important. No clue too big. No clue too small," Sergeant O'Hara interrupted in his fast-paced, brusque manner.

Talking to the American detective, in a hurry in everything he did, left Lady Elizabeth out of breath. She and Thompkins relayed the housemaid's comments.

Sergeant O'Hara stared openly at the cellist. Perhaps he sensed the extra scrutiny because, at that moment, the cellist looked up from his music and locked eyes with Sergeant O'Hara.

"I'll be a monkey's uncle." O'Hara let out a low whistle.

Thompkins stiffened and cleared his throat.

"Out with it, man. I take it you know the man?" Lord William banged his hands on the arms of his chair.

O'Hara smirked. "Oh, yeah. I know him. That's Sticky Fingers Johnson, that is."

"Sticky Fingers?" Lord William frowned.

"Trigger man for La Cosa Nostra and the Simpliano family. That's our killer or I'll eat my hat."

Sergeant O'Hara looked more likely to eat a certain cellist than a hat. With a determined stride to his step, he made his way toward the orchestra. Weaving around the dancing couples and careful to keep his eyes on his target, Sergeant O'Hara approached the cellist like a hungry tiger stalking his prey.

"Dear me. I hope there won't be any unpleasantness," Lady Elizabeth said. "Thompkins, perhaps you should find Detective Inspector Covington. I believe Lord Rumpagle had him cornered in the billiards room."

Thompkins nodded and silently left to find the detective.

Penelope joined her aunt and uncle. "What's going on?"

Just as Sergeant O'Hara reached the orchestra, Sticky Fingers reached down into his cello case and pulled out a large Tommy gun.

He knocked over the music stand, threw his cello at the detective, and pointed the large machine gun at the crowd. "One more step, copper, and I'll blow all these people to smithereens."

Sergeant O'Hara stopped in his tracks. Women screamed. Sticky Fingers fired a round into the ceiling. The staccato roar of the machine gun silenced the guests.

"Everyone against the wall." Sticky Fingers used the gun to indicate the wall and the direction. "Move. Or next time I won't aim so high."

The guests fell over each other in their rush to obey. All except Sergeant O'Hara, who stood rooted to his spot.

"You too, flatfoot."

Sergeant O'Hara marched defiantly to the wall and stood with the others.

"Good. Now, I'm just gonna walk outta here. As long as you all stay here, no one gets hurt." The gunman sneered and slowly backed away, careful to keep everyone in sight. He swung his gun from side to side, like a pendulum on a clock, ready to fire at any minute.

"You'll never make it out of here alive, Johnson," O'Hara yelled.

"You better hope I do, copper."

O'Hara stepped forward and gunfire erupted feet in front of him. Someone screamed. Lady Honorah Exeter fainted. Her husband caught her before she hit the ground.

At the door, Johnson stopped, smiled, and made a formal bow.

Just as he turned to run from the room, Detective Inspector Covington jumped into the doorway and grabbed the gunman. James and Victor also leapt in and tried to wrestle the gun away. Sergeant O'Hara ran toward the fight.

Lady Elizabeth and Penelope helped to usher their guests out onto the terrace and away from danger.

Lord William hobbled forward with his cane, prepared to enter the fray. By the time he made it to the door, Sticky Fingers was disarmed and on the ground.

It was early morning before the police finished all of their questions and the guests were allowed to leave. Lord William and Lady Elizabeth were still dressed in their finery, although Lord William's tie was askew and his leg was back on the ottoman. Victor and James had removed their ties and suit jackets. Daphne had kicked off her shoes and sat on the sofa with her legs curled underneath her. Curls escaped their clips and cascaded onto her forehead, making her look very young. Penelope sat on the window seat and rested her head on Victor's shoulder.

Thompkins brought a fresh pot of tea and left without a word.

When Detective Inspector Covington entered the study, Lady Elizabeth started to rise.

He motioned for her to remain seated. "Please, don't trouble yourself. I just wanted to thank you for everything you did to help us tonight and to apologize to Mr. Carlston."

Victor rose and shook the detective's hand. All was forgiven.

"Would you care for tea?" Lady Elizabeth asked.

"No thank you. I've got to get back to the Yard."

Penelope sat up straight. "But you can't go yet. You can't go until you fill in the holes."

"Certainly. What do you want to know?"

"I want to know why he did it," Lady Elizabeth said.

"Apparently Charles Parker was siphoning money away from the mafia bosses back in the States."

James smoked and glanced at Daphne. She appeared unbothered by any talk of Charles Parker. "We know Parker was a . . . Juice Lender."

Daphne scowled at this term. "What's a Juice Lender?"

Daphne hadn't been present when this was discussed previously, so James explained.

Daphne shuddered but showed no other sign of concern.

Detective Inspector Covington continued with his story. "That's true, but Parker was skimming money off the top. The bosses got onto him, and they ordered a hit."

"Oh my," Daphne said.

"Joseph Johnson, also known as Sticky Fingers, tracked him here. Apparently, Sticky Fingers is quite a good cellist and managed to get in with the orchestra."

Lady Penelope frowned. "But how? I mean, I thought he was a police officer."

"He claimed to be a police officer when we interviewed him after Charles Parker was murdered. Turns out he just said that to try and deflect suspicion away from himself. He had to know we'd question why an American was now playing in the orchestra when Charles Parker, another American, was murdered." Detective Inspector Covington looked down and shook his head. "I hate to say it, but we missed the mark on that one. We should have verified with the American authorities, but it never occurred that anyone would be so bold as to claim to be a policeman."

Lord William mumbled something under his breath that sounded like, "impudent blighter."

Lady Penelope still looked puzzled. "Wasn't it a bit of a coincidence that he plays the cello and there happened to be an opening for a cellist?"

"Yes. We thought so too." Covington said. "After a little checking, we learned the previous cellist had an untimely accident. He was struck by a car. I suspect the car was driven by Johnson. Fortunately, he survived, but he won't be playing the cello for quite some time."

"So, this Sticky Fingers person came all this way to kill Charles Parker?" Daphne asked.

"It appears so."

"But why did he stay? Why didn't he leave after he'd killed him?"

"Apparently, he enjoyed playing with the orchestra." Detective Inspector Covington grinned. "They're booked to play for a royal dinner party during Ascot week. He seemed quite keen on performing for the king. He didn't think anyone would suspect him and was safe to stay here another few months."

"Bloody cheek if you ask me," Lord William said.

"Thank goodness you caught him." Lady Elizabeth patted her husband's hand.

"We couldn't have managed without all of you." Inspector Covington bowed politely, made his apologies, and left.

Lady Elizabeth beamed at Penelope with Victor and Daphne with James. All was right with her world.

Lord William squeezed her hand and leaned close. "Well, dear, I think we shall have to start planning another gathering," His tone was grave, but his eyes sparkled.

"What are you talking about?" Lady Elizabeth gasped.

"Well, my dear, I think we shall have to plan a wedding. Maybe two."

"I think I shall enjoy planning another gathering," Lady Elizabeth said.

Chapter 25

Good news traveled fast and bad news traveled even faster. Within a day, the entire town knew of George Parker's arrest. Traffic at the bookstore increased. Maybe murder was good for business.

The Sleuthing Seniors met to discuss *The Unexpected Mrs. Pollifax*.

"I liked that book you recommended, Sam," Ruby Mae said. "I picked up two more." She held up the next two books in the series.

"I was happy to see an older person doing more than sitting around knitting," Nana Jo said. "Most of those cozy mysteries just depict elderly women gardening or knitting. I like a little more action. I think this Pollifax woman and I would get along quite nicely."

I was pleased the group liked the book.

In the corner, Irma coughed. "I liked it too, but I wish there was a little sex."

I laughed. "Typically, you won't find explicit sex in cozy mysteries. However, I will tell you that Mrs. Pollifax gets a romantic relationship."

"Hot d—"

"Irma!" everyone yelled.

Irma coughed. "Sorry. If there's going to be romance, I might check out the next two books too."

Dorothy leaned against me and whispered, "I hear we have an aspiring writer in our midst."

Nana Jo swatted Dorothy. "Big mouth. I told you to keep quiet."

"I think that's wonderful," Ruby Mae said.

"When are we going to get a chance to read it?" Dorothy asked.

"It's just something I did for fun to kill time." Their encouraging faces made me want to hide. I knew they meant well, but the thought of anyone reading my book still filled me with dread.

"Leave her alone." Nana Jo stepped in. "She'll show you when she's ready."

"When you get it done, I'd love to read it." Dorothy got up and poured herself another cup of coffee.

"Me too," they all said at once.

Dawson brought in a plate of cookies that distracted them. His timing was excellent. I considered giving him a raise.

I stuck out my tongue at Nana Jo. I'd forgive her later. I might even let her read the manuscript, since I'd finished the first draft. She'd made notes on the pages she'd read and pointed out a few inconsistencies and grammar problems and made some suggestions that were good. My book might never see the light of day, but that didn't mean I didn't want it to be as good as I could make it.

I watched as Dawson and the girls ate cookies and realized that even though there was a Leon-shaped hole in my heart, there were people in my life now to fill the gaps.

Nana Jo stood beside me. "I make a pretty good sidekick, huh?"

"You make an excellent sidekick." I gave her a squeeze.

Nana Jo hugged me back and whispered, "You know, Ruby Mae has a second cousin whose daughter is a literary agent in New York."

I smiled. "Of course she does."

Please turn the page for an exciting sneak peek of
V. M. Burns's
next Mystery Bookshop Mystery

READ HERRING HUNT

coming soon wherever print and e-books are sold!

Chapter 1

"Did you see the getup that little floozy had on?"

"Shhhh." I glanced around to make sure the "little floozy" was out of earshot. Tact wasn't Nana Jo's strong suit.

"Don't shush me. I've seen Sumo wrestlers wearing more fabric."

Nana Jo exaggerated, but not by much. Melody Hardwick was a supermodel thin, heavily made-up college senior who had attached herself figuratively and literally to my assistant, Dawson Alexander.

"Surely that boy knows she's nothing more than a little gold digger." Nana Jo had taken an instant dislike to Melody.

"You don't know she's a gold digger. You just don't like her." I locked the door to the bookstore. "Besides, it's not like Dawson has any money."

"He may not have a pot to pee in now, but the boy has PEP." Nana Jo wiped down the counters and bagged the trash.

"What's pep?"

"Potential Earning Power. That boy is the best quarterback MISU's had in at least a decade. They're undefeated and if things keep going like last week, they have a shot at a bowl game and maybe a championship."

My grandmother had always been a sports enthusiast, but ever since the Michigan Southwest University, or MISS YOU as the locals called it, quarterback started helping out in my bookstore, she became more of a fanatic.

"He was embarrassed. Did you see how she clung to him?"

"Dawson's a big boy. He can make his own decisions."

Based on the look she gave me, she wasn't convinced. Frankly, I wasn't convinced either. I was concerned about him too. School was a challenge for Dawson. At the end of his freshman year he was placed on academic probation. Thanks to a lot of hard work and tutoring from me and Nana Jo throughout the summer, he'd raised his grades, avoided academic suspension, and turned his life around. He didn't have to work at the bookstore anymore. His football scholarship covered room and board. I never wanted to charge him for staying in the studio apartment I created in my garage, but student athletes had to pay the going rate for housing and get paid fair market wages for work.

"Girls like that ain't nothing but trouble. You mark my words. Just like Delilah, she'll come after him with a pair of scissors first chance she gets. That woman is nothing but trouble."

Nana Jo's words broke my reverie and brought back the worry I thought I'd eliminated. I tried to shake it off, but it lingered at the back of my mind.

We cleaned the store and then she hurried off for a date with her boyfriend, Freddie.

I took a quick tour around the store. I looked at the books neatly stacked on each shelf. It was still hard for me to believe I owned my own mystery bookstore. Market Street Mysteries had been a dream my late husband and I shared for years. After his death over a year ago, I was finally living our dream. I walked down each aisle and ran my hands across the solid wood bookshelves that still smelled woodsy and fresh and shined with the oil polish Andrew, my Amish craftsman, gave me. After six months, the store was doing well and I still got a thrill walking through and realizing it was mine. My four-legged companions on these strolls trailed along behind, toenails clicking on the wood floors. Toy poodles, Snickers and Oreo, may not share my love of mysteries, but they definitely approved of the baked goods that made their way under tables and counters.

The back of the bookstore was enclosed to provide a yard for privacy and an area for the poodles to chase squirrels and bask in the sunlight. As fall hit the Michigan coastline, the weather had turned cool. The leaves were starting to darken from bright shades of yellowy green to deeper, rich hues of amber, burgundy, and russet. Lake Michigan was also undergoing a change from the deep, blue calm of summer to the pale blue that blended into the horizon and was only discernible from the sky by the choppy white swells that danced across the surface and pounded the shore. Autumn was my favorite time of year, and I lingered outside and enjoyed the sunset until Snickers reminded me she hadn't been fed by scratching my leg and ruining my tights. I needed to remember to make an appointment with the groomers first thing tomorrow or give up wearing skirts.

When my husband, Leon, and I dreamed of the bookstore, we planned to make the upper level into a rental unit to offset the cost. After his death, I sold the home we'd lived in and turned the upper level into a two-bedroom loft for me and the poodles. Nana Jo moved in after a dead body was found in the back courtyard, but she still had her villa at a retirement village. I never dreamed how much I'd enjoy living in the space.

Next week would be one year since Leon's death. The pain was less crippling. The bookstore kept me busy during the day. But the nights were still difficult. I started writing to help occupy my time and my mind. Six months ago I'd finished the first draft of a British cozy mystery and spent the last few months editing. Nana Jo wanted me to send it out to an agent, but that would involve allowing someone besides me and my grandmother, who loved me, to read it. I wasn't ready for that type of humiliation and rejection yet. Besides, in the unlikely event that a publisher was interested in my book, they'd want to know what else I had. What if one book was all I had in me? The only way to find out would be to try again. So after dinner I made a cup of tea and headed to my laptop.

⁓

Wickfield Lodge, English country home of
Lord William Marsh–November 1938

Thompkins entered the back salon where the Marsh family was having tea and coughed. "I'm sorry, but the Duke of Kingfordshire is on the telephone."

Lady Daphne was in her favorite seat by the window. She started to rise but was stopped when Thompkins discretely coughed again.

"His Grace the duke asked to speak to your ladyship." He turned toward Lady Elizabeth.

Lady Elizabeth Marsh glanced at her niece, Daphne, noting the blush that left her cheeks flushed. She placed her teacup down and hurried out of the room. In the library, she picked up the telephone. "Hello, James dear, is there—"

"Thank goodness you're home. I'm sorry but I don't have time for pleasantries. Time is of the essence." Lord James Fitzandrew Browning, normally calm and composed, had a slight tremor in his voice, which reflected the urgency of his call even more than his words and lack of propriety. The duke took a deep breath and then rushed on. "This is going to sound strange, but I need you to trust me. You're going to get a call from the Duchess of Windsor asking for permission to move her hunting party to Wickfield Lodge this weekend. It's vital she be allowed to do so."

Whatever Lady Elizabeth expected, it hadn't been this. She stood frozen for a moment before recovering herself enough to respond. "Well of course, James. We . . . we have no plans this weekend."

James released a huge sigh and she could almost see him wiping his brow.

"James, you know we're happy to help any way we can, but you mentioned this was 'vital.' Vital to whom?"

James hesitated a moment before responding. "Vital to England. The Crown. Maybe the entire world."

Chapter 2

Saturdays were busy days at the bookstore and I was thankful my nephews, Christopher and Zaq, were home from college for fall break and helping out. The twins were invaluable in getting the bookstore up and running over the summer. The boys were twenty and while they were identical, their personalities were so different it was very easy to tell them apart. Both were tall and slender. Christopher was business oriented and preppy, while Zaq was technology inclined and edgier. Neither was a mystery lover, but they each had their own gifts and I was thankful they were willing to spend time helping out their aunt and to earn extra pocket money.

Nana Jo was a mystery lover and was great at helping match customers with authors and mystery subgenres like hard-boiled detective stories, cozy mysteries, or police procedurals.

Today was a home football weekend for MISU and a bye week for the twins' school, Jesus and Mary University, or JAMU to the locals. When Dawson started working at the bookstore, I toyed with the idea of putting a television in the store so we could watch him play on Saturdays. However, a television in a bookstore seemed paradoxical. I compromised by foregoing the smooth jazz I normally piped in and tuned into the sports channel instead, at least for MISU and JAMU games. I expected complaints from people who liked to sit and read in peace and quiet. But so far the comments were all positive. I suspected the lack of protest was due to the customers' desire to support a hometown boy combined with their affection for Dawson's baked goods. They were willing to give up a little peace and quiet to support someone they knew.

Thankfully, Dawson and the MISU Tigers had today's game well in hand with a healthy lead of three touchdowns. Home team wins made for happy customers, and happy customers spent more money. As locals discovered Dawson lived and worked here, I'd noticed an increase in traffic. Many were football fans who wanted to congratulate him, talk sports, and get autographs for wide-eyed kids. The others were infatuated young girls who glanced shyly at him when he was working and then hid behind books, giggling whenever he looked at them. Regardless of the reason, the extra traffic was good for business.

MISU won handily and I had a very good day in sales. The twins had dates and hurried out immediately at closing.

"You should go to the casino with me and the girls," Nana Jo said.

"Thanks, but I think I'll stay home. I want to get some writing done." We reshelved books and cleaned the store.

"Great. You started working on the next book in the series? You know, I'm really proud of you. But you still need to start sending your book out to agents. I hear getting published is a long process. I read somewhere Agatha Christie was rejected for five years before she got her first book deal."

"I know. I—"

The alarm system I'd installed this summer startled me and I dropped the books I was shelving. The alarm buzzed whenever a door or window was opened, even if the system wasn't armed. Nana Jo stepped around to see who had entered and I picked up the books I'd dropped.

I placed the books on a nearby table and headed for the front of the store. I could have sworn I'd locked the door. Just as I came around the corner, I heard Nana Jo.

"We're closed."

"Oh, I know. I just thought I'd wait for Dawson."

I struggled to recognize the voice. As I got to the main aisle, I saw Dawson's scantily clad girlfriend, Melody. Today's ensemble included more fabric than the one she wore yesterday, but not by much. A short black skintight miniskirt with a deep V-neck mesh cut top with fabric that barely covered her breasts and red, six-inch heels that Nana Jo's friend Irma called hooker heels.

"Lord have mercy. What're you wearing?" Nana Jo stared openmouthed.

The shocked expression wasn't lost on Melody, who laughed and twirled to insure Nana Jo got the full effect. "You like?"

"Is someone watching your pole?"

Melody flushed and cocked her head and took a step forward as though she were about to say something insulting.

Younger people often thought of the elderly as feeble and weak. However, my Nana Jo was over six feet, two hundred pounds, held a green belt in Aikido, and could shoot a bat off the top of a building at three hundred yards. *Don't ask me how I know that.* Despite the difference in their ages, in a fight, my money was on Nana Jo.

"Dawson isn't here and the store is closed." I stepped in between the two women. "If you're looking for Dawson, I suggest you try campus."

For a moment, Melody looked at me as though I were gum she'd scrapped from the bottom of her shoe.

"What's going on?"

I was so intent on preventing an altercation between Nana Jo and Melody I hadn't heard Dawson enter through the back door.

Apparently, Melody hadn't either. "Dawson. How long have you been there?" She smiled big.

"Long enough." The chill in his words made me turn to look at him. His eyes were hard and his face was set like granite. "What're you doing here, Melody? I told you we were finished yesterday."

Melody kept her smile in place as she sauntered around me. "I knew you couldn't really mean that. We both said things we didn't mean yesterday." She stood inches from Dawson and placed her hands on his chest and leaned close. "Let's go up to your room and talk things over."

Dawson didn't move for several seconds, but I could see the vein in the side of his forehead bulge with each breath. Finally, he grabbed Melody by the wrist.

She winced in pain. "Ouch. You're hurting me."

Dawson turned and walked out the way he came, dragging Melody by the wrist along with him.

"I guess he was smart enough to see through that little cheap hussy after all," Nana Jo said. "I think that's the last we'll see of her."

I hurried to secure the front door. Something in the way Melody looked and a flutter in my spine told me Nana Jo was wrong.

Normally, Sundays were spent with my mom. Church, lunch afterward, and girl time. This Sunday was no different. Today we were shopping in downtown South Harbor.

Unlike North Harbor, South Harbor had a bustling downtown with picturesque cobblestone streets and brick store fronts that sold everything from fudge and truffles to over-priced coffee. Mixed between quaint soda shops and antique stores were clothing stores with shoes that cost more than a month of my salary when I was a teacher.

"Honey, isn't this cashmere sweater lovely? It would look great on you." My mom held up a bubblegum pink garment that looked as though it might fit one of my thighs.

"Mom, I couldn't fit my imagination in that sweater."

"They have larger sizes, dear. I really think you need to up-grade your wardrobe. Everything you own is black or brown. You look like you're still in mourning." She placed the fluffy concoction up to my neck.

I glanced at the tag and nearly choked. "Are you joking? That sweater costs more than my house payment."

"You really should put more effort into your appearance. You've really let yourself go since Leon died. I think you're hiding behind your mourning and it's time you started living again, and maybe dating."

I stared openmouthed. "Not all of us can live the life of a princess. I don't have the time or money to waste getting my nails and hair done and buying overpriced sweaters. I have a business to run."

The salesclerk, who had walked up with a bright smile on her face, turned and walked away.

My mom sighed and replaced the sweater. She walked to the back of the store. That sigh spoke louder than any words could have. Obviously I had disappointed her again. I stood there for a moment and then sorted through the rack of sweaters, looking for one that would fit over my head without making me look like an overstuffed sausage. I could afford the sweater. That wasn't the problem. Finances had always been tight when Leon and I were working. A cook and an English teacher didn't buy cashmere sweaters. But I'd sold the house and used the insurance money to buy the building. The bookstore was doing well, not *Fortune* magazine worthy, but thanks to low overhead, frugal spending, and hard work, it was making a profit. One cashmere sweater wouldn't break me, and it would make my mom happy. But, as a grown woman in her mid-thirties, I shouldn't have to buy a sweater I didn't want to make my mom happy. I wished Nana Jo had come with us today. She would have understood and helped intercede between me and my mom.

My mom was so very different from Nana Jo; it was hard for me to imagine my grandmother gave birth to her. They were polar opposites. Josephine Thomas was tall and hardy. My mom, Grace Hamilton, was five feet, less than one hundred pounds dripping wet, and delicate. My mom was like a dainty porcelain figurine you keep on the tallest shelf behind a glass door, locked away from harm for fear of breaking it. Nana Jo blamed my grandpa, who always called my mom his little princess, for planting the "princess seed" in her head. In her mid-sixties, my mother had never had a job outside of the home. She'd never paid a bill until after my dad died. She was the princess.

I dropped my mom off at her South Harbor condo and headed back over the bridge to North Harbor, where I belonged. I glanced at the pink shopping bag on the seat that contained a white cashmere sweater I would be too afraid of spilling anything on to ever wear and swung my car into the parking lot of a nearby liquor store. I glanced at my watch. Thankfully, it was after twelve, when alcohol could be purchased. I looked at the license plates of the cars parked in the lot, noting the majority were Indiana residents who had escaped across the state line into Michigan, where they could buy alcohol on Sunday. We were all escaping from something, but I didn't have the time or energy to figure out what at the moment. A bottle of wine would have to substitute for therapy for now.

★ ★ ★

During the summer, I saw quite a lot of Dawson. When the fall semester started, we barely saw each other, despite the fact he lived in the apartment over my garage. Twice daily football practices, weight training, and classes took up a lot of his time. But Dawson loved baking and he was really good at it. His apartment was a tiny studio with only a one-burner stove, which made it challenging to bake on a large scale. Dawson had gotten into the routine of using my kitchen to bake enough goodies to get us through the week at the bookstore. So, when I entered through the back door, I smelled a sweet, delicious aroma wafting down the stairs to greet me.

I climbed the stairs without my normal escorts. Snickers and Oreo usually heard the garage door and bounded to the bottom of the stairs to greet me. However, the possibility of a cookie or treat dropping to the floor was a greater enticement than seeing me.

I placed my pink bag on the counter with less care than I used for the bottle of wine. Dawson had his back to me as he lifted a tray of cookies out of the oven and placed them on a rack on the counter.

"What an amazing smell." I breathed deeply and allowed the smell of vanilla, almonds, and sugar to fill my senses.

"Thanks. You're just in time to try one." Dawson turned to face me.

"Oh my God! What happened to your face?"

He didn't say anything, merely hung his head. I hurried around the counter and turned his face toward the light to get a closer look. Three red scratches trailed across both cheeks. There was a gash under his left eye and a bruise on his forehead. His eyes were bloodshot and dark circles underneath indicated he hadn't slept.

He tried to turn away, but I held his chin and forced him to look at me.

"What happened to you?"

We stood like that so long, I didn't think he would answer.

Eventually, the silence grew too much for him. "I'm fine."

I snorted. "Well, you sure don't look fine."

Dawson shrugged. "It's nothing." He forcefully, but gently, pulled my hands away and walked to the back of the kitchen. He leaned against the wall and folded his arms, providing a barrier.

I took a deep breath and tried to steady my breathing. "Was it your father? Is he out of jail?"

He shook his head.

"Then who?"

He hung his head. "Let's just say Melody didn't take our breakup well."

"You should go to the doctor. Those scratches look deep, you—"

He was shaking his head before the words were out of my mouth. "If I go to the doctor, the newspaper might find out."

Sad that at nineteen you had to be concerned about the newspapers running a story about a girl who lashed out when her boyfriend broke up with her. But this season the MISU Tigers were getting a lot of publicity, Dawson in particular.

I went to the bathroom and got a cold compress and mercuric acid. He didn't balk when I made him sit at the dining room table and didn't say one word when I started to treat the cuts. "Newspapers are the least of your worries. Wait until Nana Jo finds out!"

He winced, but I wasn't sure if it was the mercuric acid or the thought of what Nana Jo would say.

"What an unusual request. James didn't have any other information?" Lord William asked as he absent-mindedly broke off a piece of his scone and fed it to Cuddles, the Cavalier King Charles Spaniel positioned at his feet.

"Not that he told me. Although, I'm sure he'll fill us in when he gets here." Lady Elizabeth picked up the knitting she kept nearby, which she said helped her think clearly.

"Is His Grace coming too?" Lady Daphne Marsh picked at an imaginary string on her skirt and avoided making eye contact with her aunt.

"Well, I suppose so, although I didn't ask him. I just assumed he would." Elizabeth looked at her husband. "You don't mind do you, dear?"

"No. No. Of course not." Lord William tossed the remains of the scone down to the dog and pulled out his pipe. "I'm sure James wouldn't have asked if it wasn't important."

"My thoughts exactly." Lady Elizabeth resumed her knitting.

"I don't suppose you know anything about this?" Lord William asked his niece.

Lady Elizabeth Marsh sighed. Sometimes her husband could be rather slow to read the signs or he would have noticed his niece, Daphne, had said very little since Lord James Browning's name was mentioned. The two met six months ago when he came to help out his friend and old classmate Victor Carlston, Earl of Lochloren, who was accused of murdering one of Daphne's beaus. At the time, Victor believed he was in love with Daphne and chivalrously stepped in to protect her by allowing the police to believe him guilty of murder. The duke helped to reveal the true killer and insured his friend's freedom. Victor was now living in wedded bliss with Daphne's sister, Penelope, down the road at his family estate, Bidwell Cottage. The Marshes hoped another announcement of marriage would be forthcoming as James and Daphne seemed destined for the altar. However, the duke's visits of late had been fewer and far between.

"No. I haven't spoken to James . . . ah, the duke in nearly two weeks," Daphne said almost in a whisper.

"I suppose you better tell Thompkins and the rest of the staff to prepare for guests," Lord William said.

"I would, but I want to wait until we're sure," Lady Elizabeth said. "Technically, she hasn't asked yet. I don't even know how many people to expect."

"Do you suppose David will come too?" Lord William asked.

Lady Elizabeth knitted. "I have no idea. The last I heard, he was in France."

"I don't suppose there will be a problem with the Queen Mother and the rest of the family," Daphne asked.

"Well, I guess that depends on what type of problem you mean." Lady Elizabeth knitted silently for a few moments. "Bertie and Elizabeth are still very angry and the Queen Mother is disappointed in David. I still feel rather badly that none of the family attended the wedding."

Lord William sputtered. "But really, how could we attend? It would have been a sign the family agreed with his abdication to marry a divorced woman—an American." Lord William waved his pipe while he spoke, flinging ashes across the sofa.

Lady Elizabeth looked up and shook her head. The sofa was starting to show bare patches from the maids brushing off tobacco. It would have to be recovered soon. "Well, I don't know if the fact she was twice divorced or an American was the objectionable part. I might have considered attending if the wedding were one day earlier or one day later."

"I agree. It was as though they were thumbing their noses at the family by getting married on King George's birthday," Daphne said. "Really, his own father's birthday."

"Bad form." Lord William refilled his pipe.

"Regardless of the circumstances, David and Bertie are brothers, and I believe they'll work things out in the end," Lady Elizabeth said. "Besides, James said it was vital to the Crown that she hosts her hunting party here. So, that must mean the king is at least aware of the event."

Lord William nodded and puffed on his pipe.

"At any rate, it doesn't appear we'll find out how the Crown feels about things. The duchess hasn't called. What if she's found another place to hunt?" Daphne asked.

Thompkins entered the room silently and coughed. "Her Grace, Wallis Duchess of Windsor is on the telephone for your ladyship."